Down the Dirt Road

RASPBERRY RIDGE
BOOK THREE

JESSIE GUSSMAN

Contents

Acknowledgments

Cover art by Julia Gussman
Editing by Heather Hayden
Narration by Jay Dyess
Author Services by CE Author Assistant

Listen to the unabridged audio for FREE performed by Jay Dyess on the Say with Jay channel on YouTube. Get early access to all of Jay's recordings and listen to Jessie's books before they're available to the general public, plus get daily Bible readings by Jay and bonus scenes by becoming a Say with Jay channel member.

One

Amara Jardine reached for her phone, pulling it out of her pocket as it continued to ring.

She stood on the steps of the mansion she had been raised in up until she'd been a teenager before her parents had moved the entire family to Chicago.

Memories, mostly good, but nostalgic and sad at the same time, swept through her.

She swiped her phone. "Hey, Olive. I was going to wait for you to get here before I go in."

She stood on the steps of the back porch. They never went in the front door. Guests did that. But she'd been sitting on the steps for a while, waiting for one of her other sisters to arrive. Going into this house by herself did not feel like something she was up to at the moment.

Even if she was a high-dollar marketing executive and one of the youngest in her company, at twenty-eight, to be promoted to manager of her own team.

"I'm so sorry. I got delayed again. I'm not going to make it. The flights out of Ecuador are notoriously bad, and I'm honestly not sure how soon I'll be able to get another one."

"You're still in Ecuador?" Amara said, tamping down the bit of panic that information caused her.

Her other sister, Mertie, was still at a ladies' meeting she was speaking at in Oklahoma City. Or thereabouts. It was going to be another week until Mertie made it up. The meeting was going to last three days, and then she had something else that she had to go to.

After that, Mertie said she had six weeks off, which was why Amara had taken all of her vacation as well, and the three sisters planned to spend six weeks at their parents' mansion, cleaning it out and getting it ready to put on the market.

She swallowed. "You be safe down there, okay?"

"Yeah. I'm no stranger to third world countries, but I think I'm ready to come home for a long time."

Olive had been the world traveler, and somehow she'd made it work. Amara wasn't quite sure where she got her money, although she worked wherever she went, from stewardess on airplanes to an au pair to well-off folks in Chile and South Africa.

She backpacked across the Alps and walked on the Great Wall of China.

Amara was a little jealous, but if she hadn't worked as hard as she had, she wouldn't be where she was at her job.

Not that she liked it that much. She honestly didn't, but it was a job, and it provided a paycheck and a rather luxurious way of living, and she loved the competition and the challenge.

"I'm ready to have you home for a long time." She wanted to say more. About how losing their parents had made her long to pull in and huddle with her sisters and be a family with them. It just...felt like they lost their bedrock or something, and she wanted to go back to feeling like she was still on solid ground and not have her family scattered all over the globe.

Maybe she was ready to come home.

No. She worked too hard to be where she was, and while she had worked hard to pay off her college loans, because her parents had felt that it was important for their kids to work for things, her share of the sale of her parents' condo in downtown Chicago would more than cover them.

Selling the mansion would set her up for a long time.

The idea that she wouldn't have to work had never crossed her mind, but as she sat there on the step, holding the phone to her ear and praying that her sister would get home safely, she couldn't help but think that maybe it wouldn't be a bad idea.

She could get an easy job, something with no stress to get her out of the house.

"Be safe, okay?"

"I'm always safe," Olive said easily, but it sounded like there was a new note of strain in Olive's voice as well. Maybe Olive was feeling the same kind of pressure. The pressure to...get out from underneath the pressure.

Except she'd been trotting the globe for the last ten years, surely there was no pressure in that. But maybe it was the pressure of longing for a home and family. A soft place to land. A place where people knew you and loved you anyway.

"I love you," Amara said, wishing she could hug her sister through the phone.

"Love you too. Be good, little sis." There was laughter in her voice. And it made Amara smile.

"You too."

She swiped off, and Amara sat there, looking out over the amazing view of Lake Michigan, the view she'd taken for granted when she was a little girl sleeping upstairs in her bedroom.

She hadn't been back in...years. She'd always visited her parents in their condo. And they always talked about how they should go back up to the house at Raspberry Ridge, like it wasn't a mansion, and have Christmas there or something.

But her parents, stockholders in multiple companies and on the board of multiple other companies, were way too busy to take the time to drive the whole way to Raspberry Ridge, even over Christmas.

Lots of families who were as wealthy as her parents were took extravagant vacations, but Amara's family never had. Her dad was a workaholic, and her mom worked right alongside him. There seemed to be a competition between the two of them, as to who worked the most, but she felt like there was love between them too.

She pushed the thought aside, since love hadn't happened for her, although she was only twenty-eight.

But how much longer did she want to wait? Did she want to be fifty before she finally found someone? And the guys that she dated in Chicago were...rather girlish.

She wanted a manly man. Someone who could protect her and wasn't afraid to stand up for her either.

Not someone who talked about the latest fads and fashions and TV shows.

Deciding that she could put off going into the house for a little bit longer, she stood and walked back down the steps.

She could go into the town of Raspberry Ridge. Fran's store was still there. And she heard that someone was thinking about putting a restaurant in. One of her sisters had told her that. Probably Mertie, she was the one who kept track of everything and was always on top of it all.

Amara walked down through the fields behind their mansion to the trail that met the dirt road that went down to the beach. There were a couple of old fishing docks there, and her siblings and she had hung out there a good bit when they were younger. Although they hadn't been allowed to talk to the Gilcrest boy.

She wasn't even sure where he lived. Down there somewhere, but their mother had forbidden them to speak to him. Or his family.

Which wasn't hard, since she never saw him. The area was poor and run down and difficult, though not impossible, to get to except by boat. Still, Barry Klein had his fishing boat down at the docks and scraped out a living from it somehow.

She thought he lived on his boat, if she remembered correctly. She spent hours down there, watching him mend his nets, listening to the stories of storms on the lake and more stories from back when he worked on a freighter on Lake Superior.

Those were some of the happiest memories of her childhood, and it was no wonder her feet automatically took her in that direction.

She went down the trail, which turned into a dirt road.

It didn't look well used but looked a little bigger than she remembered from childhood.

It was longer too, or she was just not used to walking, since she didn't remember it taking this long.

She was active at the gym, going three or four times a week, but maybe she needed to work on her legs more.

The lake breeze ruffled the grasses and lifted her hair off her shoulders, lifting her burdens as well, it seemed like.

She had six weeks off, six whole weeks where she didn't have to worry about her job or coworkers or what time she got up or when she went to bed at all.

She couldn't believe how freeing that felt. Although, she was also tempted to call the office and check in. After all, she worked hard to get where she was, and she didn't want to go backward by taking an entire six weeks off.

She never took days off, but her office hadn't been surprised. Since her parents had died, they knew that she would be cleaning out the mansion in Raspberry Ridge. She talked about it a good bit around the water cooler.

She hadn't needed to take off when they were cleaning out the condo, since she'd done it on the evenings and weekends, although she'd always taken work with her and tried to work and clean at the same time.

It irritated her sisters.

She closed her eyes, lifting her head and allowing the breeze to push her hair back off her shoulders, opening her eyes and allowing her gaze to fall on the pristine blue waters of the lake.

It was unbelievable how big they were, how massive, how they changed weather patterns because of their immense size, and yet she felt like she knew them intimately.

At least Lake Michigan.

It seemed different up here than it did down near Chicago, although she enjoyed walking along the lake there too.

It just wasn't the same. Wasn't this wild, wasn't as...fresh, clean, pure.

Maybe she was just romanticizing it since the lake held the memories of her childhood, back when she was young and innocent and knew exactly what she wanted out of life, and her moral compass pointed due north all the time.

She finally reached the beach area and the docks that she remembered.

It actually looked like someone had been fixing them up. The way someone had widened the road.

Interesting. It would be nice if there was a little fishing industry going on in Raspberry Ridge. It would be good for the local economy. And good for her pocketbook if she could buy fish from her hometown. That would be neat.

Feeling lighter and almost happy, she smiled when she saw what looked like Barry Klein's boat.

Someone had repainted it or refinished it, or whatever someone did to a boat, and it looked a lot less dingy than it did in her memories.

As she watched, someone came out from below the deck, walking up through the hatch and closing it behind him.

Not Barry. This was a younger man, tall and lithe, with the brown skin and ropy muscles that came from working on a boat day in and day out.

If Barry had a son, she didn't know about him. But she looked a little closer and saw that the boat was named *The Berry Princess*, which was the name of Barry's boat.

The man spied her as she walked down the dock, shielding her face from the sun as she looked up at him.

"This is Barry Klein's boat?" she asked, although she knew she probably should have introduced herself first.

"Used to be," the man said easily, coiling up a rope while he spoke.

"Interesting. I used to spend so much time down here, listening to his stories, watching him mend his nets and check his ropes. He would always tell me how important it was for a sailor to have good ropes."

"And to tie good knots," the man added, and she smiled.

"You knew him too?" She didn't have to say anything more. Barry always said good ropes and good knots.

"I do." The way he said it made her tilt her head to the side.

"Is he still around?"

The man nodded. "I bought his boat, but he still hangs around some. Although, he's older than the rest of us, and slower." He lifted his shoulder. "Sometimes he goes out with me, although not as often as he used to."

As he used to. It sounded like the man had owned the boat for a while.

Two

"When did you buy his boat?" Amara asked. Not that it really mattered, she supposed.

"About ten years ago," the man said, and she nodded. That was about the time she graduated from high school. She hadn't been in Raspberry Ridge for a while before that.

She didn't know why her parents hadn't sold the mansion long before.

"Do you mind if I watch you for a little bit?" She knew that was a weird question, and as deserted as the pier was, he probably didn't have too many people asking, but he shrugged his shoulder again.

"Suit yourself," he said.

Then she would. She walked out onto the wooden planking, past the boat, and sat down with her feet hanging over the edge.

It was far enough off the water that her feet didn't dangle in it, but she could see the schools of fish swimming about.

"You new in town?" the man asked after a few moments of silence as he continued to work.

"Kind of." She wasn't sure why she didn't want to say exactly what she was there for. Maybe because she didn't want to go into her parents' death and how they owned the mansion on the hill, which was a far cry from what this man had, if he indeed lived on the boat.

For once, she just wanted to be a normal person. A normal person taking some time off, and enjoying the bright sun, and not having any worries.

"I see."

"Do you live on the boat?"

"I used to."

"But not anymore?"

"Nope."

Well, maybe he had things he didn't want to talk about either.

She turned her eyes away and looked out over the lake, wishing she had brought her sunglasses. Bright sun would give her a headache, and she was going to be facing it directly as it went down.

"This brings back so many memories," she said.

"Good ones," the man said, not a question, throwing another rope down in a neat coil on the deck of his boat with a slap.

He climbed out and stood on the dock. "Mind if I join you for a minute?"

"You done for the day?"

"Yeah. I'll be going out around two AM, so it's a good idea to get to bed early."

"Aren't you bringing your catch up?"

"I sold it down at Blueberry Beach. It was a good catch for the day. A couple more days like today and I'll be able to buy groceries."

She laughed. "You can just eat what you catch."

"You know, I don't think I'd ever get tired of eating fish. Fried perfectly, roasted over an open fire. That's probably the best way."

"Yeah. I've only had it once or twice like that, and it was Barry who made it for me."

"What are you doing for supper tonight?"

Her eyes flew to his. Was he asking her out on a date?

He held a hand up. "You just sounded like you're a little nostalgic for things that used to be. I'll be eating with Barry, and you're welcome to join us." He grinned. "And if you're going to, I'll be sure to roast some fish over the fire."

She believed him, believed that's all it was, just him inviting her to do something she hadn't done for a really long time.

"Thanks. Although, I don't think I can go to someone's house to eat if I don't bring something along with me. What should I bring?"

"You'd have to go get something, wouldn't you?"

"Yeah." And there were no stores in Raspberry Ridge, other than Fran's, which probably wouldn't have much of anything. Unless she wanted to take a bag of sugar or a tube of toothpaste.

"Just come. You can pay me back the favor sometime."

"All right." She imagined trying to invite him to her mansion to eat. He probably wouldn't feel comfortable.

Not in his ragged jeans, the T-shirt with the sleeves cut out of it, and his rubber boots that looked like they were one hundred years old.

Not that she wanted to judge someone by the clothes they wore, but there was some truth to you are what people see when they look at you.

"Just so you know, that invitation was for tonight."

"Thanks. I guess I assumed it was."

He didn't say anything and just stood over her, his arms crossed over his chest, as though he were looking out over the lake.

She didn't get the feeling that he was looking for something to say. She got the feeling that he was standing there quietly being company for her.

After all, she was the one who chose to come out here and sit down where he was working. Maybe he figured out that she wanted to be by the lake, but she didn't want to be alone.

"May I sit down for a bit?"

"I should have asked you to. Please."

He smiled, and she noticed the crinkles at his eyes. They were brown eyes, warm and with a twinkle of laughter in them, and she figured a person could get caught in them pretty easily.

He had a straight nose and a strong jaw, which was covered in stubble.

He sat down beside her, a good ten inches between them.

"I used to fish off this dock," he said.

"I did too. I never caught much of anything other than sunfish."

"Sunfish are actually pretty tasty. One bite at a time though and you need a whole string of them in order to make a meal for one person."

"Yeah. I never bothered. No one ever showed me how to skin them, although Barry offered."

"Just didn't have the stomach for it?" he asked, with no censure in his voice, as though it were normal. Although he must have cleaned thousands, if not tens of thousands of fish in his time, he didn't seem to judge her for it.

"No. I don't know. It just makes me ack." She made a sound that showed disgust and being grossed out at the same time.

"Um, no offense, but we're kind of getting away from the whole knowing where our food comes from. Knowing that we have to skin it, gut it, clean it, scrape it, whatever. Even vegetables. People don't do their own vegetables anymore either. They just rinse them off and chop them."

"I always wanted to have a garden. But it's kind of hard to do that in Chicago where I live."

"Hmm. Chicago."

He didn't say anything more, and she wondered what he was thinking. "What's wrong with Chicago?"

"Nothing. Just, up here, it's a lot slower, a lot..."

"Cleaner. Quieter. More beautiful." She looked out over the lake again, surprised that she'd forgotten how nice it was with no traffic, no people, or at least just one person who seemed to be friendly and nice and not...feminine.

"You love it here," he said softly, kicking his legs a little.

"I'd forgotten how much," she said.

She put her hands behind her and leaned back on the dock, lifting her face to the sun.

"It definitely grabs a hold of you," he said, and then they lapsed into silence.

She wouldn't sit on a bench with a stranger in Chicago, looking out at the lake, just chatting.

In fact, if a stranger sat down beside her, she was liable to get up and move. If she didn't, they might awkwardly give each other a half smile, but they certainly wouldn't have a conversation.

She realized she'd never introduced herself and then thought that maybe it was just as well. It was kind of...a fitting thing, in a place where everyone knew everyone else, that she didn't know who he was.

"Did you grow up here?" she asked, knowing that he'd said that he bought the boat from Barry, but that didn't mean he was around here.

"Yeah. I grew up right here."

He seemed to be indicating the dock. But she assumed that he meant Raspberry Ridge. Because obviously, kids didn't grow up on the dock.

"You lived in a boat?" she said instead, thinking that she should know him. Maybe if she introduced herself, he would recognize her name.

"I can tell you, but just know that if I answer, when I ask about you, I'll expect you to do the same. Fair enough?" he asked, grinning.

"Touché," she said, figuring that he was right.

It was nice to not have any of the pressures of the world, including having to figure out what his name was, where she knew him from, and how they had grown up together.

It was almost like she was young again, and those kinds of things didn't matter.

"Did you fish with Barry for a while before you bought his boat?" she asked, figuring that was a safe and easy question.

"I did. I...hung around the dock so much, he started taking me with him when I was barely old enough to remember. I don't know. I must have been four, maybe three. You can ask him tonight when we eat."

"I will."

"He taught me everything he knew, from a young age up. Of course, I couldn't do everything at first, but...there's a lot to learn and a lot of wisdom that is passed down from generation to generation. It falls by the wayside when there's not someone to pick up the mantle and go forward."

She nodded. In her business, that really was nothing. But she could see how it was out here. It wasn't like a person could Google fishing and get an in-depth instruction manual, and they certainly couldn't learn to do it in college.

"Did you always want to be a fisherman?"

"Yeah. Always wanted to be on the water. I still love it. It's the best place to be. I love pitting myself against the lake, although I don't really think of us as competitors. I think of her as more of a challenge. You know, one of those good things where she challenges you enough to make you work for it but not so much that you get discouraged and want to quit."

"Really? You never want to quit?"

"Not really. I suppose there are days where it feels hard, but I love what I do."

She wished she could say that. She didn't, not at all.

"Do you take passengers?" she asked, remembering after the words were out of her mouth that he had said that he was leaving at two o'clock in the morning.

Did she want to get up that early?

And go somewhere with someone she didn't even know?

But it was Raspberry Ridge, and there wasn't anyone she didn't know in this town, even if she hadn't been back for a long time.

Unless it was Hobert Gilcrest, which she had to admit quite possibly could be. He lived around here somewhere, although she didn't know exactly where. She hadn't been allowed to go any farther than the pier, by her parents' orders, and she had obeyed her mother's wishes.

But she didn't know why she wasn't allowed to talk to Hobert Gilcrest. She didn't know why her mom hated the whole entire Gilcrest family.

She supposed it would be a simple matter of asking the man his name and offering hers to find out if that was really who she was talking to.

She would be able to tell by his reaction whether or not he recognized her name and possibly even whether or not there was some kind of stigma attached to it. Maybe he would even know why her mom forbade them to talk to him.

Did she really want to know?

Three

"You know someone who's interested in being a passenger?" the man asked, glancing over at her and giving Amara a speculative look.

"Yeah. I do," she said, returning his look with one that was sure, because as much as she loved Raspberry Ridge, and as much as she lived by the lake all of her life, she hadn't ever gone out on a fishing boat.

She'd have thought that the schools would have had field trips for that type of thing, but they didn't. Most of the time, they went to Chicago, like going to the city and experiencing that type of thing was the only thing that was interesting to the adults.

But they didn't understand that the city couldn't heal your soul. Not the way God's nature could.

Maybe He'd made it that way on purpose. More and more, she'd wondered that. That she lived in a place that seemed artificial, and while they did their best to create parks and trees and grow flowers, it just wasn't the same.

"All right then. I am leaving at two, you heard me, right?"

"How long do you wait for people who are late?" she asked with what she hoped was a charming grin.

"I probably will pull out a few minutes early, unless you need me to wait for you."

"Are you serious?"

He nodded. "I don't usually have a problem waking up. Even if I get to bed late. I always wake up eager to get out."

What would it be like to leap out of bed, eager to get to work, loving what you do?

"So how long are you going to be out?" she asked.

He grinned. "Chickening out?"

"Not exactly. I just want to know exactly what I'm getting into. That seems smart. Do I need to pack a lunch?"

"You better. I quit early today because it was a good day, and I was full. But that doesn't happen too often."

"How often does it happen?" she asked, thinking that maybe she would be a good luck charm, but then she almost snorted. She had never been anyone's good luck charm.

"This is the second time since I started, ten years ago."

"You'd think you'd be celebrating," she said with a laugh, straightening up and looking at him.

"Who says I'm not?" he asked, a dimple winking in his cheek, as his brown eyes twinkled at her.

"This is hardly a celebration."

"I dunno. It's the best time I've had in a while." He flashed a smile, and her heart did something odd, slow and deep in her chest. Which shocked her. He was a fisherman, who barely made a living wage. Actually, she didn't even know if he did make a living wage. His smile should not make her heart flip over, not that how much money he made should matter. It was just... She didn't want to be ensnared by a man who couldn't support a family.

She had a good job, it was true, but there was just something in her that felt like the man should be the provider. Maybe because the Bible said so, but she could hardly use the Bible as her defense since it wasn't something she had lived by for years.

Maybe it was time she got back to it.

"What are you thinking about? Maybe how can I be so pathetic that sitting on the dock in the sunshine, enjoying a midsummer day with a pretty girl could be a celebration?" He smiled and laughed a little, as though laughing at himself. "I couldn't have picked a better way to celebrate."

"And I'm coming over for supper tonight."

"Yeah. And you're coming over for supper. We'll have three of those fish I saved from my second full load in ten years."

"What time should I come?" she asked, looking at the sky and figuring it was probably about five.

"I'd be cooking them right now if I hadn't got distracted by something a lot more interesting than fish."

"I'm more interesting than fish?" She blinked her eyes at him. "You better be careful, you're going to turn my head with all these pretty compliments and that fisherman charm."

"I haven't even turned on the fisherman charm yet," he said, making her laugh. He had been laying it on pretty heavy, since he called her a pretty girl and hadn't missed an opportunity to compliment her.

It really was going to give her a big head. Of course, it was Raspberry Ridge, and she was probably the only female his age within a twenty-mile radius, unless there was a cruise ship out in the water she didn't know about.

"Well, you better not, because I probably can't stand it," she said, allowing the sarcasm to show through in her words.

"All right. I'll go easy on you for today, but when you come back tomorrow, all bets are off."

She laughed. "You're assuming that I'll be able to get up at that time in the morning. I'm not sure I can. I've stayed up that late, but I've never gotten up that early."

"Well, if you're really afraid that you can't, you can sleep on the boat. I didn't clean anything up though. Not any more than I usually do."

Now that was an idea. She wouldn't have to go to the mansion at all tonight. She wouldn't have to sleep in her lonely bed, wouldn't have to try to figure out how to deal with the memories that were surely going to descend upon her when she walked in.

A skeleton cleaning crew came through every two weeks, and so she wasn't expecting there to be a lot of dust or dirt, and her bedroom was probably ready to sleep in, but it was the memories and the feelings that she wanted to avoid.

"You know what, I think I'll take you up on that," she said, surprising herself as much as she surprised him, as his brows went up, and he said, "Really?"

"Really."

"Maybe you want to check out the digs before you agree to it. They might not be quite up to your Chicago standards."

She had forgotten that she told him she was working in Chicago. Interesting that he remembered, although she supposed it wasn't that long ago. It just felt like it.

"All right. Go ahead, give me the tour. Then I'll make the decision."

Without saying anything more, he rose to his feet gracefully, like a jungle cat, and held his hand out for her.

She took it, although she tried to not pull on him too much as she rose to her feet as well. He was stronger than he looked, and his hand was bigger than she expected, rough with calluses, which wasn't unexpected, but gentle somehow as he touched her.

Like he showed a deference to her that seemed to be missing in the city.

It wasn't that she hated Chicago, she actually really loved it. At least... She thought she did. Maybe it was just the newness of being back in Raspberry Ridge that called to a wilder part of her that she'd forgotten about. Maybe that would rub off, and this would feel just as old hat as Chicago did.

"Follow me," he said as he stepped up on the boat and then turned around to offer her his hand. "Watch your step. It shouldn't be wet, but if it is, sometimes it's slippery."

"Is what I'm wearing okay?" she asked, looking down at her capris and fitted shirt along with her flip-flops. It seemed like a good outfit to drive home in. But she hadn't expected to go fishing in it. Not on a boat.

"That's fine, although boots would be better. You're going to have some trouble walking around on those if we get any kind of choppy water, but you won't need to do anything, if you don't want to, so if it's choppy, you might just have to take a seat and pretend to be the captain or something."

"Oh, so this charter tour doesn't include actual membership on a crew?"

"You want to be my first mate tomorrow? Is that really what you want?" he asked, and his tone was a little bit like he was talking to a five-year-old.

She ignored it. "Yeah. I want to be first mate. I want the uniform, the name placard, the whole nine yards."

"She doesn't ask for much." He pretended to think. "The uniform is right here, like this." He indicated the sleeveless tee and jeans he wore. "I'll let you have one of my sleeveless T-shirts, but it's not going to be a modest thing."

He was interested in modesty?

She narrowed her eyes, reevaluating him.

Had she known him growing up? She knew everyone in Raspberry Ridge, or so she thought. And she didn't recall a gentleman with a keen sense of humor who had manners and a self-deprecating humor that was endearing and masculine at the same time along with a morality that was lacking in almost every man she met.

The church was closed now, but there had been a few kids her age who went, although not enough for the church to go through the trouble of having a youth group. The kids had just done everything the adults did, and no one ever thought anything about it. She didn't realize there were actual youth groups until they moved to Chicago.

She actually kinda liked it better in the country church, where she knew everyone, and everyone knew her, and the church seemed like a happy family. Of course, it was nice to have preaching directed at her specific issues, rather than generic sermons that applied to everyone.

Of course, maybe that was part of the problem, where she was used to everything being about her. And in life, it just wasn't.

He opened the hatch and then said, "Would you prefer I go before you or after you?"

"How about you go first." It looked dark down there.

"All right. That would have been my preference too, but manners dictate the lady goes first."

"It's duly noted. The man has manners."

He laughed as he disappeared down the hole.

He seemed to do it with so much ease, while she tried to figure out how she was going to hold on as she started stepping down and then realized she needed to turn around, and basically it was an awkward dance of where did she hold, where did she step, she couldn't see anything, and how much farther until she hit the bottom, until she finally made it down.

By that time, he had a light on, and she was intrigued to see that there was a sleeping berth, a rolltop desk, and a small kitchenette.

Nothing fancy, but a person really could live on a boat if they didn't need a whole lot.

"Here's the bunk. It…isn't the most comfortable thing you've ever slept on, but when you're tired, it works. It's better than the deck, unless you want to look at the stars, and then the deck is pretty nice, especially if you put a blanket down first."

He reached in a drawer underneath the bed and pulled out a folded blanket. "This one's clean, if you want to wrap yourself in that. The other one, I can't remember the last time I washed it." He shrugged his shoulders and laughed at the look of disgust and astonishment on her face. "Just being honest."

"I guess there's no washer and dryer in the boat."

"No. There is not. And I don't stay on here very often anymore."

"Anymore."

He grinned but didn't say anything else regarding that. "You can make the decision. It's totally up to you. If you stay, you'll be here when I leave, and if you don't, you'll just have to make the trip down."

"There is a way to reach this with a car, right?"

"Yeah. Did you come down the trail from Raspberry Ridge?"

"Yes. This is the way we always came."

He nodded. "Right where the trail becomes a road, you can see where it bends around and goes east. If you follow that for a ways, it eventually comes out onto a paved road, and if you turn left on that, you come out on the road that leads into Raspberry Ridge. You just turn left, and the town is like half a mile."

"Wow. I didn't realize that."

"It actually wasn't there when we were kids."

"You're saying that like you know who I am."

"I have suspicions, but...I think tonight will be nicer if we don't know, don't you?"

So he was thinking along the same lines as she was. Just easy companionship, with no pressure, no stress, just good company and good food, hopefully.

"I agree." She looked around again, thought of the big, lonely mansion, and suppressed a shiver. She would definitely rather sleep on the boat. "If the offer is still open, I'm going to take you up on it."

"All right then. I'll walk you back here after we eat. Do you need to go home first?"

"Not unless I need to pack a lunch for tomorrow."

"Got some dried fish we can take along, and I'll make sure we have water. I always have water." He opened up the refrigerator to show it was mostly full of bottled water, along with what looked like it might be a salad.

"Rabbit food?" she asked, surprised to see that in his fridge. He just didn't seem like the type.

"Sometimes I throw my dried fish over top of it. It's pretty tasty that way."

"So everything you eat is about fish?"

"I like to keep my profession in business."

She laughed as she turned and started up the stairs.

She didn't feel any more comfortable going up than she did down, and fumbled around a little bit for something to hold onto as she emerged and stepped up the last few steps.

"It gets easier. Although, you should try doing it when it's stormy out."

"Do you go out when it's storming?"

"Not on purpose. The weather forecast is a little better now than it used to be. But there have been a few times, especially when I was younger, where I felt like I needed to stay out. You know, bills to pay and all that. But after I almost died once or twice, I found out that maybe it's not really worth it."

"Yeah. Something about dying just negates the need to push yourself that hard."

They laughed together as he walked over to the latch for the hold where he kept the fish.

"Wow. That was a little bigger than what I thought it was going to be when you said you caught a couple of little fish."

"Probably only six or seven pounds each. They're coho salmon."

"I'm not going to eat a whole six-pound fish."

"No, but Barry'll dry them, and we'll eat them this winter. Or I'll use them for lunch when I have a pretty first mate along with me."

"Nice," she said. And they shared another smile.

She liked this, not knowing him, not having any expectations, feeling completely at ease, like he didn't expect anything out of her, and she didn't expect anything out of him. They...just got along well together, with no pressure.

She'd actually had a fun couple of hours with him and was looking forward to her day tomorrow. Although it still hadn't quite sunk in that she was going out on a fishing boat.

Her coworkers would think she was nuts. Although, they would probably be intrigued as well, since she bet none of them had done it either.

She thought she had lived, but maybe she hadn't lived quite as much as what she thought.

Four

Hobert Gilcrest walked along the dirt road, back away from the lake, toward the shanty where he and Barry stayed.

Barry had lived on the boat as long as Hobert had known him, so when Hobert bought the boat from Barry, he invited Barry to stay in his shanty.

His dad had long passed away; alcoholism would do that to a body, and it was just him and Barry.

Barry talked once in a great long while about his wife, but he had never said what happened to her. Hobert had asked about her once when he was around ten. Barry had told him he wasn't old enough to know and said to ask again when he got older.

Hobert had never forgotten that, but he'd never asked again either. He didn't really know how. And he assumed that it was probably a painful topic to Barry, and Barry might have just given him that answer to put him off.

Regardless, he found himself exceptionally happy with the pretty lady beside him and the best day of fishing he'd ever had.

Not that he thought tomorrow would be the same. It varied so widely from day to day that he couldn't be sure, although he had been tempted to empty his hold and head back out on the lake.

But life had taught him not to be greedy.

Tomorrow was another day, and it most likely would be like all but two of the days before it, when he didn't catch much of anything, but enough to get by.

It was days like today that made everything worthwhile.

Except today was unlike any other day. Today was different, because of the lady beside him.

"How far is your house?"

He looked away because she was assuming he lived in a house. She was going to be surprised, and he almost regretted inviting her to eat.

But he wasn't going to pretend that he was something that he wasn't, and a rich dude who had a ton of money was not him.

It was probably best she learned that immediately, not that he thought that there was going to be a future between them. She was from Chicago and probably had some kind of upscale job, something that kept her working all the time and made her antsy with the slower pace of life along the lake.

"We should be able to see it here shortly," he said easily. He wasn't going to be embarrassed because of the way he lived. Except, he kind of was. He supposed he could have gone off and "made something of himself" like his uncle had suggested years ago. But he didn't want to give up the life that he had in order to strive for money and prestige when he didn't really value that.

He valued being able to be out in the nature God created, being his own boss, living slow, communing with the Lord as much as he wanted to. No one told him he couldn't or that he had to take his Bible somewhere else because it wasn't allowed.

Of course, nowadays his Bible was on his phone.

He wasn't that backward.

"How long are you going to be in Raspberry Ridge?" he asked, curious despite himself.

He had thought that it was probably a good idea for them not to know each other's names when she didn't introduce herself right away. He didn't want to be tempted to think that there could be more between them than there was. Companionship, maybe friendship.

He didn't make friends very easily, but once he did, he was loyal for life.

She probably wasn't, but that was a judgment on his part, and he tried not to do that to people.

"I see a shed. Is that yours?" she said, ignoring his question and looking at the shanty that he and Barry shared.

"That's where I live," he said simply.

Her face was still turned toward the shanty, but he didn't need to see her expression to guess at the shock on it and the repulsion that was likely there as well. The way her entire body stiffened gave that away.

Yeah, she was definitely not impressed with his digs.

And that's why he didn't want to know her name. His life was not hers, and she would not want it. Not in this century.

He didn't want hers either, but he knew in order to have a girl like her, he would have to give up the life he loved and live a life he hated.

"You live there," she said, low and slow.

"That's right." His words were spoken easily, like there wasn't anything to be embarrassed or ashamed about, and he wasn't. He hadn't chosen this life. It had chosen him.

He hadn't fallen into it, which is kind of how he felt about his dad. His mom, on the other hand, maybe she was still around, he didn't know. She hadn't been interested in the son that she'd left behind. Hadn't bothered to contact him through his childhood, and his dad had probably been sober long enough for him to ask, but by the time he figured he could get an answer out of him, he was too old to care. Knowing that she hadn't been in touch and obviously she didn't want him.

The woman hadn't said anything more, and he was disappointed, even though he had expected that reaction.

He tried to look at the shanty where he lived with her eyes. Eyes that were used to the splendors of the buildings of Chicago. Glass and metal flying up into the sky and sleek lines, pristine and impersonal.

While the shanty sloped a little to the north, it worked out well, because it helped the rain fall off, and the roof didn't leak, which he was grateful for, although a lot of that was because about this time of year every year, he got up and put a fresh coat of tar on it.

Speaking of which, he needed to get some, get that done for this year. It had to be on a hot day with the sun shining down.

July or August were his choices, here in Michigan.

They didn't have a whole lot of junk lying around, but there were some paint cans, and an old lawnmower, and an even older lawnmower that they used for parts, an old car, and an even older car that sat off to the side, and they didn't really use for parts, since that car was a Chevy, and the newer one was a Ford.

He figured he would try them both, and then he'd know what he was talking about if anyone wanted to debate the subject.

There was an old pickup, circa 1971 or so. It was Barry's, but Barry had sold it to him along with the boat. When he sold the boat, he didn't need the pickup anymore, as long as Hobert would agree to make sure he had the necessities.

Considering that Barry considered the necessities bread and the occasional splurge of shrimp, and maybe some flour and sugar, and of course salt, it wasn't hard.

Hobert actually considered the necessities slightly more. But he didn't argue with Barry about it, he just made sure he brought home what Barry liked.

Regardless, the pickup wasn't much to look at, although he didn't really think that it was a dump either.

But from the silence of the woman beside him, he thought she probably did.

And that's why it was a good thing not to exchange names.

"And you're happy here?" she asked, her eyes narrowed as her head turned toward him, tilted a little like she was trying to understand.

"Are you happy in the concrete jungle? Stressed to death, always behind, always trying to fit more into your schedule, a slave to the alarm clock, sitting through meetings from hell where you talk about nothing important, and your work doesn't really matter. Are you really happy with that?"

She pressed her lips together, particularly when he said her work didn't really matter. He didn't mean to hurt her feelings, and he wasn't knocking her at all. But he had a lot of time to sit around and think, particularly in the winter when he wasn't fishing. Unless the lake froze enough for him to go ice fishing. Some years it did, some years it didn't.

"That's a good question," she muttered, then she looked back at the shanty. "Don't you get cold in the winter?"

"It's actually pretty cozy. It's just one room. We've got a stove in the middle, see the pipe going up?"

She nodded. It was hard to miss.

"I just move my bed a little closer to the stove if it gets cold, and that pretty much does the trick."

"You don't have air conditioning. Do you even have electricity?"

"We have a gas stove, and a gas washer and dryer, a gas refrigerator. We don't need electricity."

"What about lights?"

He laughed at her, then looked up toward the sun, squinting, before he looked back down.

"You're kidding."

"No. Although, we do have a little bit of solar power that I use to charge my phone if I'm not on the boat. It's kind of new. I've only had it for the last five or seven years or so."

"Bet that was a big change for you, getting a phone."

"Not sure if it was a change for the good, but it does keep me updated a little more. Although, I don't read as much as I used to. Too busy surfing the web and finding out all the interesting things." Then he paused. "Half of them are wrong, just so you know."

"Really. And how do you know?"

He lifted his hat and ran a hand over his hair before settling it back down on his head and noticing how her honey-colored hair floated in the breeze.

"Mostly because they don't get the life of a fisherman right at all. And they don't get the intricacies of the lake down either. She's a lot more dangerous than they give her credit for."

She nodded slowly, and he figured that he probably didn't need to elaborate. People had a tendency to romanticize things and not realize how dangerous they could be.

"Do you have a lifejacket on your boat?" she asked in a soft voice.

"I'll bring one with me." He laughed at her wide eyes. "I have one on there, but we'll need two if things get choppy. I can swim, and pretty well too, but I'm not going to swim the whole way across the lake or even partway."

She moved her brows.

"Have you decided that it's okay to come in? I don't want you feeling uncomfortable. Truly. I'm not joking."

"I'm just a little surprised. I...expected a house at least. Not something that looks like a shed, and a run-down one at that." She closed her mouth abruptly and looked over at him. "Am I being unkind?" she asked, softly, as though she were really concerned about the answer.

"You're being honest. Which a lot of people can't be."

"Can't? Or won't?"

"I suppose it depends on the person, but both can apply."

"I really would like to see Barry again. It's been years."

"So you're coming in?" he asked, still holding the fish that he carried from the boat.

"I am."

"All right then. I'll leave these outside, but I'm going to introduce you to Barry before I come back out and clean them."

"Are you going to show me how?"

"I thought there were just some things that the lady didn't want to do."

"Maybe the lady wants to know, in case she ever has to...feed herself."

He grinned a little at her making a little bit of fun at what he had said earlier about people not being able to feed themselves. It was true, people depended on grocery stores, butcher shops, and bought their meat already packaged. Which was fine for them, but...if anything ever happened, they'd have no clue how to survive. People seemed to have a lot of faith that nothing was ever going to happen.

Five

Hobert opened the door, stuck his head in, and called out, "Hey, Barry, we've got a guest," and then stood back, waiting for the lady to walk in first.

Her eyes widened a little bit, and she gave him a questioning look before she seemed to take a breath and walk almost tentatively through the doorway.

"Hey there," Barry said, sitting up from his cot where he had been napping.

Hobert wished he could see the room through the lady's eyes, see what she thought. It was neat. He and Barry both kept things picked up and put away. He supposed they learned it on the boat, and he probably learned it from Barry because his dad had never kept anything super neat, but Barry had said everything needs to have a place and be in its place, because when the sea got choppy, he didn't want to have stuff flying all over the place.

That just spilled over to when they were at home. They put everything in its place, that way they knew where it was when they wanted to find it. Not that there was much to find, neither one of them owned a whole lot. And he thought both of them were happy that way. He was.

Regardless, his cot was neatly made on the other side of the room, and straight ahead there was the woodstove that he had been talking about. Beyond that was a small kitchen.

Over on the left, behind his cot, was a washer and dryer.

They had everything they needed, including a small freezer that was on the other side of the room behind Barry.

There was a small table with just two seats, but there were more places to sit outside. Typically when it was nice, they'd do pretty much everything outside.

If it hadn't been the middle of the afternoon, Barry would have been outside, sitting on his chair, looking out over the lake. In the summer, he often napped outside, but with the rain shower they'd had around noon, he must have decided it would be better to be in.

Napping and resting was how he filled his time on the days he didn't go with Hobert, and those days were fewer and fewer and farther between.

"Who'd you bring home? Where'd you find her? Don't tell me she's a mermaid." Barry rubbed his eyes and threw his legs out over the edge of the cot.

He had been sleeping on top of the covers, so it was made as he stood up, grabbing his cane.

He walked with a slightly spraddle-legged style that was typical of a man who had spent his life on a boat.

Hobert doubted he even noticed, but his shoulders were stooped, and his back didn't quite straighten anymore, but he didn't complain about his aches and pains. He just took them the way they came.

"I don't know her name. And I don't think we need it. She's just someone I met at the dock, and she agreed to have supper with us. I left the fish outside." He paused for a moment, just to get the full effect, and then he said, "Got a full load today."

Barry had been looking at the woman, squinting his eyes as though trying to figure out whether he recognized her or not, but at Hobert's last statement, his head snapped around, and his eyes drilled into Hobert.

"You don't say," he said, his brows going up, a little smile tilting the corners of his mouth up. "It was a good day," he said, nodding his head the whole time.

"It sure was," he said, the twinkle in his eyes matching the twinkle in Barry's.

Neither one of them really needed the extra money that a full load would bring, but it was just the idea, it was a good day of fishing when the hold was full.

"I wondered why you were back so early."

"Almost went back out, but I didn't want to be greedy. I'm leaving tomorrow at two AM, and she's going with me. She's going to sleep on the boat tonight."

"She's gonna sleep on the boat." Barry seemed to be still waking up, and then his brows came together. "Did she see the accommodations on the boat?"

"I took her down and showed it to her before she agreed. I think I'll have to take a lunch tomorrow though. Something tells me she's used to eating breakfast, lunch, and supper, and she's probably used to eating it morning, noon, and night."

"I don't have to if you don't." It was the first she'd spoken.

"The kid should," Barry said. "I'll make sure you guys have something. I have some dried fish put back."

Hobert cut his eyes to the woman, who grinned at him.

"I think we're going to go out and fry up these fish. I promised her we'd cook them over an open fire outside. I figured you wouldn't have a problem with that."

"No problem at all, although if you told me she was coming, I would have made her my famous shrimp and grits dressing."

"I didn't know she was, 'til I met her after I docked the boat and got everything put away."

"How's a man supposed to be ready for guests when they pop up unexpected like this?"

"I'm sorry, I didn't mean to put anybody out."

"Aw, you didn't put me out. It's nice to have company. I just...like to be able to put out a spread for them."

Hobert tried not to laugh. He couldn't remember the last time they'd had guests, let alone conjure up the idea that Barry was going to put out a spread.

Maybe he should ask him exactly what he was talking about, but that could involve a story that would delay supper, and he was hungry. He hadn't taken anything along with him this morning; the salad that he'd had in the fridge had turned out to be slimy and rotten, and he was starving.

"All right, I'm going to head out and get these fish done up. And if you don't have the fire started by then, I'll do that. So don't worry about it. There's no rush."

"If you're going out early tomorrow, you want to get to bed in good time tonight."

"I figured I'd leave at two. But that doesn't mean we have to rush," Hobert said again. Rushing was one of his pet peeves. He hated doing it and typically dug in his feet when he had to. Unless it meant rushing to get to one of his lines when he had fish on it. That was a kind of rushing that he really didn't mind.

They walked back outside, with him pushing the door open and allowing the lady to go through first.

He probably should get her name just so he could stop calling her "the lady" in his head. But she reminded him of someone, and he thought that maybe once he knew her name, or more accurately, once she knew his, things might change.

Even more drastically than they changed when she saw where he lived.

He went to the leather pouch where he kept his fillet knife, grabbed it, and took the fish over to the boards that were lying on top of two overturned fifty-five-gallon drums.

It made it the perfect height for him to clean any fish that he brought home to eat.

No matter what he caught that day, he almost always brought something home for supper.

Sometimes when he'd get off the boat at Blueberry Beach, or even more rarely when he sailed the whole way down to Chicago, he'd grab something at a store or market near the dock.

Even more rare than that, they would go into town. And they would have town food, like they called it. Inevitably it was when they were out of flour or sugar or coffee, and they'd pick up some shrimp too, since Barry really did love making his shrimp and grits dressing, although it wasn't something that he made for guests, since they never had any.

Details, and Hobert wasn't going to correct him in front of their guest.

"This is a fillet knife," he said, holding it up.

"Are you going to do all three of them, even though we're not eating them all tonight?"

"Yeah. Fish spoil pretty fast, and although we do have a refrigerator, it's better to do them all up right away. I'll actually fillet all three of them. Barry will probably come and get the first two and season them, then set them on the rack in order for them to cure."

"You just set them outside?"

"Yes. He has a rack he uses, and yeah. They naturally dry. Although, you can do them in the oven, from what I understand."

"I think there are dehydrators that are made specifically for that type of thing."

"Actually yeah, I've seen those." He set the first fish on the board and made a careful slit down the stomach, making sure he didn't grab the guts and accidentally rip them open.

Even after gutting fish his whole life, he still took his time and was careful with it. It didn't take much to...not exactly ruin a fish, but make it so that he wished he would have slowed down and done it right.

He supposed there were a lot of things that just worked better if he did them slowly.

Six

It didn't surprise Amara in the slightest that the mysterious man was good with the filleting knife.

He explained what he was doing as he was doing it, but it felt like he was doing it in fast motion.

He spoke about how to carefully cut into the fish so one didn't catch the intestines, and then, after he had cut off its head, he dumped the fish head and the intestines in a bucket she had noticed was sitting beside them.

"There are a lot of interesting things we can do with that, but I'm guessing you probably don't want to hear about them."

"Maybe not today," she said, surprised that she'd lived beside the lake all her life, and yet this was like a foreign world to her. She had no idea what someone might do with fish heads and fish guts, and that was a good thing. It just made her feel like she'd missed out on so much by not knowing such simple things.

"Now, I'm going to do this one a little slower than I normally do, but not as slow as I just did."

"That was slow?" she asked, in disbelief. She couldn't believe that there was a faster way to do that.

"Yeah. That was really slow. Especially considering how hungry I am," he said, laughing as he started to do the next fish.

She smiled along with him, but she was starving, and she had had lunch. If what he had said in the house... Was it a house? She wasn't sure whether to call it a house or not. Shed?

Anyway, if what he had said earlier was true, then he hadn't had anything to eat so far all day.

"No wonder you're so skinny," she murmured, not really meaning to say it out loud, but she felt almost...uninhibited while she was talking with him.

Not in a promiscuous kind of way, just that she didn't feel like he judged her. Not even when they had been talking about her job. He had just known how things were and had proven his point that he had chosen something different. It might not look better to her, but maybe that was because she wasn't looking at it the way he was, and he had gotten his point across. He was living for something different than what she was. Except, she wasn't sure whether she liked what she was living for or whether she would wake up one morning and think that she wasted her life. She didn't want to do that.

"Oh, why is that?" he asked, glancing at her and then back at his work. The knife looked sharp, if the way it was slicing through the fish was any indication, and she could imagine it could do pretty good damage to his fingers if he wasn't paying attention.

"Because you haven't eaten anything all day."

"Sometimes I do. Sometimes when I dock to sell my catch, I go to a shop or something and pick up a few groceries or something for Barry and me for supper. And I grab a bite then. Especially if it's in Chicago, that's a long ride home."

"Do you really go that far?"

"It depends on what's selling, how prices are. Now that I have a phone, I can make better decisions. Although, going to Chicago takes five times as much fuel, and it's expensive. Although, interestingly, it's cheaper to buy it in Chicago than it is in Blueberry Beach, so that complicates the equation a bit."

She had never thought about things like fuel. "It's your biggest expense?"

"Boat maintenance, that's a big one sometimes, and sometimes not much at all. Insurance, that fluctuates, but it pretty much goes up every year."

"But we all have to have it."

"Sure. That's probably my biggest expense after fuel unless something goes seriously wrong with the boat."

"Like you hit something?"

"If you think I'm that kind of driver, what in the world are you doing thinking you're going to go with me tomorrow?"

"I don't know. I guess... There's not much to hit out there, but you could always have a collision with another boat."

"I'm laughing, but on foggy days, that's a real possibility. I don't have all the sophisticated sonar and radar equipment that everyone else has."

"Don't you want that?"

"Well, there's a trade-off. You get all the latest equipment, and then you have to catch the fish to pay for it. Would I really be further ahead?"

"I don't know. Have you run the numbers?"

"Well, thinking about it, I just know that it means that I would have more stress and pressure. It probably would mean buying a bigger boat, because it probably couldn't work with the boat that I have. I don't know that it's big enough. If I'm going to have that kind of equipment on my boat, I want to have a boat that's not going to sink and is a little bit more trustworthy than *The Berry Princess*." He looked over his shoulder and lowered his voice. "Don't tell Barry I said that."

"He's a little attached to her."

"Yeah. You could say that."

"So the reason you don't get another boat is because of Barry?"

"No. That might be a little bit of it, but like I said, a bigger boat means a bigger payment, more money, more pressure, more stress. One of the things I really like about my life is the fact that I don't have to catch fish every day if I don't want to. I mean, it's not that I don't want to work, because I do, and I work hard. And long hours. We'll leave at two tomorrow morning, and if we get back at two tomorrow afternoon, it's early. That's a twelve-hour day. I put in eighteen-hour days when the fish are biting and we need the money."

"Why might you guys need the money?" She didn't understand how they could looking at how they lived, unless they went on some kind of spending spree. What would they buy?

"Well, we can update our tackle, that's a big thing, even with an old boat. Ropes. Good ropes are expensive. Especially the kind of ropes we need."

He held up the pieces of the second fish. "You want to try the third?"

"I better not. I'll watch again."

"All right. Not long ago, I fell and broke my leg. There was a hospital bill, and then there were six weeks where I couldn't work."

"Just six?" she asked, thinking a broken leg should take longer than that to heal.

"Well, I still had a cast on two more weeks, but I was able to go out and catch a few fish. It was enough to bring in a little bit. But you never know. Sickness, illness, accidents, and there's always the chance I could be lost in the lake somewhere. I want Barry to have something to live on if I'm not here."

"Doesn't he have retirement or something? Social Security?"

"He never paid into any of that. He didn't have enough. I mean, I don't know. I think he gets about two hundred dollars a week or something."

"You're kidding," she said.

The man lifted his shoulder. "It's okay. I'm here to take care of him. Isn't that what family is for?"

"So he's your dad," she said, thinking that she had figured things out. But when she was younger, she hadn't realized Barry had a son.

"No. Not my real dad, but he's like one. He was a mentor to me and took me under his wing, and I learned a lot from him. Now that he's too old to work, I take care of him. I kind of feel like that's what you do. You take care of people. But we're such a throwaway society."

"I guess I knew that." And it applied to her, although she never really thought of herself that way.

"People as well as things," he muttered, doing the fish with a speed that she could only be amazed at. It was like his hands were a blur.

"Aren't you afraid you're going to cut yourself?"

"Usually I focus hard when I'm doing this. I can do it faster, but these knives are pretty sharp. That's something that Barry really takes care of. He makes sure that any knife I have to use is as sharp as it can be. So yeah, I like to keep my fingers out of the way."

"Haven't you ever cut yourself before?"

He stopped and held up his fingers. He didn't have to say anything. She could see the scars.

"So more emergency room visits to get your finger stitched up when the knife slips."

"If you just wrap it up real tight and hope it doesn't get infected, it heals up pretty good," he said.

"Have you ever got an infection from that?"

He nodded. "Once when I was a kid, I ended up in the hospital over it." He grunted. "Took a long time to pay that bill off."

"No health insurance?"

"No."

Wow. She couldn't imagine. This was such a different life than hers. It was...almost inconceivable to be so unconcerned with money, so dependent on the weather and whether or not the fish were biting.

So dependent on God to provide.

And yet, there was something really nice about it too. Something so free, to be released from the constraints of society, not having to listen to a boss or job or the commute or the traffic or the frenzied pace and the stress, not to mention not worrying about what anyone in society thought of one.

Still, no life was easy. No life was without its worries or cares.

He had just chosen different ones.

"All right. I'll take these two and get them started." Barry came up, grabbed the two fish, and took them back to the...shelter. She still didn't know what she should call it.

"Thanks," he called over his shoulder.

She noticed the manners and thought about that. He had opened the door for her, walked slowly beside her, and apparently filleted the fish slowly so she could watch. He also asked her whether she wanted to go down first or him when they were going down inside the boat.

She supposed, looking at the shack, she would have thought that he would have been uncouth and surly, perhaps a heavy drinker. But she hadn't seen any alcohol in the house, and there hadn't been any on the boat. Not in the refrigerator anyway. He was breaking through the assumptions—judgments—she would have made about him, based solely on where he lived.

"Have you ever been anywhere other than here?" she asked, and she meant Raspberry Ridge, although she didn't specify.

"I stop in Chicago and Blueberry Beach regularly." He grinned at her. "And I go out on Lake Michigan all the time."

"Anywhere else?"

"I went to the desert once. Arizona. I just wanted to see what it was like. I figured it was about as different as it could get from here."

"What did you think?" she asked, although she figured she probably should have asked why he went.

"I thought it was pretty sandy."

She laughed. "So you found there is sand in the desert?"

"Are you saying I've been somewhere you haven't?" he asked, surprise in his voice.

"Yeah. That's exactly what I'm saying. I've never been west of Minnesota."

"You haven't been south?"

"I went to Florida for spring break once."

"Bet that was fun," he said, without any inflection in his voice at all.

"The same way swimming with sharks would probably be fun," she said, and it made him turn his head to look at her.

He grinned. "You hated it."

"Yeah. I did."

"Maybe you're not so different from me than what you imagine," he said, his words coming out as he worked, preoccupied a little, as though he wasn't thinking about them a whole lot. So again, she didn't feel judged.

"You're right," she said, and she couldn't believe as the words came out of her mouth that she was agreeing with him.

He started the fire and cooked the fish with a competence that impressed her. They were things that she had never done.

Of course she'd cooked fish before, but never over an open fire. She wouldn't have had the slightest idea how to do it, but he not only knew, they were the best fish she had ever eaten.

"This is salmon, but...different over the fire, a little smoky, but...so good."

She didn't even care that they didn't have anything else to eat other than fish.

"It tastes like it's cooked over a campfire," he said with a grin.

"Yeah. I guess, it's just been so long since I've had it like this, and it is amazing," she said, putting another piece in her mouth. She had a fork and plate, and so did he, but Barry ate with his fingers.

She wasn't sure whether the man had a fork and a plate because of her, or if he'd be eating with his fingers like Barry if she weren't there. Maybe she didn't want to know.

They ate the entire fish, and it turned out to be just enough.

"If there had been any left over, I would have stuck it in the refrigerator and taken it along with me for breakfast in the morning."

"Oh, no. I'm so sorry. I didn't mean to come and eat your breakfast."

"I could have cooked two fish."

"But you brought three before you knew I was going to be here."

"He usually only brings two. So he brought a little extra, almost as though he had a suspicion," Barry said.

She remembered the stories that Barry used to tell and how much she enjoyed them, but she hadn't asked him about them, because he might have been interested in her identity and started asking questions she didn't want to answer. Not until after she'd gone on the boat the next day.

Maybe not even then. Although she figured that she probably wouldn't be back, since her sisters would be arriving and she did have a mansion to clean out.

She kinda forgot the whole reason she was here, and she hadn't gone so long without thinking of her parents' death since they'd been killed in the car accident.

Today had been a good escape, although she hated to use the man as an escape. He was much more complex than that. Although she wouldn't have guessed it to look at him to begin with.

Barry talked a little as they finished eating, just about the way things used to be. How, back in the day, he roasted fish on a stick, rather than having a frying pan over the flame. And how things were better now that they had a refrigerator, even if it was powered by gas.

Seven

But as the fire died down and night began to fall, Amara's new friend stood to his feet.

"I'd probably better start walking you back down the dirt road to the boat. You're going to want to get some rest, unless you plan to sleep the day away tomorrow."

"What's the weather supposed to be like? Maybe I won't be able to."

"Good point. It might be a little windy, so there could be some swells... Do you get seasick?"

"I don't know. I was out on the lake a few times when I was younger, but it was mostly just something pretty we looked at. It wasn't really anything we did."

"All right. Well, maybe I'll bring my bucket just in case."

"In case I throw up?"

"Multiple times."

"I don't know why you think that's so funny," she said as he grinned at her.

She was only pretending to be upset though. She appreciated him thinking about it.

"Can I just throw up over the side of the boat?"

"And scare the fish away? Did you not hear I catch them for a living?"

"Will that really scare them away?"

He laughed and shook his head. "It's just a little awkward to do that, and you don't want to lose your balance and fall over. Not that I would leave without you, it's just...not safe. Plus, the fish probably would eat it."

"Now you're just trying to gross me out," she said, shivering.

"No. I was being honest. But you don't have to worry about there being sharks, so there's that."

"All right. That's a good point, although I bet the water's cold."

"Even in the summer. It doesn't warm up a whole lot. But I don't think it's ever frozen the whole way over, that we know of anyway."

"Really? I remember winters when it was frozen."

"Not the whole way. I think forty percent is an average number, maybe less, and I think that it has frozen up to ninety or ninety-five percent, but never quite the whole way."

"Interesting. I did not know that."

Barry had started to snore a little in his chair, and the man looked at her and said, "Are you ready to go?" He lifted his shoulder and smiled a little ruefully. "Not that I'm trying to rush you or anything."

"No. Of course. I've just gotten so...comfortable. I suppose I'm enjoying it, because it's not what I usually do."

"What? You're usually rushing from the office and grabbing something that's quick so you can run home to your apartment and work all evening?"

"That sounds familiar. I have to admit it." He was right. If she even left the office at all. She might order takeout and sit and work in her office.

Back when she still had a cubicle, she would have gone home, most likely. Now that she had a luxurious office all to herself, she was much more likely to stay and work in it.

She rose to her feet beside him and held up her plate and fork. "I feel like I should offer to wash the dishes since you did the cooking."

"I'll get them when I get back. It's only four pieces."

"So if I hadn't been here, would you have eaten with your fingers too?" she asked, and maybe she shouldn't have, but she was curious.

The man smiled knowingly. "Barry doesn't have feeling in his fingers or something. I use a plate and fork. I know I look like a mountain man who'd probably just put my whole head in the skillet, but I actually do have some civilized manners. It's kind of surprising, isn't it?"

She laughed. "I didn't mean to come across like that."

"It's okay. I was just teasing you mostly." They stepped around the plastic chairs they'd been sitting on, and he pointed to the boards where he had done up the fish. "You can set them there. I'll come home and clean the boards and wash the dishes while I'm at it."

"All right. Are you gonna tell Barry that we're leaving?"

"No. He'll know where we are. It's kind of disappointing that he fell asleep. I thought you might be interested in hearing some of his old stories."

"Well, I hated to ask, because I didn't want him to start asking who I was. I...like the idea that we don't know. It's less pressure."

"I have an idea who you are," he said with a bit of a grin as they started walking down the dirt road.

"Oh really?"

"I shouldn't have said anything. Now you're gonna want to know who I think you are. And I'm like you. I prefer anonymity. It feels...safer."

"Yeah. You're right. You made me curious, and I want to know why you would choose the word safer. That's odd."

"Odd, but a good choice, I think," he said, and they took a few steps in silence as they each walked in a tire track.

Now she understood why the road looked the way it did, partially grown up, with grass under their feet. There weren't too many vehicles that traveled it. It ended at their shed, and while they had three or four vehicles, it didn't look like they drove them much at all. He used his boat to get around. It was interesting.

"Have you ever thought of getting a pleasure boat?" she asked.

"I have one."

"Where?"

"You were on it."

"But you work on that. I mean, like a speedboat or a boat you take out for recreation."

"I get to go out every day. It's recreation. Sure, I work too, and I work hard, I'm not trying to say that I don't, but I enjoy it. I get a boat ride every day. Sometimes I go to Chicago, just because I want to ride a little bit more."

"Wow. Okay." She hadn't thought about it like that. But she supposed he was right. He did get a boat ride every day. Wasn't that the point of being on a boat and going out? To just enjoy the wind and the waves and the lake and the view and the feeling of being all alone in the world, just you and the Lord.

"You go out alone?"

"Unless Barry goes with me, which he hardly ever does anymore. He doesn't say anything, but his back hurts, his hips hurt, and he doesn't keep his balance very well."

"How old is he?"

He shrugged his shoulders. "I honestly don't know. He seemed like he was an old man when I was a kid, and the older I get, the older 'old' looks, but he still seems old."

She laughed. "I'm with you. The harder I look at thirty, the younger it seems."

"I don't think we ever feel as old as what we are."

"No, I feel like a teenager at heart. Except, my job makes me feel like an adult. But you're right, it's...not really a job I take a lot of pride in, because it doesn't make the world a better place." She just worked on making ads to sell things to people. Things that they didn't need or want, until she tried to convince them that they needed them and wanted them. Things that wouldn't necessarily make their life better. It would just make a company richer.

Occasionally she sold things that were beneficial to people, but still, the idea was to make them discontent with whatever they had and feel like they needed something new.

"How old are you when you start not wanting to be older anymore and actually want to be younger? Or stay the same age?"

"About eighteen? Maybe twenty-five. I think it's in your twenties that you're like, I'm the perfect age, and then once you hit your thirties, you're always wishing you were younger."

"What if we were happy about growing older? What if we viewed it as a good thing?"

"What's good about it?" she asked, a little flippantly, because she never really thought about that before. Surely there was something good about growing older. But come to think of it, everyone always tried to look younger, including her.

"Well, wisdom, for one."

"That's if you learn wisdom. Sometimes I don't think I'm any wiser than I was when I was a kid. I sure don't feel like it sometimes." There were other times where she was proud of herself for the decisions that she made. "Okay. Maybe wisdom is one," she conceded.

"That was the easiest argument I've ever won."

She laughed. "You can think you won it if you want to. If it makes you feel better."

"So she says," he teased.

"What else? One thing isn't really enough to make me decide that growing older is good."

"When you start slowing down, and you do it eventually, you have to use your head more than your body. That's a good thing."

"It is? What if there's a lot of pain in your body?"

"Isn't it a good thing to have to try to use your brain to circumvent the pain? If I figure out ways of doing things, whether it's stretching or yoga or whatever, to try to alleviate the pain, or you raise your toilet so you don't have to bend your knees as much or something, that's using your brain and something you don't necessarily have to do when you're younger."

"All right. It makes you have to figure things out. That's kind of weak, but I'll give you that, so two points for you."

"All right then, two to zero."

"Oh, wait! You mean, I'm supposed to be listing reasons why it's good to stay young?"

"Sure. We could hardly have a discussion if you and I are both on the same side. Plus, I don't think you believed me when I said that I thought it was a good idea for us to think about reasons why it's good to get older."

"All right. Let me catch up then."

"No. You only get one suggestion each round. You missed your first turn. Sorry."

"Wait! That's not fair! I didn't realize this was a competition."

"Hmm. The city girl is coming out in her. Can't stand to be bested by somebody who lives in a shack and might not have graduated from high school," he said, with a little bit of mystery in his voice.

It hadn't even occurred to her that he might not have graduated from high school. But now that he mentioned it, he might not even have gone to high school.

"You have three seconds, then I automatically get another point in my favor if you can't come up with something."

"No pain," she said quickly.

"That's a good one. It's true too, and I can't argue with that."

She beamed. "I'll catch up. You'll see."

He lifted a brow. "Getting older means you have more friends."

"Unless your friends start to die," she said.

"You have a longer life to make friendships. They don't all have to be your age. They can be any age. Like Barry and me. He's my friend."

"I thought you said he was like your dad."

"Yes. But once a child becomes an adult, the parent-child relationship is more like friends than anything, isn't it?"

He sounded like he was guessing at that, and it made her wonder about his father and the relationship they'd had. Why was Barry like a father to him? Was that because he didn't have a father of his own?

She tried to think of anyone in town who didn't have a father when she was growing up, but no one came to mind.

"I guess you're right." And then her face fell. Her mom was so busy with her businesses that she didn't really feel like a mom, but she didn't really feel like a friend either. Maybe a distant friend.

"You keep almost missing your turn," he warned her.

She laughed again. "Good hair," she said, saying it like she was on a game show and had to get her answer out before the buzzer.

"All right, that's a good one actually. I hadn't thought of that one."

"You're a man. You don't have to worry about whether your hair is good or not."

"Maybe not the way you define good, but to me, good is not bald, and things are getting a little thin up there." He ran a hand over his head before he settled his hat back down over it.

"It didn't look that thin to me."

"Well, I don't really get to see it much, but it feels thinner. But on that note, you have less maintenance to do in the morning when you have less hair, so that's a benefit of getting old."

"Actually, that's only a benefit for men. Women have more maintenance to do, because you have more things you have to hide, so more manipulation of makeup and poofing your hair out to cover the bald spots and that type of thing."

"What do you know about that?" he asked, lifting his chin a little, as though expecting her to answer.

"A woman never tells her beauty secrets. Especially to a man whose name she doesn't know."

"I'm almost tempted to give you my name, just to learn your beauty secrets."

"Who says I would even tell you?"

"It'd be worth a shot," he said, and then he said, "I think you're stalling."

"I am not!" she said, knowing that there were far more benefits to being young than there were to being old. "More energy."

"I don't know." He pretended to think about it for a while, but she knew she was right.

"Barry was napping whenever we got there. You were up early, and you weren't napping."

"That was because I couldn't, which is a benefit of being old. Retirement."

She laughed. He thought fast, faster than she did. Which was kind of impressive, because she wouldn't have thought that if they were matching wits, he would win.

"Good eyesight," she said triumphantly.

"I don't know. You're coming up with some iffy ones. There's surgery that can be done to make your eyesight perfect in your old age."

"You still have to have the surgery."

"All right. I'll give it to you, but only because you need it."

"I do not!"

"I'm still beating you by one," he said, lifting his hands up and then allowing them to drop to his side.

"That's only because you—"

"Haven't you ever heard that you're supposed to take responsibility for your actions? Personal responsibility, right here."

"Fine. I'm behind by one," she said, being a little bit bratty about it.

"More financially secure," he said.

"Worse hearing," she said.

"Now just hold on a second. That can all be under the umbrella of physical decline. It's not right to be nitpicking here, nitpicking there, otherwise I could break down all the wisdom that you gain in old age. Now, are we going for the nitpicky, or are we going to go in a generalized way?"

"He's changing the rules mid game. I knew there was going to be a catch. Another one, since he started the game without me knowing it."

"You hold a grudge, don't you? That's nasty. That'll eat you up inside," he said with pursed lips and a teasing glint in his eye.

"I'm not holding a grudge! But you did start without me."

"You are going to gnaw that bone until it's gone, girl."

"You cheated!"

"I did not cheat. Do you want me to give you a point? Would that make you happy? A point that you didn't earn, by the way."

"Wow. So you cheat, then you change the rules mid game, and now you try to make me feel guilty for insisting on what should be rightfully mine."

"Okay, fine. You get another point, and then no more health issues. Because that's pretty much your entire argument. And it should be one point. Eyes, ears, hair, creaking bones, pain. So you get old, and things start to break down in your body. One point."

"Wow. Fine. That's fine. I can still beat you."

"More appreciation for things," he said, without any prelude.

She thought about that one for a minute. She supposed that was true. Back when she was younger, she didn't realize what her parents had gone through raising her, and maybe she still didn't entirely. She also thought that most of her peers did not appreciate the college education that their parents paid for.

Since she was paying for hers herself, she appreciated it.

"All right. That's probably true."

They walked for a few moments.

"I'm waiting," he prompted

"I'm thinking."

"Yeah, because you were going to say knee replacements, then hip replacements, then ankle replacements, then shoulder replacements—"

"I was not. I was just doing it with knees and hip. I forgot about the ankle and shoulder." She paused, then said, "Less death."

There. He couldn't argue with that one.

"Yeah. That is one, isn't it?" he said in a subdued voice, and she was kind of sorry that she said it.

It made her wonder whether he was sad for himself or sad because he knew her, knew whose death she was talking about.

Or maybe it was something completely different. Maybe Barry had lost all of his family to death, and that made him sad.

"Okay, while we're on the death subject, the closer you get to death, the less you fear it," he said.

"That's not true for everybody," she said right away. "Death doesn't look less scary now than it did when I was younger." She thought about it for a minute. "Actually, I probably fear it more."

"Maybe you're just not old enough yet. After all, you have all of those years to realize it's coming, and prepare for it, and get ready. Psych yourself up, I guess, if you're not a believer. And if you are a believer, get ready to meet Jesus. I've found the older I get, the more eager I am to get to heaven. Maybe not to die, necessarily."

"All right. You're more eager to get to heaven. I think the more you live your life, the more boxes you check, so to speak,"

"Exactly. You want to get your driver's license, have a real job."

"Make money," she added.

He looked at her with his brows raised as though he were saying, *I told you so*, but he didn't say that. "Get married, have kids."

"Travel, see the desert," she said, adding onto his list.

"See Florida," he said, and she thought he might have winked at her, but she wasn't quite looking at him and wasn't sure.

But it would have made sense; he already knew that she hadn't seen what he had.

"It's your turn," he prompted her.

"I thought we were talking about things we wanted to do when we were young."

"We're young?" he asked, then continued without waiting for her reply. "I would like to see Florida. Although, I'm a little afraid of alligators."

She laughed. "You're joking, right?"

"No. Not really. After all, they're dangerous."

"But it's not like they're everywhere," she said. Spreading her arm out, encompassing everything, she realized they were almost at the dock. The walk had flown by. "They're like...porcupines. How many porcupines have you seen in your life?"

"Three too many," he said. "I think they're more numerous than porcupines."

"They're like sea creatures. How many monstrous sea creatures have you seen out on the lake?"

"I actually did see one once," he said seriously.

"You're kidding," she said, her tone turning serious as well. She thought he might be messing with her. She supposed there was that possibility. But he seemed like he was being honest.

"No. I'm not. It was a few years ago, when I was having a lot of money trouble after breaking my leg. I was out more than I should have been and was running myself ragged. I was sitting on the boat, my lines out, one from each corner of the boat. And—"

"You use lines, not nets?" Somehow, she imagined he'd fished with nets, although she didn't know where she got that idea.

"Yes. I don't typically use the net to catch fish, although it depends on what I'm fishing for, honestly."

"You don't use traps?"

"I think people who catch things off the floor of the ocean use traps, for things like lobster, maybe shrimp."

"Oh." It made sense. She had no idea. "I'm sorry I interrupted you. I was just surprised. I really want to hear about the sea monster."

He chuckled. "Lake monster, right?" Their eyes met, and she looked away first, unsure what she felt but sure that she enjoyed being with him. "No problem. Doesn't really have anything to do with the story, other than I had them all out and I was just sitting there, nothing was biting, and I was worried. Worried about bills, worried about Barry, worried about pretty much everything."

"I hate times like that."

"Oh. I wouldn't have thought you'd know about that."

"More than I want to admit, although I have my student loans paid off now, so that was a big burden off my chest."

"That would stink if the government decides to pay them off now," he said, and he surprised her. Again. She would have thought that he wouldn't have been up on politics.

"You're right. I could have picked something else to pay or invested that money. I'll be mad if that happens!" She smiled to give less bite to her words, although she probably would be annoyed. "I'm sorry, I keep interrupting you. So you were in a really bad time..."

"Yeah. Just one of those times when you're sitting there going, 'Lord, what are You thinking? I feel like I've done all the things You wanted me to do, living the life You want, trying to live right, and here I am, I've got all these huge bills, and it just feels like You keep hitting me when I'm down, and You don't even let me get back up. I haven't gotten up from the last blow before another one comes.' I was sitting there looking at the lake, feeling a little sorry for myself, when I looked up and there was a big long neck coming out of the water, a short head like something that doesn't have teeth. Its mouth was closed... I don't know, just didn't look like it had any teeth. Although, it didn't smile, so I don't really know."

"Oh. It didn't smile? So it wasn't happy to meet you."

"I think you're making fun of me."

"No. I'm not. I believe you think you saw that."

"Well, I wasn't sure what it was, so I started reeling my lines in. I didn't want them to get caught on it. As long as that neck was, if there was a body half as big attached to it, it was gonna take my boat down with it."

"I see. Your rods are attached?"

"They are, although I can detach them and hold them in my hands if I want to. But they have electric reels on them."

"I see. That's one of the things the generators are for."

"Yeah. Among other things."

"All right. Was that it?" she asked.

"No. It didn't take long to realize this was something odd, and I'm not old yet, so I don't have the wisdom of age." He grinned at her. Their argument about which was better, being younger or being old, was fresh.

She grinned back.

"So I started motoring toward it a little bit."

"Yeah. Okay, rethinking my decision to go tomorrow."

He laughed. "It never came out of the water more than that, but I could see a huge shadow under the water. The shadow was maybe a hundred feet long? Thirty feet wide? It was narrow and long, rather than a box shape."

"Interesting. Did it have feet?"

"I couldn't tell. The part that was out of the water was like a gray blue. And I could just see a big black shadow under the water. I couldn't really see whether it was swimming with legs, or whether it was more fishlike. But I'm pretty sure there were nostrils in the head."

"You believe this," she said.

"Different people have seen them. I don't know if my description is the same as what other people have seen. I didn't have a cell phone at the time, or I would have taken a picture. That was probably the reason I got a cell phone, and maybe, that was what God intended. Because I was able to be more efficient in my business when I could figure out which dock it was better to take my fish to."

"So... It was a help in a way?"

"I feel like it was the Lord saying, 'Hey, look at this. Look what I can make. I can make a creature like this, I can make it and I can let you see it, when lots of other people can't. And people won't even believe you when you say you saw it.' It was just...like a special little thumbprint in my life from the Lord."

"That's an interesting way to look at it."

"Yeah. Maybe it's the wrong way, but I just felt like He was telling me something, you know. Like a little bit of encouragement. And I decided I was going to go back home and go to bed. I thought, this is nuts. The whole reason I'm doing this career is because I like the relaxation. I don't like the pressure. I didn't want a job where I was constantly pushed to do more and be bigger and all that. I know it probably should scare me, but it didn't. I just waited until it was gone, which I probably saw it for ten or fifteen minutes before it left. And then I turned the boat around, and motored slowly back to the shore, thinking that I would enjoy a leisurely boat ride. That is why I fish. Because I enjoy it."

He laughed and looked at her. "Would you believe, the entire way back, I caught fish as fast as I could really reel them in and throw them in the hold? Fish after fish, some of them pretty big. By the time I was almost to our little dock, I realized I had so many fish in the hold that I needed to go somewhere and sell them. It was too many for me to just take home for us to process ourselves. It would last us for five years."

He lifted a shoulder. "That was probably an exaggeration, but you know what I mean. I ended up making a thousand dollars that day, when I didn't think I was gonna make anything."

"Was it enough to pay the bills?"

"It was enough to buy a phone." He grinned, one side of his mouth curving up and that dimple winking at her, while his eyes twinkled. She looked at him, stopped by a feeling in her chest, just looking into his face, the humor there, the common acceptance of life, the...wisdom that came with age.

She didn't know any man in Chicago like this. He was most definitely different.

"Kind of the way God's putting on a show for us this evening," he said, pointing toward the sunset, which she hadn't even noticed.

"It's beautiful. I forgot how pretty it is on the lake."

"I'm sure the sun setting with the buildings of Chicago outlined against the sky is pretty too, but I guess I wouldn't trade this for that."

"I think you probably would make the right decision," she said, wondering when the last time was that she noticed the sunset? She couldn't remember when. She'd been so busy running from one thing to the next, trying to get this done and keep up with her job, not just keep up, but excel, to be the best. Was that really what she wanted for her life? To be constantly struggling and striving to do more than everybody else?

So that she could be better than everybody else? So that she could have the cushy office with the door closed and eventually maybe move to the corner office or up a couple of floors to upper management?

That was the career trajectory she had planned for her life. But did she want to get old with that behind her and nothing worthwhile to show for her life?

They stood, their eyes on the sunset, as the sky exploded in color, and then it slowly faded.

The lights hadn't quite faded completely when he said, "Here, I'll walk out on the boat and take you down. You can leave the hatch open if you want, or I'll show you how you can close it and lock it so that no one can get in. You...can have light, but it pulls from the battery when the motor isn't running, and you don't want to completely drain the battery, so I would suggest not using lights unless you absolutely need them."

"I have my phone. I suppose I should have charged it, because it's gonna be dead by sometime tomorrow."

"We'll probably be back sometime in the afternoon, although...do you want to go get it?"

She looked at the sky. It was almost dark with the last of the light fading. "No. I'll just live. I haven't been using it anyway, so maybe it'll be fine."

"I can bring my charger tomorrow, and we can plug it in and charge it if you need it, how's that?"

"That's perfect. Thank you. I never thought about that."

"Me either. I'm sorry it took me a bit. I'm not used to two phones, but I assume your charger fits with mine?"

She held her phone up, and he looked at the end of it.

"I'm not sure. I guess it doesn't matter. If it fits, you can charge it, if it doesn't, you won't."

"I guess that's boiling it down to as simple as it gets," she said.

"Yeah. All right, let me show you this," he said, opening up the hatch and going down first.

Nine

The man had the light on already when Amara got down there, and she suspected that he had known it would be pretty dark, since it was dark outside and the light that had filtered down earlier when they had gone down was gone.

"Here's a light you can reach pretty easily from the bed. Again, you want to try to make sure that you don't use it too much, because I want to be able to start my boat in the morning."

"What are you going to do if you can't?" she asked.

"Well, if it doesn't start, I have a portable battery charger, with jumper cables, but I have to go back to the shanty and get them and bring them out. It would probably be a delay of at least an hour and a half."

"Well, there you go, if I don't want to get up at two, I can run the lights all night and sleep in until three thirty." Who would have thought she would ever call three thirty sleeping in?

"You could do that, but I probably won't be in as good a mood then as I am now."

"You are in a pretty good mood," she said, again thinking about how they had just chatted together, with no pressure or strain. Maybe that was because they didn't know each other's names, or maybe that was because he was just that kind of easygoing guy. The kind of person anyone could talk to and who never got upset about anything.

"Right here's where you hook the hatch, once you close it. In order to grab it, you don't have to walk up the ladder, of course. You pull it over and then make sure that it doesn't hit you on the head on its way down."

He smiled like it had either happened to him, or he'd seen it happen to someone, and she nodded.

"Got it."

She wanted to say that she was probably good, except she really didn't want him to leave.

As though he could read her thoughts, he said, "Are you sure you're going to be okay? If you want me to, I can still walk you home."

She really couldn't ask him to stay. That would be...uncouth. And a little ridiculous. She was an adult woman. The hatch would be locked down tight.

"If I have the hatch locked, how are you going to get down here in the morning?"

"You're going to have to open it up for me. Are you a deep sleeper?"

"Not normally. But I've never tried to wake myself up at two o'clock in the morning either."

"All right. I guess we'll see how easily you wake up. But I'll probably just stomp on the hatch a little. I would yell your name if I knew it, but I'm probably gonna say, 'Hey, lady, get up!'" he said.

"If you're trying to get me to tell you my name, it's not gonna work. My lips are sealed."

"That really wasn't an effort, but I can respect someone who's able to keep a secret."

She gave him a saucy smile. "I guess you can respect me, because you're not finding out."

"And maybe I already know," he said, raising his brows, before he put his hand on the edge of the stairs and one foot on the bottom step. "You don't know my name, but I'm tempted to offer you my phone number, just in case you have any issues. I'm not expecting it, but you might feel better."

The idea of having his phone number was...reassuring. Not just because she would have it that night, because she didn't really think anything was going to go wrong, but...she couldn't shake the idea that this was just a mirage or a once-in-a-lifetime meeting, like his meeting of the lake monster. Whatever he had seen, he'd never seen it again.

Why couldn't she talk to him? Enjoy time with him, have more fun with him than she could ever remember having before with a man, and that was the truth, she realized suddenly. And he was just going to slip away?

"Do you mind giving it to me?"

"As long as you don't ask for my name," he said, waiting for her to pull her phone out.

To her relief, she had more than seventy percent battery. She had plugged it in in the car a little on the way down, and she hadn't been using it nearly like she usually did. Not like she did on a workday.

He rumbled off his number, and she plugged it into her phone.

"Thanks," she said.

Maybe she should have offered to give him her number, but something kept her from it. There wasn't any need for him to know, and he didn't need to get in contact with her. If she offered, it might be obvious that she wanted to be more than just two ships that passed in the night. She smiled a little at the imagery.

"What's so funny?"

"You and me. Two ships that pass in the night."

"It's gonna take us two days to pass each other, right?"

She nodded, laughing.

"I guess it doesn't apply," she said airily.

"Good night. I'll see you in the morning."

"Two AM is technically morning, I guess."

He laughed as he disappeared out the hatch. Then he said, "You want me to close this for you?"

"Would you mind?" she asked, and then before he could, she added, "How do I open it? Just push up?" She didn't know if there was some kind of latch that would hook, and the idea of being trapped down there without being able to get up was scary.

"Yeah. Just push up." He stood there for a moment, with the hatch sitting straight up in the air, as he held it, and then he said, "I'm gonna run home, clean up my mess from supper, and take a shower. I'll be back. That way, I think you'll feel a little better."

"Where are you going to sleep?" she said, panicking a little, because she didn't want him down with her. But he was going to close the hatch, and she was going to lock it.

"I'll sleep on the deck. It's a clear night out, and the stars will be pretty."

"But there's no mattress. It's going to be hard."

"Well, you haven't tried that bed down there yet. It's not that much softer. But I'll bring a blanket, and I'll be fine. I do it in summer all the time. Not only does it make it easier to get up and go to work when I'm sleeping on the floor of my office, but it's pretty."

"All right," she said, wondering if she should admit how much better his words made her feel. She figured it couldn't hurt. After all, he was going to spend an uncomfortable night on the hard floor for her. "I was actually a little nervous. Thank you."

"You ready for this to come down?"

"Actually, can I just leave it up? If you're coming back, and you're going to be sleeping up there, it's safe, right?"

"It sure is, as long as you think I'm safe."

"Well, you haven't tried to touch me at all, and you haven't made any suggestive comments, not even an off-color joke. So, yeah. I think I'm okay."

It was true. He'd been as polite as...another woman might have been, although he was unlike any woman she knew.

He set the hatch back down, and she could hear his footsteps as he left the boat, feeling it bob up and down in the water as he climbed off the side, and listened to his steps echo on the dock as he walked away.

He was walking back in the dark.

He didn't seem scared about it either.

She took a breath, feeling a little bit of anxiety swirling in her stomach. She wasn't used to being this alone. He was the closest person to her, and as she stood there, he was getting farther and farther away. If she wanted help...she had his number.

Walking over to the light, she turned it off.

She hadn't thought about a shower, hadn't thought about a change of clothes. Hadn't thought about anything. She was going to sleep in the clothes she wore all day and then spend the day tomorrow with him.

Suddenly, that bothered her. And not because she didn't like being dirty, which she didn't, but because she didn't want to smell bad and be dirty and frumpy in front of him.

Which was ridiculous, because the man lived in a shack. He had nothing. Not even a car. Unless she counted the old beaters that sat in his driveway.

He didn't even have health insurance.

And yet, he had a kindness about him, a loyalty, a compassion when he spoke about how he helped Barry and how he wouldn't leave Barry but would take care of him until he died.

He had a sense of humor, and made her laugh, and challenged her at the same time.

He had...everything she wanted in a man, except money. She wanted a provider, but he would provide for his family. Wouldn't he?

She didn't know why she was thinking about that. She wasn't interested in a man who owned two pairs of clothes and was content to just...exist, apparently.

Except...maybe she was.

No, she told herself, it was just that he was so different from everyone else she knew. Of course that was attractive.

She used her phone light to find her way over to the bed, and as she sat down, she realized he was right. It wasn't much more than a glorified blanket. But she realized as she sat down that she was actually tired. She'd driven from Chicago, and that was after she had closed up her apartment and done everything that she needed to do in order to leave it for six weeks.

And the last six months had been stressful, dealing with everything including her parents' death.

She thought about that for a little bit. She wouldn't have thought that they could be gone so soon. It was so final. She hadn't had a chance to say goodbye, not that she and her parents were that close, but they were just a family unit. They were there. Maybe not unconditionally supportive, but still her mom and her dad.

Her mind had moved on to other things, and she was half asleep when she felt the boat rock again and then heard footsteps above her.

She wanted to call out his name, make sure it was him, but first of all, she didn't know his name, and second of all, if it was someone coming to steal something, she didn't want to alert them to the fact that she was down there. Just in case that would give them an idea of something else they could do besides steal.

"It's just me, in case you're still awake." His voice came softly down the hatch that he left open less than an hour ago. He must have done things really fast.

Maybe he could feel her anxiety and had done everything quickly, just so he could ease her mind.

"Thank you," she said. Not going into the big list of things that she was thanking him for. Least of all, coming back fast.

"Good night," he said.

"Good night."

Ten

The woman hadn't said whether she wanted Hobert to wake her up before he started in the morning, but he assumed that since she wanted to go along, she wouldn't want to miss anything. If he woke her up, she would have the option as to whether or not she wanted to go back to bed.

Hoping he was right, he got up from where he had lain on the deck of the boat, glanced at his watch, and saw that it was one fifty AM.

He grinned. The clock in his head was right on.

He had been able to do that since he'd been little. Set his head for a time and wake up at that time.

He didn't know anyone else who could do that, although he hardly thought that he was that unique. It wasn't like he met a lot of people.

And the woman, she...she knew everyone. A ton of people. He probably seemed like a backwoods hobo or something to her.

He did his regular pre-trip checks, wondering if maybe his footsteps above her and the shaking of the boat would wake her, but if it were him, the rocking of the boat would lull him into a deeper sleep. There wasn't too much he loved more than lying in the bunk while the boat was out on the lake, not in big waves, but big enough that it would make a normal person seasick. That was just about the way he liked it.

She hadn't gotten out by the time he was done and ready to start the motor, so he went over to the hatch, wondering if maybe he was looking forward to this day a little bit more than he should. He didn't have any pressure to catch a lot of fish. What he hadn't told the woman yesterday was after he had broken his leg, he had seen the wisdom of having a savings account and getting a little bit of money ahead.

He hadn't exactly been working himself to the bone to do that, but he had consciously tried to save a little more money and not give so much away.

Of course, Barry had money as well, and Hobert was pretty sure that he could have asked Barry when he broke his leg to help him out, and Barry would have.

But there were no guarantees in this business, and he might not be around when Barry needed him, and Barry might need that money to pay someone to take care of him.

However, he would have taken it if Barry offered.

At any rate, it wasn't necessary for him to be serious about fishing today, although he'd probably fish just like he did any other day. He could afford to take the time to show his guest whatever she wanted, and if she ended up wanting to take a ride down to Chicago and see the city from the water, they could do that too. He enjoyed looking at the sand dunes, since they were an unusual feature that a person typically only saw on the ocean.

Bending down, he said softly, "Lady? Lady, I told you I was going to get you up."

"What?" she said in a voice heavy with sleep, like she didn't quite know where she was.

"Lady, I'd use your name if I knew what it was."

That seemed to do it, because she said, "Oh. It must be two already?"

"Time flies when you're having fun," he said.

"I was sleeping," she said, sounding more like herself.

He laughed. "Not anymore. I just wanted to get you up. If you want to stay down there, that's totally up to you, but I'm going to close the hatch."

"No, I'm coming," she said, as though she were afraid to be down there with the hatch closed. He smiled a little. Maybe she was.

She came up quickly, like she didn't want to be down there any longer than she had to be and risk him shutting the hatch on her.

"You know I wouldn't shut that while you were down there if you didn't want me to, right?" he said as she scrambled up the steps, a little awkward because she was still trying to figure out where to put her hands and how to balance herself as she came up.

He had been on the boat so long that that was just second nature to him, and he couldn't even remember when he had to scramble for purchase.

Maybe he never did, because kids seemed to have better balance than adults did, which he was not going to mention to the lady, just in case they revived their competition of old versus young.

He couldn't believe how much fun he had with her yesterday. Just talking. They hadn't done anything. Other than him filleting fish and cooking them over the fire while she watched in admiration like she'd never seen anybody cook before.

And maybe, maybe she never had eaten fish that had been caught that day. There was something rather tasty about them, and adding the open fire made everything better.

At least in his opinion, but his opinion wasn't the one that mattered.

Except, her opinion wasn't supposed to matter to him either. If she was who he suspected she was, she probably wasn't going to talk to him after she found out his name.

He'd seen her plenty of times from a distance, and they'd even ridden the bus together until her family had moved away. To be perfectly honest, he wasn't exactly sure which sister she was.

Not that it mattered. Any of the three wasn't going to want to have anything to do with him.

He wasn't quite sure why.

"Is there anything I can do to help?" she asked as she stood on the deck, her hair flowing in all directions, the crease of the pillow still on her cheek.

Her clothes were rumpled, and he had to admit, he'd never seen anything more beautiful.

The glow of the moon on her just seemed to enhance the beauty that he'd seen yesterday in the glare of the sun.

"I mean, I know you do this all the time by yourself. But, just asking?"

"There's really nothing. I'm going to start the motor. I've already done my pre-trip inspection, making sure everything is good before we go. I also brought a life vest down, and I'll put it right here. I suggest you wear it at all times."

"You suggest... But you're not wearing one?"

"It's kind of hard to wear one while you're working."

"I see." She narrowed her eyes as though something had just occurred to her. "Technically, am I supposed to be on here?"

"I suppose technically, a commercial fishing boat is not supposed to have passengers, so yeah, I christen you first mate, for today."

"Just today? You mean I'm not welcome to come back?"

"Let's see how you do."

"Wow, he's tough."

"That's right. I can't hire just anyone. You want people who are conscientious about the job that they do."

She laughed. "All right. I'll put the life vest on. Where should I sit so I'm out of your way?"

"Come on up here, you can stand beside me at the wheel, if you want, or you could sit anywhere you can find a spot."

"I'm not going to get in the way somewhere?"

"No. If I need you to move, I'll let you know."

"All right. Can I follow you around and you explain what you're doing?"

"So, is this interest in commercial fishing new, or is this something you've always had and just haven't had a convenient stranger to pester about it?"

She laughed. "I've actually never had a convenient stranger to pester about anything, so I'm enjoying the opportunity."

"I would think Chicago would be filled with convenient strangers."

She was quiet for a bit, and then she said, "None of them are like you."

He wasn't sure what that meant, that he was an oddity? Was that good?

She seemed to be enjoying herself with him. After all, she was still there, and no one was making her.

Unless there was something she was avoiding. He really didn't keep up with the gossip of Raspberry Ridge, and even if he did, she hadn't been in town in so long that he didn't have a clue what was going on in her life, and he doubted that many people in Raspberry Ridge did either. Unless of course she wasn't who he thought she was.

The temptation to ask was strong, but he figured they'd wait until they were on their way home. Maybe after supper. Maybe she'd stay for supper, and he'd wait until after they ate.

He kept putting it off and putting it off. Because then he was thinking that maybe she'd go with him again tomorrow.

Something told him, the more she went, the lonelier his boat was going to be when she stayed on shore. And his boat had never been lonely. He'd always enjoyed it, even when Barry didn't come. He enjoyed having the old man along, but he had fun the first few times Barry had trusted him enough to go by himself, and then when he bought the boat, he had the opportunity to go alone whenever he liked. It...made him feel like a man.

He kept up a constant stream of explanations as he started the motor, untied his boat, and guided it out away from the harbor and into the lake.

"Do you have a certain place you go?"

"I fish all over. But yeah, some places are better than others, and then sometimes you just get lucky."

"Or blessed."

"Yeah. Although, some people have sonar, and they can tell if there are schools of fish below them."

"Can they tell what kind?"

"No. And they can't tell whether they're going to bite or not either, so there's a little bit of an advantage, but they can see a school of fish, stop to throw their lines out, and get nothing. Which is pretty much the same as me boating right over top of them."

"But they can throw their lines out and get all kinds of bites. So, it's kind of a tossup. A 50-50 chance?"

"Yeah. 50-50."

They talked some more until he motored out to a spot that was usually pretty good for him, and he threw his lines out, explaining to the woman exactly what he was doing as he did it.

"And now?" she asked as his fourth line hit the water and he put the rod in its holder.

"Now we wait," he said, nodding to the bench and then going and sitting down, his arms crossed over his chest and his legs stretched out in front of him.

He already explained to her how he knew that there was a bite, and she shrugged her shoulders, knowing that nothing was moving yet.

"So you have whole days when you don't catch anything?" she asked.

"I do. Not a ton, but it happens."

"That must be so discouraging and disgusting."

"Why? I get to sit here. Under the stars."

She was looking at him, not at the sky. And he didn't know why she would be, because the sky was where it was at. The Milky Way stretched the whole way across, with bright stars on either side, twinkling down.

"Wow."

"They're there all the time. You just never get to see them."

"All right, another advantage to living in the country versus the city. You don't have to tell me that. I definitely wouldn't mind seeing this every night, except my apartment isn't exactly conducive to stargazing."

"No windows?" he asked, surprised.

"Oh, there are windows. But they look out, not up, and it isn't easy to get outside, even if I could see anything through the lights of the city."

They sat in silence for a little bit, and then she stirred, almost as though she were getting sleepy.

He figured maybe he'd try to pick up where they left off yesterday. So he said, "The older you get, the better stories you have to tell."

It took her a second, as she sat there, not saying anything, her mouth open.

"Oh!" She laughed. "That's actually true."

"I know."

"He is so humble. I think it's the early morning hour that does it, just brings out that humility that lurks under the surface at all times."

He laughed. "I can't pretend to be modest when I know I'm right."

"Yeah. False modesty is not a good look on anyone."

"You are the queen of stalling."

"No, I think you're just trying to press your advantage because you're used to being up at this hour in the morning, while I am not."

"Haven't you ever been up at three o'clock in the morning?" he asked. The sound of the waves lapping at the edge of the boat was familiar and relaxing. He loved that sound. Loved the soft shake of the boat, the early morning hour while it was still dark out, the lake shimmering with the stars, and somehow it was better with this woman beside him. He hadn't thought until this point that he was lonely or that he needed companionship. But maybe he was and he didn't notice it, because everything seemed better with her beside him.

The morning didn't seem as dreary. He woke up with more energy, and he realized he hadn't even made coffee.

"You can eat whatever you want and not get fat."

"That's not true for everybody when they're young."

"Did you have issues?"

He shook his head, not saying that he'd never had so much to eat that getting fat could have been an option.

"Me, either."

"I'll give it to you, because it's mostly true."

"It's true for the majority of people."

They didn't argue about it anymore, and he said, "I forgot to make coffee. You want some?"

"I would love to have some, although how much can your bathroom down there hold?"

"It'll be fine." He grinned.

"Just checking. I didn't want to sink the boat or anything."

"Well, trust me, I definitely don't want you to sink the boat either.

But that would be more like don't drill a hole in the side of the hold or anything."

"Oh. So I'm not supposed to pound nails in the floor?"

"That's right. Very good."

"Maybe you shouldn't trust me?"

He laughed. "I'm going to trust you to keep an eye on things while I make coffee. You'll have to let me know if there's any action up here. After all, you're the first mate, and you need to do something to earn your paycheck."

"I'm getting a paycheck?" she said, looking excited.

"If we catch fish. If we don't, you just have the pleasure of my company for a day."

"You don't have to pay me. I was kidding. But I will keep an eye on things."

Eleven

Hobert shook his head as he disappeared down the steps, taking his time to make coffee and trying to do a halfway decent job at it. He didn't really care what it tasted like. He just drank it to get the caffeine, but he thought that she might be a little bit more picky than he was, so he spent some time working on it and then came up with two mugs.

"It's a good thing I accidentally left a cup on board the other day. Because normally I only have one cup."

"You should have Styrofoam cups," she said.

"I try not to use anything that's disposable. I mean, I can't get away with not having any garbage. Obviously, I need something to put the coffee grounds in. But the less trash to take off the boat, the better."

She nodded. "I hadn't thought of that."

He sat down, blew a little on the top of the coffee, and then just held it in his hand. He didn't like it when it was so hot it burned his mouth going in. That's how Barry drank it, and he thought the man must not have pain sensors or something.

"You have enough years to learn to like yourself." He started playing their game again, and she caught on right away.

"Is that true?"

"Well, let's put it this way, you have more years to try to turn yourself into someone that you like."

"Okay. That makes sense. Although, I don't know if I like myself better now than I did when I was younger. I've turned into what I wanted, but...I don't know if I like that."

"You have a chance to change it. Every day is a chance. You make a choice every single day, multiple times sometimes."

"That's true." She grew silent for a bit. "So Barry is not your dad. Is your dad still alive?"

"No."

"What happened?" she asked.

"What about your parents?" he countered, figuring that was fair.

"Six months ago, they died in a car accident. Instantly killed, both of them, when Dad ran a stoplight, and a tractor-trailer coming the other way hit Mom's side of the car, pushed it across the intersection at an angle, and a car coming the other way T-boned Dad's side."

"Ouch."

"Yeah. I'm... I spent some time the last six months cleaning out their condo."

He noticed that she didn't mention any other family, and he wondered again if maybe he was wrong about her being one of the Jardine sisters.

"That's a hard job."

"It was. Although, I spent my high school years in their condo, but it didn't hold the memories that you have when you're little, you know?"

"Yeah." He knew all about memories when a kid was little. His were a little bitter.

Maybe a little angry too.

"And your parents?"

"My mom left right after I was born. I never knew her. Maybe she's around, maybe she's not, but I realized that she didn't want me, obviously, she was able to walk away from me, so...there's that."

He hated that he had to talk about his family. Hers had been so perfect. Two parents, a neat car accident, and they're gone, and yeah, that was sad, but it wasn't sad like not being good enough for his mom.

Except he knew that wasn't the case. It wasn't his fault that she didn't stay. There wasn't something lacking in him as a baby. It was his mom's lack of character.

Maybe, maybe he had gone through so much effort to take care of Barry because he wanted to make sure that the lack of character wasn't inherited.

"And your dad?" she prompted.

He realized he hadn't finished. "My dad was an alcoholic. That shack that you were in last night is where I grew up with him. He really didn't amount to much. I'm not even sure what he did. Sat around and drank a lot. Worked enough to buy booze. And, I don't know, fifteen years ago, thirteen, something like that, he fell down and broke his hip. Went to the hospital and never came out."

"That's terrible."

"Yeah. Pretty big bill to pay over that."

"No. Losing your dad."

He knew he sounded a little bitter. Maybe he was. Why couldn't his dad have been a little more responsible? Why did he have to become an alcoholic? And of course, Hobert knew that people didn't make those choices. He didn't choose to be an alcoholic. He didn't choose to be a terrible dad, it was just little choices that he made that allowed him to sink further and further and further until there wasn't much further to sink.

"He really wasn't much of a dad. I was angry for a long time."

"And you're still angry?"

She could probably tell.

"Sometimes. When I forget what Jesus has done for me. When I live in my flesh. When I think about how my childhood could have been a lot different if my parents had made different decisions. But then, I remember that I'm flesh just like they are. And I've made mistakes too. Plenty of them, and lots of dumb ones. I just don't happen to have a kid who's affected by them. Not yet anyway. But someday I will, and I suppose I'm going to want him to look at me, know I'm not perfect, and forgive me anyway. You know?"

"And have you?"

"I think so. I don't wish ill on them. And I suppose if my mom came back and apologized, I'd be okay with it."

"But she has to apologize?"

"That's a good question. I often wonder about that. After all, as far as I know, she's not sorry for what she did. Birthing me and then abandoning me. I... Most of the time, I know that is not in my hands, you know? I have to forgive her and give it to the Lord. It's not an easy thing to think about, and I'll probably always have some scars from my childhood, but if it hadn't been for Jesus, I would be in a lot worse shape."

"Really? You seem so responsible."

"I think that's the way a lot of kids of alcoholics are. You know, the parents can't keep it together, so they have to."

"Now it makes sense," she said, like she figured him out. Maybe she had. "That's why you're so resistant to the big job in the city, the idea of working for a living, of having more than what you need, all of that, is because you're afraid you'll become a workaholic, because that's what your true nature is, after growing up with your dad the way he was."

He tilted his head, trying her logic on, running it through his mind. "You're probably right. It's a deliberate step that I take to keep myself from overachieving. Not that I think overachievers are terrible, it's just what I do, because...I was never good enough."

"So you said."

"I don't believe that anymore. I mean, Jesus loves me. And that's the only thing that matters. Even if my parents didn't, or they didn't know how to show it, or whatever the popular excuses are anymore. I just... know that I can't allow their mistakes to ruin my life. And since I know that I have tendencies, I can try to combat them."

"It's pretty impressive how well you turned out."

He was going to say something to counteract what she said, but just then, he had a bite on two lines at once.

"We'll reel them in, and you can see what it's like to land a fish, hopefully."

"Could they be salmon?" she asked with excitement in her voice.

"I don't know," he said, laughing.

After that, his fishing lines were busy for an entire hour, and she got to the point where she could almost help him, bending over the edge and using the net to grab the fish, but she didn't volunteer to take any hooks out.

She would, however, take the fish that he had caught and throw it in the refrigerated hold once he had gotten the line free. Which might have saved him a few seconds anyway. He could cross the boat much faster in his rubber boots than she could in her flip-flops, but he was free to immediately start baiting the line and throwing it back in.

And then, just as fast as it had started, it was over. And things were quiet again.

The sun had just started to lighten up the eastern horizon, and he took a minute to enjoy it before she came over and stood beside him following his gaze.

"You know, I don't know how long it's been since I've seen the sunrise?" she asked softly.

"That's too bad. In Chicago, it would rise over the water."

"I know. It's probably gorgeous, but I never once, in all the years I've lived there, not a single time, watched it."

"You missed a lot of beautiful ones. I can tell you that."

"You probably see it every day."

"Pretty often," he agreed.

"Is that how it usually goes? Frantic activity followed by bouts of doing nothing?"

"Yeah. Some days, I burn a little more fuel than others trying to find a good spot, but I pretty much learned that burning fuel and running here and there isn't really more profitable than just chugging along, hoping to find a good spot and throttling down when you do."

"So maybe that's where sonar would come in handy? If you find a school of fish that are biting, you could use your sonar to follow them and continue to see where they're going so you can continue to catch them."

"Yeah. I suppose I could. Would I sound weird if I say that sounds a little bit like cheating? Like going hunting at night with night vision goggles or something."

She smiled. "I suppose it does give you an unnatural advantage.

Although, you could argue that the boat is an unnatural advantage as well."

"That's true. It could be an unnatural advantage, since man wasn't really made to be on the water. Except, the Bible does have that one instance of a boat, ark, being built. Then of course the disciples were fishermen, and they used boats, so I would say whether it's an unfair advantage or not, it's sanctioned by God."

"All right, you got me beat on that one."

"I'm all about beating you. You're so competitive."

"I am kind of competitive. And yet, I wouldn't say that I was being competitive just now."

"Well, it's okay. I like you anyway, and I won't throw you overboard just because you can't stand to lose."

"That's a relief. I guess I should have asked to read the fine print before I agreed to go."

"There's always some tricky language in the fine print."

And that's the way their day went. They had a few more times of frantic fish biting, a few more times of sitting around, and a few times of a bite here and there.

She seemed to enjoy herself, and it was on the tip of his tongue to ask her to come back.

But he didn't, because... He wasn't sure why. Maybe he figured they had to get through the exchange of names before that happened.

Finally, around three in the afternoon when things had been quiet for an hour, he said, "You ready to head back?"

"Are we taking the catch to the dock?"

"Yeah. I think I'll take them to Blueberry Beach. I checked earlier, and it seems like that would be the most cost-effective thing to do. We caught more than I thought we're going to get."

"Did you think that having me along was going to slow you down?"

"Maybe. I don't know. Sometimes you just spend a lot of time explaining things and not as much time doing things, but you caught on pretty quickly and we were able to go at a good pace when the fish were biting."

"I think he just said I was a help."

"I'll have to give you your share," he said as he turned the boat around and headed for the dock.

He stood at the wheel, since they were going a bit faster than they had been, and thought about whether he wanted to ask now, or whether he wanted to wait. The drive between Blueberry Beach and Raspberry Ridge wasn't long, and he thought that maybe it wasn't enough time to ask what he wanted to, so he decided that now was probably the time. But he hated so much to ruin what was between them. Maybe if their lives had been different, if she wasn't a bigwig in Chicago, and he was not a dirt-poor fisherman living in a shanty along Lake Michigan, maybe they could have found some middle ground and had a natural relationship.

Though he hadn't even asked, maybe she had a boyfriend in Chicago.

If so, the boyfriend hadn't called her at all, since as far as he knew, her phone hadn't rung all day, except for one text she had gotten which she said was from her sister.

So she had at least one sister. There were three sisters in the Jardine family.

"I'm Hobert Gilcrest," he said and waited for her reaction.

Twelve

Amara was shocked. Her heart felt like it was going to leap out of her chest, and she wanted to be angry. To say, *why did you deceive me like that?* But he had a politely curious look on his face, like he was waiting for her to return the favor.

How could he have done this to her? How could he have made her like him so much before she found out who he was?

But then she remembered, she didn't have to listen to her mother anymore. In fact, her mother was gone. And while, for the most part, she wanted to honor her mother's wishes, she didn't have to dislike someone just because of their name.

Of course, he might have a reaction to *her* name. Maybe there was something on both sides, and her mother told them not to talk to him because she was afraid that he would be unkind to them because he was angry at them for some reason.

Although Amara had no idea what that reason could be.

"I take it you recognize it?" he finally said.

"I do. I'm Amara Jardine. I'm the youngest of the Jardine sisters."

"I kinda thought you were one of them. So I was close, but I couldn't have said which one you were."

"How did you know?"

"I saw you guys on the bus when we were in school. I got on first, since I was clear at the end of the route. The bus had to turn around and then go back into Raspberry Ridge before it went out to Blueberry Beach. I was on about fifteen minutes before everybody else. It was pretty early."

"You probably had to get yourself up, if your dad was an alcoholic?"

"Yeah."

He didn't say anything more, and she remembered what he had said about children of alcoholics often needing to be responsible beyond their age.

"My mom told us that we weren't allowed to talk to you."

"I figured there was some kind of problem there. I...noticed that you guys didn't return my greeting, anytime I spoke with you. It didn't take too long for me to quit trying. You're not the only ones who wouldn't talk to me."

"Do you think it was just because..." She hated to say it. She didn't want to rub it in.

"My dad was an alcoholic? That was a good reason for a lot of people. That we were poor white trash? That was another good reason. I...didn't always have shoes to wear. So sometimes I wore my dad's shoes to school. I looked ridiculous when I was a kid, but you could hardly go to school barefoot."

"I can't believe the teachers didn't report you."

"I had a couple who pulled me aside and asked what was going on, and I said that I had donated my shoes to a little boy who didn't have any, because I felt so bad for him, but that my family was fine."

"You lied."

"Apparently the children of alcoholics learn to lie pretty easily and early."

"But..." She wanted to say that she had thought that he was honest.

"Maybe I try to make up for that now, because it's kind of the way I try to counter my drive to achieve. By deliberately... I hate to say not allowing myself, but you know what I mean."

"You know what, I think that's true. You don't allow yourself to live up to your potential."

"Or maybe I just like my life the way it is. Maybe I don't want to take the risk of having more and turning to alcohol, like my dad did."

"Is that what he did?"

"I have no idea. He never told me. He took the secret to the grave, along with some other ones. Like why your family won't talk to me."

"I thought you said there were a lot of people who wouldn't talk to you? Although... My parents just really weren't the kind of people who hated people just because they didn't have a lot."

"Yeah, I don't know. It did seem like you guys were a little extra, but like I said, there were a lot of people who wouldn't talk to me."

"I'm sorry," she said.

"I was too afraid to tell you my name because I thought that maybe that would change things, and you'd remember that you weren't supposed to be talking to me."

"No. I don't know why my mom told us we weren't allowed to talk to you, but she forbade it. And there wasn't anyone else in the world that we were forbidden to talk to, other than you."

"It sounds like something major."

"I always wondered what it was. You don't have any idea?"

"My dad made enemies. Maybe it has something to do with that, but I don't know how we'd figure it out."

"Maybe Barry would know?"

"He might. For being on the docks all the time, he sure knew a lot of the gossip from Raspberry Ridge, and he probably has some stories he hasn't told, like what he did before he started fishing."

"Maybe he'll tell them to us sometime."

"I asked once about his wife, and he told me when I was older, he would tell me, but I never asked again."

"Interesting. Maybe it's too painful for him to talk about."

"That's kinda what I figured, and I figured I didn't need to know."

Amara thought maybe it really was just because her mom felt like they were beneath him. That his dad was an alcoholic and she didn't want her daughters around a man like that. Maybe she was afraid he would be abusive.

"Just another twenty minutes until we make it to Blueberry Beach. If you're hungry, there's a good diner there, and we can eat if you'd like."

Amara glanced over at him, standing at the wheel, watching where they were going, keeping his eye on the compass. And she really wanted to say yes to eating. To spending more time with him. But she knew he wasn't exactly well-off, and she didn't want him wasting money on her. Not when she wasn't going to stay around. As much as she loved Raspberry Ridge, as much as she loved spending time with Hobert, now that she knew who he was, it didn't make a difference, but...she wasn't going to stay.

"I think maybe we should just go straight home."

He nodded, his face impassive, still looking out over the ocean.

They must have ridden for another ten minutes before he spoke again.

"Are you gonna tell me the real reason you went with me today?"

She pressed her lips together. She hadn't thought he was going to jump her about that. Or that she was going to have to answer for it. But she didn't see any reason why she should hide the truth.

"My parents passed away in a car accident six months ago, I told you that."

"Yeah. I know."

"So I got in yesterday. My sisters were both supposed to come too. I took six weeks of vacation time, and it was supposed to coincide with them being able to come, but I don't even know when they're going to be here. One is stuck in Ecuador, and Mertie hates coming back to Raspberry Ridge for some reason. I'm not sure why."

Actually, she had some suspicions about that. Mertie had some secrets that people in Raspberry Ridge might be able to uncover, and it could possibly affect her position as a prominent national Christian author and speaker.

Not that Amara really thought it would. The things that Mertie had done were far back in the past, except, sometimes the past had a way of coming out and haunting a person.

"And?" he prompted her.

"And the house felt... I don't know. I didn't want to go in. It just felt like the past was going to come down and strangle me. Which I know sounds dramatic, but I was really grateful to have this distraction."

"Do you think you're going to be able to go back?" he asked, and she appreciated the fact that he was concerned for her, even though she turned him down for lunch. Maybe she should explain why. That it wasn't because of him, or anything that he had done, or any problem on his part at all, other than she just didn't want him to waste his limited amount of money on her. But despite that, he still cared.

"I really appreciate that you care."

"You sidestepped my question," he pointed out with a wry grin in her direction.

"I don't know." Every time she thought about it, she had anxiety ballooning up in her chest. She didn't want to go back. She would much rather go on the boat with him indefinitely and even sleep on the boat, and...if she didn't shower, she didn't even think she'd care. She just didn't want to be left alone in that house.

"You want to stick around with me, you know you can."

He said it casually, like he didn't really care, but she kinda thought that...maybe he wanted her. Or maybe he felt like he was stretching his neck out again, and she'd already rejected him.

"I would like to. That would be my preference. But I think I need to be a big girl about this. An adult. I need to go face the fact that I have to walk into that house and face my past. No matter how painful it is. It just... I need to do it."

"You don't have to do it alone. If you want me to, I can walk up with you today, and we can do it together."

She wanted to. She was so tempted to say yes right away, but...what happened to the marketing exec who had climbed the ladder faster than anyone else her age and now had a private office of her own? The competitive woman who didn't let anything stand in her way when she was working toward a goal?

That was different. That was...work. It didn't matter like this did. Maybe work was easier than real life.

"I know you're tired." It wasn't an answer. And she knew it.

"I wouldn't have offered if I thought I couldn't handle it, if I was too tired, or if I didn't want to. But if you don't want me, you can just say so. I...understand if it's something you need to do on your own. But if it's something you want a friend to help you with, I'll do it."

Hobert Gilcrest was her friend. That thought sank down in a shocking way. Piercing into her conscience.

The man her parents had forbidden her to talk to was now her friend. The one offering to walk into her childhood home with her.

"Please. I'd appreciate it if you'd come."

Thirteen

Amara had no sooner said those words than Hobert felt the wheel shake under his hand, then the motor sputtered and died.

Amara turned panicked eyes to his.

"Relax. We're okay. The battery will be good for hours, so if we need to call someone, we can. But most likely, I can fix this. It just might take...more time than I'd like."

"What about the fish?" she asked, concern bringing her brows together, which warmed his heart. Why should she care about the fish? Unless she cared about him.

Hobert had thought when he told her who he was, she would freeze their relationship immediately, but she surprised him. Although, the more time he spent with her, the more he hoped that would be her reaction. That she wouldn't just hate someone because her parents told her to.

He liked that she had a brain and she used it herself. As she was able to think for herself and not be blinded by the prejudices of someone else.

That to Amara, character and integrity mattered more than some fuzzy thing in the past that no one knew about.

"They'll be fine as long as we don't open the hatch. Of course eventually they'll go bad, but they'll stay cold in there for a while. And they should be fine. If it takes me...a long time to fix it, that's a different story."

"A long time?"

"Six hours," he said. "It depends on how many fish are in the hold, what the temperature was when the cooling unit shut off, and a lot of different things. I believe regulations state the fish have to be chilled below forty degrees within an hour after they're caught. But I have to check the boat to make sure."

"I see."

She probably had no idea there were regulations about those types of things. But he had checked the temperature of the hold and logged it hourly as he was required to do.

"So you're able to work on a motor?" she said. "Or is it something else?"

He liked that she wasn't afraid to ask him. That he didn't present a grumpy exterior that made her afraid to talk to him.

"I think it's most likely the motor." He didn't mention that this happened a couple of times, and he did a temporary fix each time, putting off the more expensive motor overhaul that he knew was coming.

"Do you have tools?" she asked as he moved from the wheel and opened the hatch to down below where there was a panel he could remove to work on the motor.

"I do. Underneath that hard bed you slept on last night."

"I knew there had to be something lumpy under there."

"I think she's a princess after all. After all, if she can feel the tools underneath her bed, surely she could feel a pea as well."

"So you're familiar with fairy tales."

"Just because I was raised a little unconventionally doesn't mean I'm not familiar with what everyone else in the world knows, although...I suppose there are probably gaps in my education."

He felt that a lot, like he was missing out and had to guess what was normal for everyone else. As he got older, he realized that everyone had had a mostly different upbringing. Maybe people had TV shows in common, or music, or other things like that, but pretty much everyone had school in common. And while it hadn't been his favorite thing to do, he understood the value of a good education thanks to Barry, and he'd done okay. Not missing class on purpose the way some kids did. Sometimes he didn't figure that kids understood exactly how blessed they were, how nice it would be to come from a two-parent home where your parents cared about you, and you didn't have to fight feelings of inadequacy and worthlessness.

Of course, until a person lived it, how could they know? Unless they read a book about it, but even then, it was hard to feel the actual feelings if you didn't actually walk in someone's shoes.

To his surprise, Amara had followed him down the hatch and watched as he rolled up the mattress and took the lid off the bed which was actually a chest, with his tools and flares and other things he might need on the boat.

Once he had pulled out the things that he needed, he put the lid back on and knelt on that while he removed the panel from behind the bed area.

"I never could figure out why they put the bed right beside the motor compartment. Makes it pretty loud when a person is trying to sleep while the boat is running."

"Maybe it was so you'd wake up if someone stole your boat," Amara said easily.

"I hope I would wake up before that," he said.

But he supposed she was right, although he highly doubted the builders had that in mind.

Regardless, she stayed down with him, using her phone as a light so he didn't have to use the light and drain the battery.

He smiled a little, since she seemed very concerned about saving enough battery to make sure they could be rescued.

He could have reminded her that as long as her phone had battery, they could make a call. And they had his as well.

It took him an hour, but he was able to rig things together enough that he thought that he could limp the boat to Blueberry Beach and off-load their cargo before he took it home.

"I think we can go ahead and try to start it."

"Do you want me to do that?" she asked, and while he didn't really need her to, he thought it would make her feel useful, so he said, "If you don't mind. I'd appreciate it."

"All right. I watched you do it a couple of times, and all you have to do is push that black button, right?"

"Turn the key on first."

"Yeah. I forgot."

It didn't take much time at all for her to go up on the deck, twist the key, push the button, and the motor...it didn't fire right up, but it choked and coughed a couple of times, and he held his breath until it caught and then started humming like it was supposed to.

He grabbed a rag from where he kept them under the sink and started wiping his hands and then wiping his tools off before he put the panel back on and latched it, and then remade the bed.

He didn't know what Amara was going to do tonight. If she was going to stay in her big lonely mansion all by herself, or if she'd rather sleep on his boat.

He liked the idea of her sleeping on his boat, but whatever she chose, he wanted the bed to be ready for her in case she chose to stay, so he made sure that it was neatly made, mattress stretched back out over the top of the lid, before he turned around to walk up.

He hadn't heard her come back down, and he was surprised to find her standing on the floor beside the ladder.

"Everything good?" she asked as he stopped, surely looking surprised to see her. Even though he knew she was on the boat.

"It sure is. Thanks for your help."

"You can hardly call it help, but thanks for letting me have something to do with my hands so I didn't feel so entirely useless it was pathetic."

"If I were to go to your office building, I'd be standing around feeling useless and pathetic, so don't feel bad."

"Actually, I think you could do whatever you want to do. There's nothing stopping you."

"Thanks, but you know I'm doing what I want to do." She acted like there was something else he should be aspiring to, and there really wasn't.

Yeah, sometimes it was tempting to buy a new boat, buy new

equipment, upgrade everything, but it was like he had told her, he would have to work harder and longer in order to pay for it all. He would have the pressure of catching more fish, when now, he had the luxury of not being stressed out if he didn't have a full hold when he went to sell it at the end of the day.

But maybe having a woman like Amara beside him would make him feel like the risk was worth it for them to build a life together.

He supposed he hadn't really thought about that.

"Yeah. I know." She said it kind of slowly, and then she said, "I guess I just feel like maybe you think that because of the way you were raised, that this was all there was for you. And you know you're better than your father, right?"

"Took me a little while to figure out that it was his choices that led him to be the way he was," he said and then started up the ladder. "And my choices will determine the way I am. I have choices to make every day. I think sometimes we think life is going to be one big choice that's going to determine everything, but most of the time, there are a few choices like that in life. Most of the time, it's the hundreds of different choices we make every day, all day long."

"The choice to get up and go to work at two AM or roll over and go back to sleep."

"Exactly. That's a little choice you make, and you make it every day. Every day that you make the right choice, it strengthens your character just a little bit and leads you on the road to doing the right thing."

She looked like she was thinking about that, like she was thinking about the choices that she made every day, possibly in her normal life back in Chicago.

Or maybe she was thinking about her choice to go with him today. Instead of staying in her childhood home and cleaning out the mansion.

He personally felt like she made a good choice, but he could see the argument that she should have done what she was supposed to do, rather than avoiding it and being with someone she didn't even know.

They didn't have any more issues and pulled into Blueberry Beach a little more than five minutes later.

"I didn't realize we were so close to it."

"We could almost see it, from where we were," he said. He took care of the things that he needed to, unloading the fish and waiting while they weighed them and determined how much his catch for the day was worth. They used the going rate on the open market, minus the commission.

Still, even though they didn't get held up at all, it was almost two hours before they were back out on the water heading toward home.

Fourteen

By the time they left Blueberry Beach, Amara was wishing that she had said yes to him when he asked her if she wanted to eat.

Her stomach growled loudly just as she was thinking about that, and she put a hand over it and laughed self-consciously. "I'm sorry."

"So she's hungry after all," he said.

"Aren't you?"

"I am. But you said you didn't want anything, so I wasn't going to go get something for myself."

"You should have said something, because by the time you were done with everything, I was starving and wishing I had said yes."

"Well, they have a really good diner up in Strawberry Sands. Do you want to stop there on our way home?"

"Sure," she said without hesitating that time.

"You made that decision fast," he said, teasing her.

She accepted it gracefully. She tried to, because he was right. She had really jumped on that.

They were still grinning when they pulled into the dock just south of Strawberry Sands.

"We have a little bit of a walk. Hopefully that's okay."

"Sure. It'll be nice to stretch my legs after being on the boat all day. I...didn't really think about it until just now, but it's a little cramped."

"Yeah. You can't really stretch out, but it wasn't intended to be a place to exercise. It's a place to work."

"And enjoy the lake," she reminded him.

His eyes sparkled as he finished tying the boat to the dock. "That's exactly right. I'm glad you remembered."

"Do you forget sometimes?" she asked as he jumped off the boat and then turned around to give her a hand.

It was hard to believe she'd only known him for twenty-four hours, because she felt so familiar with him. It...felt like they'd known each other a lot longer. Maybe because of their shared history in Raspberry Ridge.

"Sometimes. Sometimes I start thinking I want more. Want something bigger and better, and I forget that in order to have that, I have to sell my soul."

"You could save up your money and buy it."

"Yeah, I have a little nest egg now, but after I broke my leg, it made me realize that at this stage, anything I have shouldn't be spent on luxuries but saved for the time when I really need it."

"I can't disagree about that," she said, although she had no nest egg to speak of. "Maybe that's your wisdom that comes with age," she said as they walked off the dock side by side.

"What do you mean?" he asked, looking down at her as they stepped onto the dirt road and headed toward Strawberry Sands.

"Just that when I first got this job, I used all of my salary to rent an apartment and buy a car, and now I have payments that I'm locked into, and...I feel like I have to keep working in order to keep up with my lifestyle, and I think the next time I get a raise, that's what I'll put in my savings account, but it seems like I get a raise and I have an unexpected bill, or something else I see that I just absolutely need and—"

"Your bills expand to eat up all of your paycheck."

"Yeah. Or most of it. I don't even understand how it happens."

"I can see how easy that would be. I don't have much of a paycheck, so I can't allow my bills to expand that much. That, and it's so unpredictable. I can't really tell what I'm going to make from day to day."

She nodded, and they followed the road around the bend. A rabbit hopped across in front of them. A bird flew out of a bush beside them, startling her.

She didn't exactly jump, although she did swerve just a bit, and her arm bumped into his.

Somehow their fingers touched, and she wasn't sure whether it was him, or whether it was her, but they melded together, and as she straightened her steps, their fingers connected between the two of them.

"I...didn't exactly mean to do that. I'm sorry," she said after glancing down at their hands and looking back up at him. Notably, she made no move to remove her fingers from his.

"I didn't mind," Hobert said, and then his dimple winked at her again as his eyes sparkled. "You don't have to apologize."

She grinned back. "I felt a little bad like you might have thought I did it on purpose, but I promise I didn't."

"It would have been even better if you'd have done it on purpose."

His eyes held hers for just a moment as her stomach swirled slowly. This was...unexpected. And inconvenient. She was only going to be here for six weeks. A friend, yes. Something more, she really couldn't.

But they were holding hands now, and his hand felt strong and capable, and it made her feel like he was someone she could depend on. Someone she could lean on when she needed to. There was no shame in leaning on someone sometimes. The Lord gave fellow humans to walk the path of life with a person.

They didn't say anything more as they continued to walk along the dirt road. And soon the town of Strawberry Sands came into view.

"Griff owns the diner, and he almost always has some kind of strawberry special going on, plus he's an excellent cook."

"Oh really?" she said. "How do you know?"

"Not that long ago, maybe a year or so, my boat broke down when I wasn't far from Strawberry Sands. After I spent six hours working on it, I finally got it going, and I probably should have gone straight home, but the town looked so inviting, and I was hoping I could find something to eat there. Barry had taken one of his rare trips to go see relatives on the East Coast, and I knew there wasn't going to be anything waiting for me at home, and I hadn't saved any fish back because I thought I was going to be home in plenty of time to make something."

She felt bad that he was all alone, but before she could say anything, he continued.

"I ended up stopping, and I found Griff's. It was so good, I stopped several times since, and he's always had something really delicious. Plus, he's a nice guy."

"A nice guy," she said, slanting her eyes over at him and wondering what kind of man Hobert considered a nice guy.

"You can tell me if I'm wrong after you try his food."

He opened the door, and she walked in the diner, bells jingling over her head as she did.

She glanced around. There was a sign that said "seat yourself," and she glanced back at Hobert with her eyebrows raised, asking if he had a preference.

She didn't need to say anything; he seemed to know what she meant as he shrugged his shoulders and said, "Wherever you want."

She chose a booth by the window and slid into it.

He slid into the other side, and she again thought about how odd it was that they just met, yet she felt like she knew him better almost than she knew her friends in Chicago. Definitely better than she knew coworkers she'd been with for years. He was just so easy to talk to and get along with.

The waitress came, took their drink orders, and told them that the special was Marry Me Chicken.

After they both said they'd take the special, she winked and said, "Be careful, because it's been known to get more than a few people hitched in a very short amount of time." She sashayed away.

Amara widened her eyes as she laughed. "Well, good luck with that, since I work in Chicago, and I have zero plans of commuting back and forth to Raspberry Ridge. That's almost three hours of driving, one way, and it's just not gonna happen." She laughed some more, to keep her comments light. "And I know you're not moving to Chicago."

There. She said it. Sure, she held his hand, but nothing else was going to happen. They were just friends.

"You know, sometimes life has a funny way of turning things on their side, and things you never thought were possible end up happening."

It made her uncomfortable that he didn't agree with her. He was supposed to laugh and say *yeah, maybe in the next life, it would be nice,* or just something silly and impossible. And a nod at the idea that they liked and respected each other, but nothing more.

He didn't know how to play that game apparently, or maybe she knew how to play it too well.

Regardless, there wasn't much idle chitchat between the two of them as they waited for their food.

Amara had to admit though, it was the best thing she'd ever eaten. It was so good, and apparently the waitress had said that Hobert was there, or maybe Griff just made it a point to come out and talk to people, because they weren't finished with their meals when Griff and his wife came out and greeted Hobert like he was a long-lost friend.

"It's been a while since we saw you. I was hoping you hadn't hung it up. I know some fishermen who have. It's not an easy way to make a living," Griff said, holding his hand out for Hobert to shake.

"It's not. But it's definitely the best way for me. I suppose I won't be hanging it up until I don't have a choice." He nodded across the table. "This is Amara. Amara, this is my friend Griff and his wife, Chi."

Chi said, "It's so nice to meet you. It's really fun when Hobert stops in. He always has some tale or another, and he keeps inviting us up to Raspberry Ridge, but we haven't quite made it up yet."

Griff grinned at her. "Someday."

They nodded at each other, and after chatting for a bit more, they moved to another table and chatted with some other patrons.

"Was I right?" Hobert said a little while later as he held the door open so she could walk out of the restaurant.

"You're right. It was definitely worth the stop. In fact, it makes me want to come back."

"They serve different things on different days, so I can't guarantee the Marry Me Chicken again, although I'm not sure it's going to have any effect on us."

She almost said *I hope not*, but that wouldn't have been quite true. It would be nice if the Marry Me Chicken truly had some kind of magical powers that made all of the obstacles between a couple disappear and made it easy for them to make a decision to fall in love and get married.

"Effect?" she asked, thinking she knew what he meant, but somehow wanting to make sure.

"To make us fall in love?" Hobert asked easily as they started walking down the sidewalk.

She wasn't quite sure when it happened, but his fingers had wrapped around hers and laced together.

She liked it and didn't try to pull away. Although it made her a little sad.

"I think so. I mean, there's attraction, which isn't really something you make a decision about, but love? Yeah. The Bible clearly commands us to love people, so we must have the ability to make a decision about it."

"Or to make the decision to not," he suggested.

She nodded, thinking about that. "Maybe the way your mother decided not to love you. It wasn't your fault, it was hers. She made that decision."

"Yeah. And I guess it was up to me to make the decision to not allow that to determine the trajectory of the rest of my life. It took me a long time to figure that out."

"Children don't have the same ability to reason that adults do. They just see things from a different perspective. And process them differently as well."

"Yeah. I suppose the thing I've worked the hardest on is forgiveness though. Forgiving her, and maybe dealing with my anger and bitterness. We talked a little bit about it. It's just that it clouds up your mind, takes over your life, and you'll be a nasty, terrible person if you allow that. And you have to make the decision to not."

"So many times we can control our actions by our thoughts."

"That's right. I had to start thinking about my mother in different terms. Maybe she had some kind of issue. Maybe there was some reason she couldn't keep me. Or maybe she just was selfish and immature. I've made stupid decisions because of my selfishness and immaturity, so I have to be willing to forgive her for making decisions because of the same thing. Right?"

"Yeah. That's a good point."

They didn't talk much as they made it back to the boat, and he helped her back inside, and it wasn't long at all until they made it back to the dock at Raspberry Ridge.

"Do you mind if we go check on Barry?"

"Not at all." She took a couple of steps on the dock before she said, "You don't have to come up if you don't want to. I know I said that it was going to be hard, and that hasn't changed, but I think I've given myself enough of a mind change that I can handle it if you don't want to come. I know you're probably tired."

"I'm a little tired. As I'm sure you are, but I'm not hungry anymore, so I'm good if you are."

"All right. Let's go check on Barry and then walk up."

He took her hand again, and that time, she did notice, but she might have grabbed at his, if he hadn't taken hers first. She kind of got used to this. Holding onto him, and while he wasn't exactly an anchor for her, he was something that steadied her, someone beside her she knew she could count on. A friend. Maybe a little more. And that was okay.

Fifteen

Barry was fine, and Hobert promised him he'd get some shrimp and they would invite Amara to eat again soon.

If things went well, Hobert was hoping Amara would go back out on the boat with him, but he knew that he was pressing his luck with what he had already. And he should be content. Not constantly striving for more. Holding her hand was probably a step further than he should have gone, but when her fingers had brushed against his and they had kind of twined together, with him thinking he might need to try to keep her from falling down, it just seemed like a natural thing to do. After that, walking beside her without holding her hand felt like the unnatural thing.

So he took it again as they walked away from the shack where he lived and toward Raspberry Ridge.

He hadn't spent a whole lot of time in town. There wasn't much there, other than a general store, although he'd heard there was a restaurant coming soon. But otherwise, the view of the lake was just as good from his boat as anywhere. And he had no reason to walk up to Raspberry Ridge.

Except now he did.

Amara was funny and smart and honest. She hadn't flinched when she told him the hard things, and she took his gentle teasing and wasn't afraid to give it back to him without being rude or competitive or mean. Maybe he just hadn't spent enough time around women, but Amara felt different to him, special in a unique way, and perfectly suited to him.

Even though that was crazy, since she was an executive in Chicago and wasn't the slightest bit suited to him. Not even a little.

"This healing garden is new since the last time I was here," she said as they walked up the trail from the bluffs and came out at the back of the garden that was enclosed by a wrought iron fence, with blooms visible through it, and he could hear a waterfall somewhere inside.

"I think there's water in there. That's always a draw for me."

"I'm sure it is, working on the lake the way you do."

"For sure. There's nothing more soothing. Whether it's still in a pond, or running in a stream, or ever-changing the way it is on Lake Michigan."

"You love it, don't you?" she asked, and he felt like she was asking more than just a surface love. Like a deep, I-couldn't-stand-to-be-away-from-it kind of love.

He nodded his head. "Yeah. I do."

She nodded, looked away, and then said, "Do you want to walk through it?" She nodded at the garden in case he didn't know what she was talking about.

"I'd love to. I can smell the flowers, and it definitely is an improvement and a complement to the lake."

"The lake by itself is rejuvenating, and it always smells so fresh and clean to me here in Raspberry Ridge, but the flowers just make it even better."

"That they do," he said as he opened the gate and they walked in, enjoying the beautiful flowers, the graceful way the garden was laid out. It really did feel healing, just a peaceful serenity that encouraged a person to contemplate the wonders of God and turn to Him.

He wasn't quite sure how the garden managed to do that, considering that it couldn't talk, and there were no signs saying, "God made this, make sure you give thanks for it," or anything like that. It was just...quietly religious.

As they moved toward the center of the garden, there was a waterfall that fell down into a soft reflecting pool. He noticed there was a woman sitting on the bench beside an older lady.

They looked up, and Amara drew in a breath.

"I'm sorry. We didn't realize there was someone else in here. We're just walking through."

"Oh, don't you worry about a thing, honey. My friend Linda and I are just enjoying the waterfall. It's our daily stroll. We do this every day before we have Bible study."

The younger lady smiled a little and then stood from the bench, putting a hand on her stomach. She came around and held out her hand. "I'm Skyler, not Linda," she said with a little laugh. "That's my mother-in-law. She's dealing with a little bit of Alzheimer's and sometimes confuses me with her friend Linda."

"It's nice to meet you, Skyler," Amara said, shaking her hand and then watching while the woman held her hand out for Hobert to shake.

His fingers entwined with hers again as soon as he had shaken Skyler's hand. "That's Hobert. He lives below the bluffs on the southern side and has a fishing boat there."

"I haven't been down that side. I always take the trail to the bluffs."

"The trail goes off to the left and eventually meets the road, and that's how you get to his house."

"It's kind of interesting sometimes the way we go off on the same trail all the time and don't realize things that are right around us. This garden is beautiful, and I didn't realize it was up here."

"It was just put in last year by the couple on the hill, Vera and Dominic Miller. In memory of the son that they lost." The woman smiled. "They're on the verge of adopting four children, and Vera just found out she's pregnant. She just told me that the doctor thinks it's twins. There are two heartbeats."

"Oh wow. That's a lot of children." Six kids. He couldn't wrap his mind around that many. He was an only child, and while he'd often longed for a brother or sister, five other siblings was not something that he ever thought would be a good idea. How would he feed that many, for one thing.

"We're hoping to open the church again, hopefully soon. We have a man arriving in a month, more or less, and hopefully he'll agree to take it."

"That would be wonderful. I have such fond memories of going there when I was little."

Hobert had fond memories of sitting outside and listening to the people sing. Not far from this spot. He could hear their voices passing over the field in the summertime quite easily. In the winter, it was a little different story, although sometimes on Christmas Eve, he'd come up to see the service with all the pretty lights and the voices and the carols and all the things that made Christmas special.

His dad, of course, never set foot in church, and Barry didn't go often either. Although he did remember Barry taking him one Christmas Eve, after Hobert had begged and begged. He had wanted to see what the inside of the church looked like, and he was afraid to go on his own.

It had been just as beautiful and magical as what he had hoped it would be. It was kind of hard to go back to the dingy shanty after that. But he kept his memories warm and sweet inside his chest for a long time when he was a kid.

The ladies were done chatting, with the older woman sitting on the bench, seeming entranced by the water, and Skyler confiding that, "The water seems to calm her. Sometimes she gets a little upset because she doesn't recognize where she is or know anyone. She wants to go home, but I'm not sure exactly where she means by home, because she's still in the only home she's lived in for more than fifty years." She paused and then said again, "She's such a sweet lady. It's been difficult to watch her go downhill."

"It's so nice of you to take care of her. I'm sure your husband really appreciates the fact that she's in good hands."

"It's the least I can do," Skyler said and didn't elaborate anymore.

Hobert was pretty sure there was a story behind that, but she didn't offer it, and he and Amara continued walking along the path, watching where the water flowed around and created a little rippling stream, then the more strident sound of the waterfall.

"Are you ready?" Amara said as they walked back to the gate.

"I am. Although, that was a nice place. I think I'll be back."

"I'll definitely be back. It was beautifully designed and planned. Someone put a lot of thought into it, although it's sad to think that it took the death of a little boy to inspire such beauty."

"Maybe that's an example of something good coming out of something bad," he said as he closed the gate behind them with a soft click.

He took Amara's hand again as they started walking up the road toward the mansion she'd grown up in. It had been a while since he'd seen it, and of course he never looked at it through the eyes of someone who knew someone who lived there.

How different their homes were. She had a mother and father who loved her. He didn't have a mother, and his father was a drunk. His best friend was an old man who lived on a boat. Beyond that, he lived in a one-room shack, while she lived in a huge, beautiful mansion with everything money could buy. Up on a hill where everyone could see them, while he was down below, and people didn't even realize he was down there.

She had been in the church. He had been outside, feeling like an outsider, but in the grand scheme of things, God loved him just as much as He loved Amara. He'd figured that out a while ago, and while Amara's life might have seemed like it would set her on a better path for success, he thought that maybe he had figured out the important things in life before she had. That it was family, or what passed for family. For him, it was Barry, and making sure he spent time with him, taking care of him, and not working himself into the ground to buy things that he didn't really need, but taking the time to appreciate his life, appreciate the people in his life, and to be content with what he had, enjoying the little things like the sunrise every morning, and the sunset in the evening, and the cool fingers of a woman he admired clasped in his, and her presence beside him.

As long as he lived, he would cherish this time.

Sixteen

Amara held tight to Hobert's hand as they took the last steps up to the back porch and she stood and looked at the door.

Feelings of anxiety churned through her, and she took a couple of calming breaths.

Knowing that talking to Hobert would ease her mind, she turned to him and said, "It's interesting to me that you and I have known each other such a short time and yet having you beside me eases my mind more than I can say. So I'm a little nervous, but I feel like I have a friend, holding my hand." She grinned, lifting up their hands. "And letting me know that everything is going to be okay. I...really appreciate you being here beside me. It's so much easier than it was...was it only yesterday?"

"Yeah. A lot has happened." He laughed. "The day feels a lot longer when you start it at two AM."

"It sure does. We're going to have a beautiful sunset. Maybe we can be sure to sit out on the patio and watch it. It's a beautiful view."

"I can only imagine. Sometimes when I come in to the dock, I see this house sitting up on the hill and think about what a glorious view they must have. But I guess I never really wanted it. I was always happy with the view that I had from the boat. I guess I never thought that there could be a better view. Maybe I'll find out differently and get spoiled."

"And it will be all my fault. Sorry about that," she said.

"No apology necessary. The company is worth whatever price I have to pay later."

She wondered if that was true. He was big on not paying prices later. He seemed to be all about paying upfront.

She would feel bad if there was a price for him to pay for this time, especially since she was the one who seemed to benefit the most from it. Although she appreciated the fact that he was there with her and clung tightly to him as she put the key in the lock, the familiar click causing her to bite her cheeks and take another deep breath.

She turned the lock, then tried the handle, and the door opened.

"Here we go," she said.

She walked in slowly, and he walked in behind her, holding onto her hand. Even when she might have pulled away, and she again appreciated the fact that he wasn't going to let go.

Everything looked the same in the small mudroom that was off the kitchen. It was a place where they kept their jackets and coats, and there was a bathroom along the side as well.

She didn't look in, assuming that it was probably the same, but if she remembered, it was painted an odd color of mustard yellow. It might be a room that she needed to paint before they could put it on the market.

They stepped into the kitchen, pushing the door open, as the familiar coolness enveloped her.

The expensive tile floor, a blue-gray color that felt cool and inviting at the same time, always kept the room a constant temperature. If she recalled correctly, there was radiant heat in the floor, and in the winter, the floor was warm, despite the tile.

It was a huge kitchen, with a double oven, a massive six-burner stovetop, and two refrigerators, one on each end.

There was plenty of cupboard space, a sink in the island, and another sink in front of the huge window that looked out over the lake.

"Wow. Barry would love to cook in this kitchen," Hobert said from behind her.

"I don't think I ever made anything in this kitchen. We had a housekeeper. She made all of our meals. If she had the day off, she'd cook something extra the day before or we went out to eat. It wasn't a room that I ever really worked in at all. But thinking about it now, she probably loved standing at that sink looking out at that view."

"It's a beautiful view. Especially in the evening, when the sun is setting like it is now."

"Let's go outside and sit on the patio," she said softly, wanting him to be able to see the sunset, which she knew he would appreciate. She had sat out on the back patio multiple times, enjoying the view and sunset, and she knew it was glorious.

As much as Hobert loved those things, she wanted him to get to experience it.

And indeed, he did seem entranced as they sat in silence, both of them in the comfortable patio chairs that had been there for as long as she could remember. The people who came to clean every two weeks or so must have kept them from getting the grime and mildew that so often ruined patio furniture. They looked like they had been freshly scrubbed. Maybe one of her sisters had told the cleaning service that they were coming, and they had spruced everything up for them.

"I think you're right. I think this view is definitely better than I had imagined. I... I might have trouble being content with just watching it from the dock from now on."

"You can come up here anytime, although...I guess I shouldn't say that because my sisters and I are cleaning it out so we can sell it. But until we do, you're welcome."

"I can't imagine you want to sell it."

"I guess I didn't think too much about it until I got here. I just wanted the money. We already sold the condo, and my share from that is enough to pay off the student loans I was telling you about and my car."

"I suppose this will be like what we were talking about that you wanted to be wiser and actually start saving."

"Yeah. I suppose it will be. Although... I don't know, I keep trying to figure out a way to be able to stay here. But it just doesn't compute," she said, not really knowing what she was trying to say other than she wanted to quit her job, but she knew she couldn't. She had the lease on her apartment, which she had for five years, so maybe her landlord would be a little understanding if she tried to get out of it, but did she really want to quit her job?

The idea hadn't even entered her mind until she'd come here.

"They say you shouldn't make any big decisions within a year of a major event in your life. So, as much as I would like to counsel you that, yeah, you need to get away from the big city and come back to small-town life, I suppose that conventional wisdom says the exact opposite. Give it six more months."

"I'll take that into consideration. Although, I loved my parents, I wasn't that close to them. It just...feels like my foundation was knocked out. But it probably wasn't as big of a blow as it would have been if we had been a tightly knit family. You know, the kind of family who actually liked each other, instead of just spending time together because we had to."

She shrugged her shoulder and tried to pretend it didn't matter. "My parents were also highly involved in their businesses, and sometimes I felt like we were...maybe not in the way, but an inconvenience at times. Not all the time. Just sometimes."

"I guess I can relate to that a little bit."

She felt a little bad for even saying anything. He had been through so much more. It didn't even compare.

"You definitely know, even more than I do. So, I know you understand how I feel, although I doubt I feel as bad as you do."

"I don't know about that. I've also come to terms with it. I... sometimes wish that things had been different, but I know I wouldn't be who I am today if it weren't for the way my childhood went. And while I wonder if maybe I'd be better, I know that those things aren't up to me. I can only use what I've been given and make daily choices that help me become the man I want to be."

"You've mentioned something like that several times, and I agree. I need to make better choices." It was full dark now, the sun had gone down below the lake, and she kind of wished she didn't have to look at the rest of the house in the dark. She also knew she had to bid Hobert goodbye. He had to be up early tomorrow morning to go back out on his boat.

"I really appreciate you coming today. I appreciate you letting me go with you, letting me sleep on your boat, feeding me, twice, and just everything. Everything. The last two days have been unbelievable for me, and I feel like I found a new friend, a friend whom I'm going to have as a friend for the rest of my life."

"Well, that's kinda how I am. Loyal to a fault, and I think you can blame my alcoholic father for that. I've read that children of alcoholics are often very loyal, although it usually comes out as loyalty to their parents to keep their family together. I don't recall ever doing that, but I do have a tendency to hold tight to the people who walk into my life and leave a footprint there."

"You definitely left a footprint. And while I don't have the alcoholic parents excuse, there's just something about you that tells me that I can depend on you. And I want to be that kind of person for you right back."

They had stood, and she opened the door to lead them into the kitchen so he could walk out the back door rather than walking around the house in the dark.

She flipped the switch, and the whole kitchen was flooded in light.

"Whoa. That was a change," she said, switching another light switch until the lights under the cupboards came on, and she switched the big overhead lights out. "There are outside lights to light the path you have to go back down."

"Are you sure you're going to be okay?"

She had been talking, working with the lights, fiddling with things, trying to keep her mind off the fact that she hadn't gone through the house yet, and now it was dark. But she'd relied on Hobert long enough.

"I'm fine. You have to get up early tomorrow and go to work. I don't want to keep you anymore. In fact, I feel bad because you're going to have to walk home in the dark. I didn't think about that when I asked you if you wanted to stay and watch the sunset. In fact, I think I insisted."

"I wanted to. And if you need me, I'll stay longer. It's not going to be the first time I didn't get a full night's rest."

"I don't want it to be because of me. You go, and if I need you, I have your number, remember?"

"You'll use it?"

"I will," she promised, knowing that she probably wouldn't unless she really, really needed to, but if she did, she would.

She thought about giving him hers. It just seemed...like something that friends would do, but she didn't want to hold him up more, after already keeping him so long. He had the long walk home, and then Barry would probably want to talk, although maybe he would be understanding and just let Hobert go to bed.

"Will I see you again?" he asked as he made it to the door, his hand on the knob.

"Come up anytime," she said, and she hoped he could see from her face that she meant it.

He lifted a hand and put it on her cheek, and she resisted the urge to press her cheek into the palm of his hand, allowing him to cradle it and give comfort that way.

He gave a little smile, and then he said, "Thank you so much. It was the best two days I've had...in my life, I think. Thank you."

In his life?

But then when she looked back over her life, she realized that they were probably two of the best days that she'd ever had as well.

"I could say the same," she said sincerely.

He searched her eyes and seemed content at the honesty there. He smiled a little. "Then we'll have to do it again."

"We will. Or something new and better," she said, lifting her brows and smiling.

"I'll be up," he said easily, opening the door and giving her one last glance before he slipped out into the night.

She remembered she was going to turn some lights on and raced around, trying a couple before she found one that worked.

Content that he wouldn't trip and fall at least going down the sidewalk of the property, she made a note to turn the lights off later and turned around to go back inside.

Seventeen

Amara turned around and looked again at the kitchen. A room that was rather unfamiliar to her. Other than coming in to take a cookie out of the cookie jar or grab something in the refrigerator to eat, she hadn't been in it much, as she'd told Hobert.

She couldn't believe that she hadn't appreciated this gorgeous room when she lived here. Of course, doing any kind of work in the kitchen wasn't something that was expected of her when she was a child. Kind of funny since her parents had insisted that she had to pay her own college tuition but didn't insist that she had to learn how to cook.

Maybe somewhere along the way, her parents had gotten their priorities mixed up.

Again, she wondered why they might have forbidden her to talk to Hobert. He was one of the most upright men she'd ever met. Why would her parents have such a problem with him?

The question nagged her a little as she walked through the kitchen into the formal dining room. They had spent a lot of time eating in there, but it typically was quiet. Sometimes her parents were on their phone, dealing with different problems that came up in their business, and she and her sisters often fought.

They had become better friends since they'd moved out and didn't share the same house anymore.

The walls were a dark green, and she wondered who in the world had decided to paint them that color. The house would never sell with walls that color, although the floor was nice, an oak hardwood that brightened the room up considerably.

A soft creamy yellow or even a light gray green would go much better than the grumpy dark color that was on the walls now.

Maybe she wouldn't have been so anxious about walking through the house if the walls had been a little more welcoming.

And then she walked into the living room and cringed.

She'd forgotten the hideous red on these walls.

Her mother was a lot of things, but a designer she apparently wasn't. She was the one who had chosen this color. It had some kind of border at the top with berries on it that went nicely with the red color except... Who wanted a living room painted in this awful shade of red?

Even the light furniture couldn't cheer up the room, and the dark walnut floor did not help.

This was definitely a room that was going to have to be painted, and as she walked out of the room and into the hall, she cringed again. Red carpet and bright orange walls.

She shook her head. The color atrocities had not struck her as a child, but maybe this was why they didn't come back to this house more often.

She walked across the hall and opened the door to the study. It was lined with books. Bookshelves, almost from floor to ceiling. They were painted an eggshell white that went nicely with the green trim and natural wood on the windows and the rustic stone fireplace.

This was probably her favorite room. But...all those books. Someone was going to have to go through them and figure out whether they wanted to keep them or donate them.

She didn't look forward to that job. There must be a thousand of them, if not more. Every single shelf was full of books. Which was a dream in a way, if they didn't have to go through them.

Through the study, there was another door that led to another bathroom and the playroom that the girls had turned into a study of their own when they had gotten older. That's where she had done her homework, and it was the room that she'd probably spent the most time in since there was a TV in there, and she and her sisters had watched plenty of movies together.

There was a sofa along the back wall, with the TV in front of it, and her desk on the opposite end of the room.

She could remember more than one fight with her sisters when someone wanted to study, and someone else wanted to watch TV.

Eventually they had posted hours for study and hours that the TV was available, and if someone wanted to study, they had to go somewhere else.

As she thought about this, her eyes turned toward the bulletin board, where the schedule was still tacked into the cork with a thumbtack.

She laughed. She didn't know which one of her sisters had made that list, probably Olive, since she was the middle child and the peacemaker.

Mertie had been very bossy and controlling and always insisted that things had to be done her way. She supposed that's the way the oldest typically was, but Mertie had mellowed out through the years, although she was still the kind of person to take charge of the situation and start barking out orders.

Most of the time, Amara appreciated that.

Sometimes she even wished she still had Mertie to boss her around. That someone would just come and tell her what to do with her life. Quit her job? Tell her sisters she wanted to buy their shares of the mansion and come here to live?

But then, could she afford it?

She didn't know how much it was worth and hardly thought that her share of the condo and the nest egg that she was hoping to have in her account would be enough to even put a down payment on it.

Although with property values in Chicago, could it be worth a lot more than property values in Raspberry Ridge?

She wasn't sure.

It didn't really matter. She wasn't going to need the answer tonight at any rate.

She decided that she would go out to the car, grab her things, and go upstairs to her bedroom. The upstairs could wait until morning. And while she was waiting for her sisters, maybe rather than going through a whole lot of things without them, she would get busy painting the walls.

She was the one with the most flair for design, and she didn't figure that her sisters would care, but she texted them just to make sure. As she figured, they both texted back almost immediately that they would be relieved if she spearheaded the painting.

With that decided, she went outside and grabbed her things. As she did so, she wondered if Hobert had gone to bed yet. If he was still basking in the glow of their fun times together as she was. If he was thinking of her as she was thinking of him. If he was trying to figure out a way that they might possibly make things work, even though neither one of them had said anything about the future.

Maybe it was just her getting the cart ahead of the horse.

With that thought in mind, she grabbed her bag and walked back into the house, going straight to her bedroom, taking a quick but welcome shower, and collapsing into bed, falling asleep almost immediately.

Eighteen

Hobert walked away from Amara's house, the light she turned on illuminating his path brightly.

He wasn't quite sure why it was so hard to leave her. As she had pointed out, they had known each other less than two days. And yet, he felt like he knew her. Like she was a part of him in a way.

Regardless, he walked down the path until he hit the driveway, and he didn't turn around and look at the house until he made it to the road.

It was lit up not quite like one of those long-ago Christmas trees in the church that he had stood at the window and admired for hours. The house was outlined against the stars in the night sky.

What would it have been like to grow up there? To not feel any more love than he had? Not much more. Her parents obviously cared about her.

The only one who ever cared about him had been Barry.

But he didn't want her to leave her job in Chicago, didn't want her to come home to Raspberry Ridge, didn't want her to give up everything, just for him. She had to do it because she wanted to.

He had to step back and not pressure her. To allow her to make the decision.

That was assuming that she felt even half for him as what he did for her.

He could hardly contain how he felt, had wanted to kiss her good night, pull her close, hold her hand as they walked through the rest of the house which he knew she was not looking forward to.

And yet, he had to walk away.

It made him wonder again how his mom could have walked away from him if she felt even a little bit of love for him. He couldn't possibly love Amara that much. He'd only known her two days, and yet walking away from her was hard. How did a mother walk away from her baby?

That would never make sense to him.

Sometimes he wished his mom would come back so he could ask her how she could do it, but he thought he would probably be angry at her, and maybe he would have to apologize for the anger and unkind thoughts that he had toward her ever since he realized what she'd done.

Didn't really seem right that he would have to be the one to apologize, especially if she didn't.

But maybe someone needed to take the first step.

Which was all speculation on his part, because he didn't know if she would ever come back. Most likely not, if history were any indication, and if she did, he had no idea how he would respond to her presence.

He supposed he didn't really care about her. Supposed it didn't really matter to him what she did. Except... A person did have a bond with their mother, whether they wanted to or not. Whether she was a good person or not. Whether they were a good person or not.

It was a bond like no other bond on earth. Everyone had one.

He turned away from the mansion and started walking down the trail toward the dirt road. Leaving Amara behind. Knowing he had to go out on his boat tomorrow. Although knowing he would probably, almost certainly, come in early and walk up to the mansion and see if he could do anything to help her.

Maybe that was one nice thing about the way he lived. He didn't need to spend long, hard days every single day fishing as hard as he could.

He could...take a day off if he wanted or come in early, if someone he loved was in town and needed him.

Surely he could do that without influencing her in any way.

Lord, help me stand back and allow her to make the decision that's best for her and not pressure her to make the decision I want her to make.

Of course, he also didn't want to stand back so far that she didn't know that he cared. Didn't know that he wanted her, didn't know that he was concerned about her and wanted the very best for her.

He didn't want to stand so far back that she didn't have a clue of how he felt.

But maybe he should just let things move along as they naturally did and not focus on how he felt. Focus instead on helping her, doing what he could for her, and making sure she had a good time when she was with him. As good a time as what he had when he was with her.

Smiling at the thought, he walked down the trail, hitting the dirt road with a happy heart. He didn't even feel that tired. He actually felt a little rejuvenated, like the good day had given him energy, rather than taking it.

Or maybe that was just being with Amara.

Barry was still waiting up when he got to the shack. He wasn't even in bed but was sitting outside on one of the chairs, his feet propped up on a log, his head tilted back looking at the lake and the stars.

"Late night," Barry said as Hobert walked into the light cast by the dying embers of the fire and took a seat beside Barry, where he could also look at the lake and the stars.

"It was a good night," he said, unashamed that he had spent it with Amara. He hadn't done anything wrong.

"You know you're probably just courting trouble," Barry said.

"In what way?" Hobert asked like he didn't have a clue that he and Amara were completely opposite from each other and didn't suit at all. And that he was most likely going to get his heart broken. Not that he ever had an opportunity to have experienced heartbreak in his life before, and he figured that maybe he wouldn't be so blasé about it if he knew exactly how much pain he was facing.

"Her parents didn't care none for you," he said softly.

"Her parents are gone. Killed in a car accident six months ago."

"You don't say. Well, I didn't know that."

"I didn't know it either until Amara told me today." Was it just today?

"Well, that probably changes things a little. If they were still alive, they wouldn't allow her to have anything to do with you."

"Do you know why?"

"Some things are better left buried."

"What happened to your wife?" Hobert asked, remembering the question that he asked years ago and Barry wouldn't answer. "You told me a long time ago that you'd tell me when I got older. Am I old enough to know?"

"I suppose, son." Barry shifted just a little as though the subject were making him uncomfortable. Hobert felt a little bit bad for bringing it up to begin with. After all, he loved Barry and didn't want to see him hurt.

"You know, in life, there's a lot of things that go wrong. Lot of things that don't work out the way they should."

Hobert hoped he wasn't just going to say that his marriage was one of those things. He knew there was a story behind it.

Barry propped his elbows on the arms of his chair and steepled his fingers. "Back before I came here, I had a house, dreams of lots of children and a woman who I thought loved me."

He paused for a moment, and then he continued. "But she always wanted more. She was never happy with what we had, always wanted a nicer car, more clothes, a bigger house, a better everything. All I knew how to do was fish, and it got to the point where I was out in my boat day and night, trying to pay for the things that my woman wanted."

Hobert didn't say anything. That was his biggest fear, and he wondered now how much of it was because Barry had beaten it into his head, teaching over the years, day in and day out, that he needed to be content with a little.

"One day, I came home, dead tired, first time I'd been home all week, been fishing round-the-clock, going into the dock when my hold was full, just to empty it and turn around and go right back out. I stepped in the house, thinking my woman would be there, give me, you know, do the things a man wants to do when he gets home, and..." Barry sighed.

Hobert could guess where this was going. He didn't know how he knew; it was like he'd heard a story like this before. He hoped Barry called out in the house, but he was guessing he hadn't.

"I had wanted to surprise my wife. I wanted...to talk to her. Spend time with her. You know, and I was hoping she wanted that with me too. But it was kinda weird that the house was so quiet. Her car was out there. The nice brand-new car I'd bought her just six months prior. All bright and shiny out there."

Barry swallowed, but his voice was still low and a little sad too.

"We were expecting a little one, and I was excited about it, it wasn't due for a while yet, but I wondered if that might be it. Maybe she was at the hospital having trouble, that was back in the day before people carried their phones around with them. There was no note on the counter, no note in the living room, no one in our big fancy dining room, no one in the study, because her house had one. It was a nice house. Best I could afford. She picked it out. Then I was working my fingers to the bone to pay for it.

"So I walked upstairs, just in case she might be taking a nap in the middle of the day, although it wasn't like she had to lift a finger to do anything. I didn't want her to have to work. I wanted to provide for her. I wanted to be the one to take care of her. I didn't want her to worry about a thing. I wanted to pamper my lady. I wanted to protect her and provide for her the way a man should. The way the Good Book tells us to. I thought I heard some noise as I was climbing the steps, but that sounded odd, that my wife would be making noises like that. It didn't really sound like sleeping noises. Sounded like...noises lovers made."

Hobert held his breath, staring hard at the lake, like focusing on trying to figure out where the water met the sky was the most important thing he could do in his life right now, and maybe that would stop the inevitable, what he knew was coming.

"The door to our bedroom was open, why would they close it? She wasn't expecting me to come home. They were in bed together. Her and some other man. I just stood there in the bedroom, in disbelief. It's like, when you see something like that, you just have to stand there and stare at it, because your brain can't quite process that what you're looking at is actually happening. It's not that I wanted to...see them."

Hobert shuddered.

"In fact, I definitely didn't. She was my wife. I loved her. There she was, with another man. I... I guess I said her name. That stopped them pretty quick, and he lost interest if you know what I mean. I think he was scared. I was younger. You know the work you do lifting fish all the time. I had the muscles to stand behind my work, and he was just a little guy. I could have taken him with my pinky finger, but if I'd taken him, would that make her love me any more? Make her love him less?"

"You're right. I'm surprised you could think that rationally while you were standing there. Sometimes anger has a tendency to make a person irrational," Hobert said softly.

"Tell me about it. I didn't feel anger as much as I felt hurt. Pain like I've never experienced before. Like a bomb had gone off in my chest, and someone was scraping the raw insides with their fingernails. I couldn't hardly stand it. But I did know that she didn't love me, and there wasn't anything I could do about it. I couldn't make her love me, couldn't make her not want that man.

"So, I remembered about the baby, and suddenly I realized that maybe it wasn't even mine. I hadn't been around a whole lot, and when I was, for some reason she was too tired. I figured that much out."

Hobert's lips pulled back. He hated that Barry had gone through this. Barry had been such a good man, a good father to him, when his own father didn't even care.

"So yeah, I asked her about the baby. She said it was his, not mine."

He shrugged a shoulder, and let out a sigh, and then said, a little fatalistically, "I guess that was all I needed to hear. There wasn't anything holding me there. So I walked back out of that house, walked back down the dock to my boat, and sailed away. I landed here. Built the pier, claimed the land. It wasn't worth anything. That was before there was much of a town at Raspberry Ridge, and no one cared about this little strip of land. I got it for a little bit of nothing."

"What about your other house and the car and all that?"

"She sold it, and he paid for her car, I guess. She sold the house. It wasn't enough to cover the loan, and I spent a year or two paying for that."

"Why were you living in your boat when I met you?"

"That's because I built this shack with your dad, then he needed it for you, and I didn't care. So, I just stayed on the boat. I kept an eye on you, because I knew how he was, and maybe there were some reasons that he was like that."

"Are you going to tell me?"

Barry looked over at him across the embers of the fire, with the fading glow of the fire on his face, and smiled a little. "I think maybe you need to be a little older before you hear that."

Hobert laughed a little, although not with a lot of humor. He really didn't want to know. Now that he knew Barry's story, he understood why Barry hadn't told him when he was ten.

"Did you ever see your wife again?"

"Nope. I have no idea whether she's even still alive. Maybe she's not with that man. Maybe she is, and they have a bunch of kids. I... I just know that sometimes a man marries a woman who's all wrong for him. A woman who's going to want him to give her more than what he can, and she's more interested in the money he can make than in the love they share together. I'm afraid that little Miss Chicago might be that for you."

"She's not that way. She's different."

"I guess you haven't been out in the world enough to know that's what they'll say. She's different. Everybody says that. Everybody thinks that. But the fact of the matter is, humans are pretty much all alike."

"Are there any women who are any good?" Hobert asked carefully. He didn't believe all women were bad, and surely Barry didn't think that.

"I think there are good women. But I think trying to find one is pretty hard. Maybe you did, I don't know," Barry said, shrugging his shoulders and flattening his lips. "I suppose the only way you're going to know is if you try and see. But a woman can lie. Just want to let you know that."

"And some people can change?" Hobert asked, since Barry had brought the subject up.

"I suppose. I don't really feel like I've ever been the same. Feel like there's a part of me that's been shot, and I've been carrying the bullet around all this time."

"Maybe you need to forgive your wife."

"What do I need to do that for? She never asked for forgiveness."

"Because forgiveness is more about you than it is her. It's about not letting the anger and the bitterness inside of you rip you up, because she doesn't care. It doesn't bother her at all that she hurt you. She got everything she wanted. The house, the car, the other man."

"Yeah, I know. Seems to me like it's supposed to be me giving you advice. Not you sounding old and wise to this old man."

"Well, you can take it for what it's worth. You know I'm not someone who's walked around in the world much at all. But I have read my Bible. Multiple times."

"I told you, son, years ago. If you just keep the Bible and use it for your road map, you won't go wrong."

"I remember that. I didn't really understand, since we never went to church or anything like that, but you're right about it."

"That's what my mother told me. She was one of the good ones. A good woman. Loyal, helpful, she wasn't out to see what she could take from my daddy and use for herself, she was always giving. She probably gave too much."

"Is there such a thing?" Hobert asked, wondering. The Bible didn't really say a person could give too much. There were no warnings or a given limit. It didn't point out the point where giving was too much, when a person needed to stop. There were plenty of commands to give, but no commands to stop giving.

He pondered that sometimes, when he brought his paycheck home, taking what he needed to buy food and groceries for them and giving the rest of it to Barry.

He didn't know what Barry did with it. He didn't know if Barry had family somewhere that he was sending money to or what, but it didn't matter. He appreciated Barry taking care of him, and as far as he was concerned, he was going to take care of Barry until either he couldn't, or Barry wasn't around anymore.

"I don't know, son. I don't know," Barry finally said, after thinking the question over for a while.

They sat there, both of them deep in thought, as Hobert considered what Barry had said.

He understood why Barry might have those concerns. Especially considering that Amara worked in Chicago, and consumerism had seemed to have swallowed America whole. With no one ever feeling like they had enough.

He really thought that Amara was different. But again, maybe Barry was right. Maybe everyone thought that about the person that they were falling for. They were different. They would never do what Barry's wife had done to him. What Hobert's mother had done to him. That she was a different kind of woman. A woman like Barry's mother. Who would give and give and give until...until nothing. Just keep giving. Because there was no such thing as too much giving. No warning in the Bible to stop giving, no limits to what a person was supposed to give.

None.

But that went for him too, Hobert realized. He was supposed to give and keep giving and giving, and never stop giving. Just like there were no limits on loving. They were just supposed to love. It didn't say unless a person betrayed you, or unless a person abandoned you like his mother had, or unless the person was an alcoholic and didn't raise you the way he was supposed to, like his father had, but the command in the Bible was just to love. Unconditionally, with no parameters. Unending, no-strings-attached love.

Did he have that kind of love?

He wasn't sure. He wasn't sure he could say he loved his mother. Or his father. Or that he could continue to love Amara if she decided to choose someone else over him, or if she were to hurt him the way Barry's wife had hurt him.

But wasn't that the command? To love. And not stop loving. Because they were to love like Jesus loved, and Jesus never stopped.

It was a radical idea, one he didn't think he had ever encountered before. No limits on loving, no limits on giving.

What kind of person would he be if he actually lived that?

Nineteen

It didn't take Amara long to realize that she had forgotten her toothpaste.

She had brushed with water the night before, too tired to root through her bag to find it, but now she held her toothbrush in one hand and went through her bag with the other for the third time.

Finally, she just dumped everything out on her bed.

No toothpaste. How could she have picked up her toothbrush and left her toothpaste in her apartment?

They were together all the time. One didn't use one without the other, so what in the world would have made her just pick up one?

She had no idea what she was thinking, but she was a little annoyed with herself.

Regardless, she knew she was going to have to stop and get toothpaste, and also order paint, and probably pick up a few groceries, so she did the best she could using water to brush her teeth again and then finished getting herself ready.

Thankfully, there was some coffee in the kitchen, which, for some reason, reminded her of the coffee that she had the day before, at two o'clock in the morning with Hobert.

Was he on the water now?

She looked out the window. The rays of sun were bright in the sky.

He was almost definitely on the water now. Was he catching fish?

She tried to shake the thoughts off. She didn't want to focus on Hobert when she had her own life to live. She'd never been so enraptured with someone that she couldn't stop thinking about them.

She poured her coffee and drank it sitting on the porch, thinking about all the things she needed to get that day. Deciding that she would walk to the store in Raspberry Ridge, buy toothpaste, and come back and brush her teeth properly before she left to get paint that she needed along with rollers and tape...

She got up and went inside and rummaged in the junk drawer until she found a piece of paper and a pencil.

The pencil point was broken, so she went into the old schoolroom/playroom and used the pencil sharpener that was still there.

Since their schedule was still tacked to the bulletin board, it made sense that no one had bothered to remove the pencil sharpener either.

Walking back out to the porch, she made a list of the things that she needed. But first, she was going to walk downtown. A walk would do her good.

Maybe it would clear her head and help her to stop thinking so much of Hobert.

She had a life to live, except... He was a good man. One it probably didn't hurt to think about, because there was a lot of integrity and character in him, despite the fact that he hadn't been brought up the way a normal person would have been. In fact, maybe the reason that he had so much integrity and character was because of his different upbringing.

But that really didn't explain it. It was almost more like Jesus had his finger on that man.

And Amara, more than anything, wanted a man who walked in Jesus's footsteps.

That was something that Hobert was obviously doing, even if Hobert didn't sit around and preach about it constantly.

He just quietly tried to do the right thing.

The way he'd worked on forgiving his dad, the way he'd worked on the anger and bitterness that he had in his own life, knowing that it was something he needed to get rid of. The way he cared for Barry. The way he made sure to keep his bills paid.

She admired the way he deliberately lived his life, according to principles and standards that lined up with what Scripture said.

She considered herself a Christian, absolutely would say that she was if someone asked, but realized that she hadn't ordered her life the way he had. In a deliberate and mindful way to make sure that she was following the Savior.

She wasn't even sure exactly what Jesus commanded, so how could she follow it?

Determining that she would start to read her Bible, she put "Bible" down on her list and then realized that she probably could get a version for her phone immediately.

So she took a few moments to do that, finding the King James Bible of her youth, the one that she had memorized back when she had done that type of thing, and downloaded it on her phone as she took her coffee cup into the kitchen and texted her sisters on the group text.

The hideous colors of these walls hasn't changed since last night. Mom had zero taste. Rest her soul. I'm going to order paint this afternoon, unless either of you have a problem with it. I'll start painting, because that definitely needs to be done. I'll wait to start going through anything until the two of you arrive. Hopefully soon. I can't stay on vacation forever. Love you.

That was all she said, and she smiled as she hit send.

Her two days with Hobert had made her a little happier with the world in a way she couldn't explain, but she just knew that before she might have resented the fact that her sisters had both promised to be there, and she, the only one with a regular job, had taken a valuable six weeks of vacation so that they would have time to do this, and then both of them stood her up. Normally she would have been upset about that, but now... She didn't really care if they ever came. She was perfectly fine waiting indefinitely for them.

In fact, maybe she wouldn't have to worry about the six weeks of vacation. Maybe they would stretch into forever.

She tucked that thought aside, because it gave her a little bit of anxiety. Who quit their job? Their good-paying, hard-fought, excellent job with a straight path and almost guaranteed raises every year and a position of management within the next ten if she played her cards right, which she had every intention of doing.

But one day at a time. Hobert was right. A person shouldn't make big, life-changing decisions after a major event in their life, and while she didn't necessarily think that the major event was her parents passing, although that made her sad, and she was still dealing with grief, the major event was...meeting Hobert.

She put her purse over her shoulder and walked out the door, locking it and putting the key back in the flower bed where she found it in case her sisters came, which she highly doubted that either one of them would, but she didn't want them to be locked out if they did.

In the meantime, she would know where it was when she wanted back in, and part of her realized that Hobert would know where it was as well.

Which...maybe that should bother her, with how little she knew about him, but it didn't.

There was a small voice in her head that said that there was a reason her parents had forbidden her to talk to him, but she just couldn't imagine that reason was anything that would cause any danger to her right now.

She hated to say this about her parents, but maybe they just didn't want them associating with an alcoholic and his son. Especially since they were basically poor white trash living in a shack by the lake.

As much as it pained her to think that her parents might be like that, she had to face the fact that it might have been true.

Regardless, she enjoyed bright sunshine and a breezy July day as she walked down the path toward town.

She decided that she would spend some time at the healing garden, just a few minutes, because it was so pretty and it drew her.

But again, someone had gotten there before her, and...the lady looked a little hassled, as she tried to open the gate, couldn't quite get it, and yanked a little harder before she stopped pulling, seemed to talk to herself for a moment, and then gently unlatched it and stepped in.

"Oh," the lady said as she turned around to close the gate and saw Amara walking toward her. "I didn't realize there was anyone else here. I hope you didn't hear me talking to myself."

"I saw you looking like you did, but I didn't hear what you said, so your secrets are still safe."

She laughed at Amara's words and turned and held out her hand. "I'm Vera Miller. My husband and I live on the hill." She pointed toward a large house that sat along the bluffs, overlooking the lake. It was closer to the bluffs and closer to Strawberry Sands than the mansion that Amara and her family owned.

"I'm Amara Jardine. I'm here in town to clean out the mansion my parents own."

"I'm so sorry. I heard they passed away in an automobile accident a few months ago." Vera furrowed her brows as though she couldn't remember how long ago.

"Yeah. It's okay. I... My sisters and I are all coming back to try to clean things out. But I had forgotten how quaint and fun this town is."

"It's a great place. For sure," Vera agreed. "My husband and I are hoping to adopt a family of children. We are looking at a family of four, which is crazy," she said, shaking her head as though she couldn't believe that they were even considering it.

"You're the one who designed the garden!" Amara exclaimed.

"I am. My husband built it. I helped a little, and actually Homer, who lives in the creamy yellow house right there, helped as well. It was a group effort."

"It was for your son."

Vera nodded, her smile not dimming as though thoughts of her son did not bring her sadness. Amara admired that.

"It really was healing. I know that's what it's called, a healing garden, but there was just something about building it and thinking of him, and...it just brought me closer to the Lord. To be honest. And maybe happy that my son's in heaven. I mean, what better parent can he have than Jesus, right?"

"He's a better parent than I would ever be, I'm sure."

"Not that there is not still sadness, not that it doesn't still hurt, but it's just so nice to think of my son in heaven. He doesn't have any of the cares of this world, and he'll never have the sadness and heartbreak. I'll never worry where he is at midnight or at one o'clock in the morning. I'll never wonder whether he's going to get a job, or get fired from his job, or whatever. He's just...happy."

"That's a really good way to think about it," Amara said. Thinking that her parents were in heaven as well and probably happier than they'd ever been, although she could see her mom feeling down the folds of her white robe trying to find her phone. "Since you designed it, I was curious about the crosses that are by the flowing water inside."

"Oh, I'm so glad you asked," Vera said as she led the way into the garden, talking about the crosses as they walked toward them. "My husband and I were visiting our son's grave, and the first time I put flowers on it, I bought them for all the other children in the cemetery. Any other kids that I saw who were under ten years old, and I just thought of them as my son's friends. It's weird what grief does to you, I guess," she said as she lifted her shoulder, as though she was a little embarrassed to be talking about it.

But Amara thought it was an awesome idea. "That is so sweet."

"That's what my husband said, that he just thought of it like our son was playing with those kids, so we ended up going through the cemetery by the church in Raspberry Ridge and getting the names of all the kids who had passed away under ten years old. And we just put flowers on all of their graves, and I had a paper where I was writing down all of their names. And the next day, my husband started building crosses for them. And at the time, I was designing the garden, and I asked if I could use the crosses, and that's how that happened. So those are my Trent's friends, and of course there is a cross for Trent as well. And then there are different kinds of flowers for each one of the boys as well. Right now, their black-eyed Susans are blooming."

"I saw the black-eyed Susans, and I noticed there were thirteen clumps of them and they were in the same pattern as the crosses, but I didn't understand the significance."

"I mean, some of them are boys, and I'm sure they don't appreciate the flowers but the idea, you know, that someone cared. And most of them passed away long before Trent was born, most of them before I was even born, but I guess when we pass away young, no one ever remembers you as old."

"Forever young, right?"

They nodded together.

"Well, I need to go. I packed my toothbrush, but for some reason, I forgot toothpaste, which is so weird, but I need to run down to the store... Fran still has a store, right?"

"Yes. Same old store. She's stocking a few more things than she used to. You might be surprised. But... Skyler and I are visiting a friend outside of town tomorrow, and I was wondering if you'd like to go with me?" She smiled a little self-consciously. "I know that's kind of weird, since we barely know each other, but I would love to get to know you a little better, especially if you're going to be here for a while. Perhaps you're staying?"

Amara opened her mouth, and then she closed it. And then she opened it and said exactly the truth. "I'd like to."

"Well, you and Norma Jean are really not quite the same age, but close, although she has a little girl. She asked me to do a little Bible study with her on how to love your husband and how to be a biblical wife, and we're going to talk about that tomorrow. It's only going to be an hour, and I don't want you to feel like you have to, but it would be a really nice way to meet the neighbors and get to know you a little bit better."

"I'd love to." And she smiled. Laughing a little, because what was it with small towns? She wasn't even here for two days, and someone was inviting her to Bible study. The neighbors were so kind and inclusive, and she felt right at home here. It was such a change from what she was used to in the big city.

Not that she didn't know the people in her apartment building... Except, she really didn't. And those that she knew, she just waved at in passing. She never thought to invite them anywhere or to take them food, like small towns often did.

"All right then, I'll pick you up... Maybe around ten?"

"That sounds good to me. I'll be ready," she said.

She could start taping stuff up, go with Vera to the Bible study, and perhaps even start painting when she got back.

But first, toothpaste.

She bid Vera a good day and walked out of the garden, carefully shutting the gate behind her and saying a small prayer for Vera and for the children that they were going to adopt.

It must have been so hard to lose her son, but she admired the fact that they had taken their grief and channeled it into something beautiful. Planting a garden, finding other kids to plant flowers at their graves, and even incorporating those kids into the garden that they built. And now, they were making a huge sacrifice in inviting four kids, all that chaos and craziness, into their lives.

Would she be willing to do that? She was afraid the answer was no. She was so used to living for herself, alone in her condo in Chicago, looking out for her own needs, making sure she performed well in her job, and not really thinking about anyone else. She had never considered that her life was...rather selfish.

She hated to admit that and resisted that determination for a while, but there really wasn't any way around it. Because any way she looked at it, she had not been very generous with her life. Sure, she gave donations to charities. Ones she felt would do a good job and spend her money wisely, but as for giving of herself, she really hadn't.

Not much.

But talking to Vera had been inspiring. Showing her that maybe there were ways that she could be a blessing to people. If it would have been her in the cemetery, would she have gotten so many ideas and implemented them the way Vera and her husband had? It was so simple and yet so brilliant. They just had their eyes open for others, rather than focusing on themselves, and considering how deep their grief must have been, it was rather amazing.

Walking on the sidewalk, she waved at Skyler, who was walking again with her mother-in-law.

They were coming in the opposite direction.

She stopped to chat for a few moments, and then they continued on, with Gertie calling Skyler Linda again.

And Skyler was okay with it, answering her and winking at Amara, like she was just keeping the lady happy and not worrying about whether or not she was using the right name.

For some reason, everything seemed to be striking her in the way of showing her that she could be better. After all, if someone used the wrong name for her, she would certainly be correcting them. Even if it was her mother-in-law.

Maybe. Except, did it really matter? Especially since the woman had Alzheimer's and didn't know.

It was just a little bit of giving up of oneself, a little bit of unselfishness, a little bit of care and consideration for others that Amara wasn't sure that she had been displaying.

She wanted to do better.

Finally she got to the store, and she opened the door, going in with the bells tinkling over her head.

She didn't think that department stores did that anymore. They had the automatic sliding glass doors, and people just walked in, and maybe there was a greeter at the front, but the stores were so large that someone was around all the time. She supposed that was the point of the bells; if the store owner was in the back or working stocking shelves somewhere, they would know that someone came in.

For some reason, the sound of the bells made her smile and feel like she came home.

Which was odd.

But Vera had been correct, the store was a lot different than it was when she had been in it last, which was more than a decade ago.

There had been the regular touristy things, which she still saw over in the corner, but now there were a couple of aisles of groceries and racks of souvenir T-shirts and sweatshirts, and she saw some beauty items, which is the aisle she walked toward.

"Good morning," a lady called from the back, where she was stocking shelves on a small stepladder. Amara didn't see her until she moved down the aisle. Was that Fran?

"Good morning. You probably don't remember me, but I'm Amara Jardine."

"Don't remember you? I remember you! You were adorable in your little pigtails and sundresses and your two sisters hauling you around. You were the youngest, correct?" the lady said as she moved her body off the stepladder and walked slowly toward Amara, giving the impression she was rushing, but her pace was still slow.

"Fran?" Amara said. She aged in the last ten years.

"The very one, darling. Remember how you and your sisters used to come in here and buy penny candy every single day?"

"I do. I don't see the penny candy anymore though."

"Well, I had to give that up over the last couple of years. Inflation made it to the point where there is no such thing as penny candy anymore. You pretty much need a dollar if you want to buy anything."

Amara felt a little bit sad over that. She had forgotten that until just then how much fun she and her sisters had as they came down, each clutching their dollar to their chest, as they walked in and spent it carefully on candy in the store.

Their mom had been rather strict about their diets, but their dad had been the one to give them the dollar every day. She thought that maybe it got them out of their hair for a little bit, but it was too late to ask.

Which made her a little bit sad again. She'd forgotten all about that.

Maybe her dad just felt bad for them because they loved candy so much, and their mom wouldn't let them have it.

She'd never know, not unless one of her sisters had an idea, because it was too late to talk to their dad about it.

"That's one of my happiest memories of Raspberry Ridge. I'm so sad about the penny candy."

"Oh, I can assure you. Me too. Me too. It was a sad day, the day that I decided that it just wasn't possible to call it penny candy anymore, and I needed to put something else on my counter. So now you can buy a candy bar or a pack of gum, and it's going to cost you a good bit more than a penny or even a dollar. Unfortunately," she said, tsking and shaking her head. "These high prices are going to put me out of business, I'm afraid, although people come in, and they seem to be willing to continue to pay. They just don't buy as much, you know?"

"I hadn't considered that..." She looked around the store, remembering how much she loved to decorate and the things she'd learned about sales and design in school and life, and thinking about some things that Fran could do to change the layout of the store that would make it more welcoming and possibly display her goods to a better benefit and induce people to buy more.

"My background is in marketing."

"I heard you had a highfalutin job in Chicago," Fran said, smiling like she was just as proud as punch of Amara for working in Chicago, like Fran personally had something to do with it.

"Well, what I was thinking was..." She wanted to be careful. She didn't want Fran to think that she was criticizing anything in the store. "What I do in my job is display things to make them ideal for customers to want to buy. In fact, I try to engage their emotions using color, design, and power words to create advertisements that make consumers want to one-click buy. As in, they can't whip out their money to get what I'm selling into their life fast enough."

"Wow. Sounds like I could use a little of that magic in here. I wish I could get people to whip out their money fast."

"Well... I'm here for six weeks. I...would be willing to try to make a few changes using the things that I use in my job that might help you a little bit if you'd be interested?" she said, hoping that her words came out the way she intended them and didn't sound like she was criticizing anything.

"How much would you charge for that, sweetie?" Fran asked, as though money was an issue.

"I wouldn't charge anything," she said, and she couldn't believe how good it felt. "I'd do it because...that's what I love. Not necessarily getting people to part with their money and plunk it down just as fast as they can, but I love designing things and making them look good together. I love figuring out what makes people tick and what makes them decide to make purchases and then trying to use that to sell whatever it is that I'm trying to sell. It's just...something I've always loved."

It was true, she loved that part of her job. The part of her job she didn't love was the part that took up eighty percent of her time. Endless meetings, endless emails, endless group sessions that led nowhere, and endless working with the right people, trying to get herself positioned in the right area so that her boss would notice her and give her the credit that was her due. Constantly trying to outmaneuver her coworkers and bring attention to herself.

Those were the things she hated about her job, and those were the things that took up most of the time.

"If you're serious about donating your time, sweetheart, you can come in here anytime you want to."

"All right. Then…if I need a few custom racks or something made, can I have Hobert Gilcrest do it?"

She was taking a chance there. Hobert hadn't agreed to anything. She didn't even know if he was going to talk to her again, although they left on good terms, she was sure of it. She had no idea if he was thinking of her as much as she was thinking of him today, but his name came out of her mouth without her really needing to put any effort into it, and she was sure that if he could fix the motor, he could make a few shelves or racks for her.

"Hobert Gilcrest. The fisherman down below the bluffs, on the south side?"

"The very one," she said.

"There was some bad blood between him and your family. Are you talking to each other yet?"

"Yes. He's a very nice man. He has character and integrity, and he loves this small town."

"Oh my goodness. I hardly ever see him, but I'll have to pay more attention from now on. Those were some pretty high words of praise there."

"I meant them. He's a good man."

She kinda felt her face glowing and thought that maybe she ought to shut up or Fran was going to think she thought he was more than a good man. She was going to start thinking she was thinking good husband.

"All right. All I came in for today was some toothpaste, but I think maybe I'll grab a long-sleeved T-shirt if you have one in my size. It's July, but the evenings still get cool."

"Especially with that light breeze," Fran said agreeably, pointing to the rack. "You look like you're probably a medium or small. I have plenty of those. The large and extra-large sell out first."

"All right," Amara said, digging in the rack until she found a dusty pink one with raspberry-colored words on it. She thought that was very fitting. And then, on a whim, she looked at the men's sweatshirts, picking out a dark green one with the same raspberry-colored wording on it, one she thought looked like Hobert's size.

Maybe he wouldn't appreciate a long-sleeved sweatshirt, but she could imagine that he probably didn't get too many new clothes. And it was corny, but she smiled a little thinking of them wearing matching sweatshirts.

She was such a ding-dong. And she didn't know where that came from. When she was in Chicago, she felt like she was just as sophisticated as everyone else. But today in her small town, all of a sudden she was corny and silly.

She bought the sweatshirts, paying for the toothpaste as well, and assured Fran that she would be there the day after tomorrow.

She had already agreed to go with Vera in the morning the next day, and she did want to get a little bit of painting done.

With that thought in mind, she carried her small bag of purchases back down the sidewalk, toward the driveway to her home, singing a little under her breath.

When was the last time she had done that? Walk on the sidewalk singing to herself?

People in Chicago would think she was nuts, or...maybe she would have fit in even better. She laughed a little to herself. Regardless, she hadn't felt like doing that for a very long time.

Twenty

H obert had intended to quit fishing early. But just as he was about ready to pull in his lines, just before noon, and start home, the fish had started biting like crazy.

He could hardly quit when the fish were biting like that, and so he spent the next two hours pulling in line after line, fish after fish, and throwing the lines back out, and barely getting the other lines taken care of before he had to pull in more.

He ended up with one of his best days of fishing ever. The hold wasn't quite full. He probably could have fit five or ten more fish in, but when the feeding frenzy slowed down, and he had all four lines out for twenty minutes with no bites, he decided he was calling it a day.

Still, with that many fish, and with the price fish were going for in Chicago, he knew a trip to the Windy City was the most efficient use of his time.

He hated to do it because he knew that would make it late afternoon until he got to Amara's house. That was if nothing happened.

But he had to. He couldn't justify taking the huge load to Blueberry Beach when the price at Chicago was much higher.

So, when he finally docked back at Raspberry Ridge, he almost didn't walk up the path to see Barry before he ran to Amara's house.

It was crazy the hold she had on him. He'd never felt anything like it before and wasn't exactly sure whether it was dangerous or just heady.

"Hey there," he said as he walked closer to the shanty and saw Barry sitting on his chair beside the completely cold fire, just enjoying the sunshine and the lake breeze and the view.

"Hey there. I thought you were going to be a lot earlier today. Figured you'd be running up to that girl's house."

"Had a stroke of good luck, and had almost a full load. So I took it to Chicago."

"He's a smart kid."

"I was taught by the best," he said.

"Well, you better get going then."

"Are you going to be okay?"

"I'm doing good. Just need a little sunshine on these old bones. I've been cold."

"Well, it is Michigan, even if it is July."

He narrowed his eyes a bit, a little concerned. It looked like Barry had lost weight. Although he had never been a big guy. He'd always been thin, with long stringy muscles that could work all day. The kind of muscles Hobert had. Although, he hadn't really thought about muscles until he thought about Amara, and wondered if she'd prefer he be a little bulkier.

Not that he could do much about it, unless he started lifting weights on his boat.

"You gonna run yourself ragged though, son. But I guess there's probably nothing I can do about it. I was young once too."

It wasn't that Hobert was that young. He was almost thirty. Too old to be acting like a teenager when it came to girls, but Amara was different.

"I'll try not to wake you up when I come in."

"It doesn't matter. I can catch up on my sleep tomorrow. You on the other hand…" Barry didn't need to say anything more. But his eyes held a warning.

Whether that was because he was worried about Hobert getting hurt by Amara or concerned about something else, Hobert wasn't sure.

Regardless, he checked on the old man one more time and said a short prayer.

There was just something that was nagging him, although he couldn't quite put his finger on it.

Thinking maybe he should take something, he left because there really wasn't anything in the shanty to take, nothing that would work for any kind of gift or anything, so he just started up the road, which eventually turned into the trail. It was about a twenty-minute walk to Amara's house.

By that time, the sun was starting to go down, although it would be another hour or so until sunset. But he felt like the day was mostly over.

He knocked on the door, and he heard a faint yell of, "Come on in!"

He smiled. Small towns. He should probably give her a hard time, because she shouldn't just be letting anyone into her house, but at the same time, he loved that it was just the way small towns were.

"You know, I could be a serial killer," he said as he stepped into the kitchen.

"If you are, you can come to the front door. I'd be able to see you there," her voice said, coming from the other side of the kitchen.

He walked through the dining room, which looked fancy and formal, although it was an ominous color of dark green. Then, into the living room, which made him gasp at the angry red that practically leapt from the walls.

Around the corner in the hall, he found Amara on a step stool, putting tape around the door.

"Hey there. I was expecting you hours ago. The fish must have been biting pretty well today."

"Actually, I had one of my best days ever, although it wasn't quite a full load. I still went to Chicago."

"Oh. I should have guessed. I...was a little bit worried, but I figured I wasn't going to call you until you didn't show up at all."

"You can call me anytime. You know, it's not like it's going to bother me or anything."

"Well, I would be, if you were jumping from line to line trying to get everything done. And I wouldn't want you to stop just for me. If you didn't answer, I might be worried. So I just thought it would be better to not."

"I would have called you, but I didn't have your number." He didn't want that to sound like he was pressuring her for her number, so he continued, "So what are you doing? What do you want me to do?"

"Well, I think there's a ladder in the garage out back, but it's pretty heavy, if I remember right. We need something so we can reach up these cathedral ceilings and tape the whole way around."

"All right. I'll go see if I can find it."

"You can use the door on the other side of the house there through the pantry. It's on the other side of the kitchen from where you came in."

"All right." He saw the pantry door and realized there was a hall there. He went down the short hall to the door and saw the shed as soon as he stepped out.

It wasn't locked, which surprised him considering that no one had been living at the mansion. He would have thought that they'd have everything all locked up. He was able to run in and grab the ladder, bringing it back to the front door. He figured it would be easier to walk it in there.

Amara must have been watching for him, because she got down off her stepladder and ran to open the door so he didn't have to put the ladder down and knock.

"Thank you so much. I was just about ready to go get it myself. I'm almost done with everything I can reach."

"What color are you painting it?" he asked as he brought the ladder in through the door, careful not to hit anything. If he broke anything, it would probably cost more money than he earned in a year.

"I thought I would do the hall in an off white. I'm going to rip up this carpet, but there will be baseboard, so we don't have to worry about painting it the whole way down to the floor."

"Got it. I don't know a whole lot about design other than I like it when it looks nice, but the red carpet with the orange walls just kind of give me a headache."

"I'd forgotten that Mom had done this. And not too long before we moved. I'm not sure if she just wanted to make sure that no one would ever buy it in case we wanted to sell it, or what was going on, but the colors she chose were hideous."

"All right. I was trying to say it a little bit more politely, but I agree with hideous."

She laughed.

"So how was your day?"

"Well, I forgot toothpaste, but I didn't realize it until this morning, so I went to Raspberry Ridge, thinking I would look at the healing garden a little bit, because it just seems to draw me."

"It was hard for me to walk by it without stopping too," he said as he set the ladder up on the side that she had already done so he could reach up and do the tape at the top. He saw she had a second roll of masking tape in the bag, and he grabbed it before he ascended the ladder.

"Yeah. There's just something about it." She sighed. "I met Vera there. She was the lady who designed the garden."

"That's neat. For her son, right?"

"Right. Remember those crosses that we talked about when we were looking at it?"

"Yeah. I think there were thirteen of them with names on them."

"Those are thirteen kids who are less than ten years old in the cemetery out by the church. They're in the same cemetery where her son is buried. He was ten I believe when he passed away, and they adopted, figuratively speaking, all of the kids in the cemetery that were younger than ten. There happened to be thirteen. And they planted flowers on their graves and gave them each a cross."

"That's an interesting idea."

"That's what I thought. Anyway, I talked to her a little bit, and she invited me to go to a Bible study tomorrow with someone else in Raspberry Ridge, and I thought I would. So I'll be starting here early."

"Well, you know where I'll be tomorrow morning."

"Yeah. I hope you're not pushing yourself too hard. I mean, you don't have to stay late tonight, because I bet you were up early this morning."

"Two. But that's kinda normal."

"Aren't you tired?"

"I am, but...it was worth it to come here to see you." He didn't know whether he should be saying that or not. He really wasn't sure how normal people acted when they were... Was he courting? That was kind of what he wanted to do, although she had said that there was no future for them because she wasn't leaving Chicago. So he supposed he was just courting with no hope of actually getting anywhere, but he didn't care. He wanted to be with her, and he wanted to treat her as well as he could. So if that was courting, and courting with no hope, then that was him.

"I'm so glad you came. I couldn't believe how disappointed I was when I thought that you weren't going to make it. I know that's ridiculous, but it's true."

"It would take a lot for me not to make it. I know that I could have sold my fish at Blueberry Beach, but I would have gotten about seventy-five percent of what I got when I went to Chicago. And with the fuel expense, it was still worth it. So as much as I wanted to come here earlier, I knew I couldn't."

"I know you made the right decision." She sighed. "I wish I was staying longer than six weeks. It seems like such a short amount of time, and I want to spend every second with you, but I know you're not on vacation the way I am."

"No paid vacation, although I do have the winter off typically. Although, not voluntarily. Also, if we get a stormy day, I'll probably not go out. The fish don't bite that well, and there's no point in risking the boat."

"Oh, I never thought of that. Should I pray for rain?"

"You can if you want to," he said. Her comment had made him smile, warming his heart.

"Anyway, after I did that, I went to Fran's store, and I realized when I walked in that I could do a lot better job of arranging her merchandise and perhaps help it sell better for her. So, while I was getting the toothpaste and, oh! I totally forgot. I got you something," she said, sounding like a little kid at Christmas, only she was excited about giving him something.

"You didn't need to do that," he said, wondering what in the world she might have gotten him. Fishing lures or something. Only he didn't use the kind of fishing lures that people bought at Fran's store.

Regardless, whatever she got him, he would appreciate it because she thought of him.

"I know I didn't, but I got one for myself, and as I was looking at them, I know it's crazy, but..." She started down the ladder. "All right. I am too childishly impatient about this. I want to give it to you now."

"All right," he said, a little uncertain as she brushed past him and ran up the stairs, he assumed, to her bedroom.

Soon she came back down, holding a bag.

"I took the toothpaste out, but I got this for myself," she said as she reached the bottom of the stairs, pulling out a long-sleeved T-shirt in a dusty pink color with darker pinkish maroon lettering on it.

"So...did you get me a pink T-shirt?" he asked, rethinking the idea that whatever she gave him, he would appreciate it. Not that he wouldn't appreciate her pink T-shirt, he would. He just wouldn't wear it.

"No. Would you want one?" she asked, tilting her head.

He grinned. "Let me see what color it is before I say no."

She laughed, pulling out a dark green sweatshirt with the same color lettering on it.

"Okay. I can wear that."

"I don't want to offend your manly sensibilities."

"I suppose that I should be manly enough to wear pink, but...maybe I'm just not there yet. Give me another ten years or so."

"How about fifty years? In fifty years, if you're still around, I know you can pull off pink with aplomb."

"All right. fifty years is good. I'll pretty much agree to anything if it means you're still going to be around."

A fifty-year anniversary. He hadn't even thought he would be thinking about such a thing, and not that that was what Amara was thinking. He just...didn't know anyone in his life who had a marriage that lasted fifty years. It was what he wanted for himself. But he needed to stop thinking along those lines, because Amara obviously wasn't.

"Do you want to try it on? I guessed on your size, just eyeballing it."

"Because you're a designer, you probably are pretty good at eyeballing things," he suggested.

"I don't know. We'll see."

He pulled the long-sleeved sweatshirt over his T-shirt, and it fit perfectly. "I'd say your eyes and your profession are in line."

She laughed.

"But I better take it off, just in case we start painting tonight. But now I won't be cold on my way home."

"That's actually what I was thinking about. Since it's Michigan, I mean, everybody needs winter clothes, right?"

"Even summer evenings get cool sometimes."

"That's how I feel. Last night, I thought it was chilly. And I felt bad that you were walking home and might be cold."

He wasn't the slightest bit cold. He'd spent the way home thinking about her and hadn't given a thought as to whether or not he was actually cold.

"That's very considerate of you. Thank you very much." He took a breath. "I honestly can't remember the last time anyone gave me a gift."

She stopped holding her T-shirt up and lifted her eyes to his. "Oh my goodness. That's...sad."

"Sorry. Didn't mean to be sad. Just stating a fact."

"I'm so glad I got it. I should have wrapped it up and made a bigger production out of it."

"Nah. This was good. It's... I'm a little speechless. I really appreciate it, thank you."

She beamed, like he had been the one to get her a gift, and he felt like maybe he should have, but it hadn't even occurred to him, other than as he ran out of his yard, that he should take a housewarming gift or something so he didn't visit with empty hands.

But he didn't have anything to take.

He folded his shirt up and set it with hers on a small piece of furniture, he wasn't even sure what someone would call it, but it looked a little bit like a bookshelf, only it had a shelf like someone could set something on it and it had cupboards in the bottom.

"Actually, we're going to need to move this furniture out of here if we're going to paint."

"Yes. I didn't even think about that. I've had so many other things on my mind."

"You seem so happy," he said, a little jealous, because obviously going into the store and finding a place to help out and talking to Vera and going to Bible study had excited her. Unlike spending the day with him yesterday.

But then she said, "I had such a good time with you. I just...never did anything like that before. I don't know why, but it put me in a whole different frame of mind. I mean, I dropped in the bed last night exhausted and didn't move until this morning. And the funny thing about it was, the empty house didn't bother me at all. Normally, I would have been like, man, I'm the only person in this house, and it's creepy, but I was so exhausted it didn't even matter."

"Well, you're welcome, I guess."

She laughed. "I'm serious," she said as she carefully placed masking tape on the ceiling, right along the edge where it met the wall. "I mean, I had a good day today, meeting Vera, agreeing to go to Bible study, and after hearing what she had done with the kids, after seeing what you did with Barry, it influenced me to try to keep my eyes open and look around to see if I can do something. So when I walked in the store and knew that I could arrange the merchandise better, because that's what I do for my job, at least it's a part of my job that I love. There's a lot of my job that doesn't involve that, that I don't like. But anyway, I felt like I could be a blessing to someone. I just had to be careful how I suggested it today so I didn't insult her or make her feel like her way wasn't good."

"I take it you were able to do that."

"I was!"

And she talked for a bit about how she wanted to do things and how she could arrange things to make it look brighter and more welcoming.

He listened with a little smile on his face as he stood on the third rung down at the top of the ladder, taping up the sweeping cathedral ceiling.

It amazed him how happy and chatty she was. He wasn't used to that, with Barry's more taciturn nature. Although, Barry could get into a story and go on for hours, regaling him with tales from when he was younger. But come to think of it, those times had gotten fewer and farther between. Now Barry just mostly sat and did a lot of sleeping. Which he supposed was normal for someone who was probably eighty or more years old. But still, he wasn't used to this happy chatter.

"And I said that you would help me out, and she said that was fine."

"So you volunteered me?" he said, bringing himself out of his contemplations to answer her. He had been paying attention, but he'd been letting his mind wander a little bit too. Admiring her. Enjoying her. Knowing that as much as he wanted this kind of time to last, it wasn't going to.

"Exactly. And she said she knew you, but she hadn't seen you for a while. Said she would keep an eye out for you."

"I don't typically have too much reason to go to the store."

"Well, maybe you can stop in, because she looked happy at the idea of talking to you. But anyway, I'll let you know what I need."

"All right. I'm glad that you assumed that I would be able to make whatever it was that you want."

He was teasing her mostly. He could do a little bit of woodworking, although he was limited in the tools that he had.

"I saw you with the motor yesterday, remember? I just figured you were good with your hands."

"I suppose there's a difference between designing merchandise to make a store more appealing and designing a building. I'm guessing you don't do both."

"All right. You're right. I should have asked. But you don't seem worried, so I'm guessing I was right."

"You are right."

They talked until late in the night, when they had the entire hall taped up, as well as moving the big piece of furniture out of it and into the living room. Amara said she wanted to paint the living room and the dining room and potentially even more rooms. She had gotten permission from her sisters, and apparently neither were expected to come in the next week or two.

Hobert was not disappointed. Her sisters might have more against him than what she had. Whatever their parents had been upset about, maybe her sisters knew better than Amara, since Amara was the youngest. Maybe they were old enough to understand what had been going on.

He didn't bother to tell her that Barry knew what the issue was but didn't want to tell them.

He did, however, remember that Barry had told him about his wife, but he didn't want to ruin the atmosphere by talking about such a sad story.

It was ten o'clock when Amara said she was quitting.

It wasn't going to give him much time to sleep, but he remembered what Barry had said about men chasing after women and foregoing sleep in order to court.

Maybe that's what he was doing, because he didn't care. He would go with no sleep in order to spend time with her.

He smiled about it the whole way home and was a little surprised to see Barry sitting in the same place, only he had built a fire at some point, and the embers were still glowing. Like they had been last night when he got home.

"Did you wait up again?" he asked, and Barry jerked awake, his eyes looking sleepy as they focused on Hobert.

"'Bout time you come home, son. Figured you'd be out late. You got it bad."

"I suppose I do. I suppose I'm not being very smart, and I know you said everyone says it, but I feel like she's different."

"Maybe she is, boy. I thought about that later. I was probably a little hard on you. It's a little scary to me that you might get married and run off. But you got a good head on your shoulders, and you're a good judge of men. I'd assume that you're a good judge of women too. Better than me anyway."

Hobert sat down in the chair beside Barry.

The little bit of praise warmed him from the inside out.

"Maybe I can learn from your mistakes. You sure tried as hard as you could to teach me. But she's a good woman. Honest and forthright. She isn't the kind of person to make up lies behind my back."

"I'll trust you on that." Then Barry's eyes narrowed. "Is that a new shirt?"

He had such a small wardrobe that even someone who never

noticed clothing would probably notice when he wore something new. Plus, he didn't have anything with pink on it. Whether it was lettering or what. He just…didn't really like the color. But because this came from Amara, he would probably wear it until it fell apart on his body.

"Amara bought it for me. She has one that matches it, only hers is pink."

"Wow. She bought you something?"

"She did. It was…nice to know that she was thinking about me today." Even speaking the idea out loud made him feel good all over again.

"Well, if she's a smart woman, she'll think about you all the time."

"Just so you know, I don't know what's going to happen between Amara and me. I mean, she still has her job in Chicago, and she's going back to it in another five and half weeks or so, but whatever happens, I'm not leaving you."

"I'm not going to Chicago," Barry said, in a voice that Hobert would never dream of arguing with.

"I didn't think you would. I don't want to go there either, although I know they do have beautiful views of the lake."

"And it's a trap. You can't get out. You're stuck there, and people living on top of people. It's…not a good place. Not where I want to be."

"All right. We're not going to go to Chicago."

Well, he just backed himself into a corner with that one. He had thought that maybe he could follow Amara to Chicago. Docking fees would probably be expensive in Chicago, and he might not be able to afford them, but…maybe he could find a closer dock, one he could afford, and…

Who was he kidding? He didn't know anything about living in the city. He probably couldn't afford any apartment or house or whatever people lived in close to Amara that was affordable, either.

And he was very much like Barry. He didn't want to. The only reason why he was even running those scenarios over in his head was because he didn't want to leave Amara. And he didn't want her to leave him. And if that meant giving up the life he loved here and moving to the city… He supposed he would do it. But he couldn't drag Barry along, and he just promised him that he would never leave him. Not that he'd been planning on ever leaving him anyway.

"We'll figure something out. Come on, morning comes early when it comes at two AM." He stood up, clamping a hand down on Barry's shoulder.

Barry pushed hard, getting himself out of the chair with difficulty. But Hobert knew better than to try to help him.

Barry got his cane, and they walked into the house together. Hobert knew the night would be short, and he would spend it dreaming about Amara.

"Okay, Holly, while I'm busy with my company, you have to be quiet and play in the room, okay?" Norma Jean said as she talked to her stepdaughter while she bustled around the kitchen, trying to get everything ready. She had managed to make a decent loaf of bread, although she hadn't cut into it, so she had no idea what it looked like on the inside.

But it at least rose the way it was supposed to, although it didn't quite look like the pictures that she had used as guidance. She was counting on it being edible. It was hot, so at least they could have melted butter on it. Which was almost enough to make anything edible.

"But I'm hungry," Holly whined.

"You just ate breakfast. I literally just cleaned up your breakfast twenty minutes ago."

"But I'm hungry," Holly said again.

"All right. I'll feed you as soon as the ladies leave. I promise, okay? But I can't feed you now, because then I'm going to have dirty dishes that I have to do something with, and I can't do that, because they could be here anytime. Please play nicely, okay?"

"I don't want to play by myself," Holly said.

"Ten minutes ago, you couldn't wait to play with your new doll. You just told me that."

Girls were so fickle.

"But I want to play with trucks like I can at Aunt Laura's house. It's better there."

Her words pierced Norma Jean's heart. Her sister-in-law was perfect in every way. Her husband thought so, and now his daughter did, too. "But you don't like playing with trucks. You like playing with dolls."

There was a knock at her door. It was the ladies. They were here. Vera had texted her earlier and told her that she was bringing a friend that she was sure Norma Jean would like to meet. One her own age.

Norma Jean was excited about it, but she didn't want her daughter to act like a monster and scare everyone away.

Not that she always acted terribly. About thirty percent of the time, she was actually likable. That thirty percent of the time was typically when she was sleeping, but still.

"You can go play, or you can sit quietly here, but I don't want you to fuss. Or I will be dealing with you whenever the ladies leave." She pointed to the room. Holly looked at her one more time with big sad, hungry eyes before she turned and walked slowly into the room.

Norma Jean didn't typically allow them to eat in the room, but maybe next time she'd have to make up little snack bags for her. Maybe that would keep her occupied.

She turned the burner on, where she already had a teakettle sitting, and then walked to the door.

She opened it, seeing Vera and a dark-haired, dark-eyed, smiling beauty.

Her teeth flashed white, a shade of white that Norma Jean hadn't seen on teeth before, and she was dressed in a style that Norma Jean had also never seen before. She thought Vera had said she was from Chicago.

And it made Norma Jean feel drab and frumpy, running a self-conscious hand down her front, where she had flour on her blue T-shirt, and wishing that she had changed out of her old, paint-stained jeans into something a little bit nicer.

She'd been too busy taking care of her daughter and trying to make sure that she wouldn't be hungry or need anything that would interrupt the ladies while they were talking.

"Welcome. Come on in," she said in a voice she hoped was welcoming and not exhausted and frustrated.

"It smells so good in here," Vera said as they stepped in. She shut the door behind her before she said, "Norma Jean, this is Amara Jardine. She lives in the big mansion up on top of the hill, at the end of the long drive, just south of Raspberry Ridge. She must have a beautiful view of the lake."

"I do. And, Norma Jean, it's so nice to meet you," Amara said, holding out her hand. "We'll have to do this at my house sometime."

"I have a daughter. I wouldn't want you to feel like you had to try to figure out what to do with her. I doubt your mansion is child friendly."

"We actually have a room where my sisters and I used to do our schoolwork. It...maybe is not child friendly, but it certainly can be childproofed. We can even sit in there and talk while she plays if we want to."

"I think it might be too hard for us to be able to get anything done if she's with us," Norma Jean said, and then she didn't know why she was arguing. She should just let it go. They would be fine. If Amara wanted to invite them to her house, she could do it.

"We can figure out that later. It's always nice to come out here to the farm, and your bread smells delicious this week," Vera said with a small laugh.

Norma Jean tried to join in, but she felt a little intimidated by Amara. She was obviously sophisticated, and probably everything she touched turned out perfectly.

"You make your own bread?" Amara said. "Like this isn't the frozen loaves that thaw and rise and then you just stick them in the oven and bake them?"

"No. I got up this morning and started it myself. It's...probably not perfect."

"That doesn't matter. As long as it tastes like bread. But wow. I'm so impressed. Maybe I can learn how to do that too."

Vera nodded. "There's just something very satisfying about making your own bread. And then, if you really want to get into it, you can grind your own wheat too."

Amara laughed. "I actually know people in Chicago who do that. I have never gotten into it to that extent. I think the wheat would go bad before I used it more than once. It's probably one of those things where I would do it once and think, 'okay, that was a lot of work. I think I'll just buy my bread from now on.'"

"But then your house wouldn't smell like this," Vera said.

Norma Jean had led them to the table and offered them seats. In the meantime, her teakettle had started to boil.

She poured three cups, set them on saucers, and set them on the table along with the assortment of tea bags that she had.

"You can choose whatever kind you want. Go ahead and root around. I have a whole range of them."

"I love different kinds of teas," Amara said.

"Me too. I understand your sister-in-law has quite a collection as well."

"We exchanged some. I gave her some of mine, and she shared some of hers with me." Laura really was the sweetest, and Norma Jean wanted to be more like her.

"That's awesome, so you guys are chatting?" Vera said with a hopeful look.

"We are. I got to thinking about what you had said last time about how I need to make sure that none of the problems that are between me and everyone else are because of me. And so I went to her and I apologized to her and explained that I was feeling intimidated by her and I allowed that to come between us and I wasn't as friendly as what I could have been."

She shook her head. She still couldn't believe that her sister-in-law, tough as nails, capable of doing anything, sat down and cried over that.

"I was shocked when she started to cry. But she explained that she didn't mean to be intimidating. That she had worked hard to be a good wife and a good mother and to do things well, but she didn't want to do them well so that other people felt bad. She wanted to do them well so that she was a good wife to her husband and a good mother to her kids. It put everything in perspective for me."

She did not mean to go on and on, and she had been mostly looking at Vera, but as she said the last line, she included Amara in her gaze.

Amara nodded. "You know, I don't know if this is what you guys are talking about or not, but I've been convicted lately that I was trying so hard in my job, making sure that I was the best, promoting myself, and I realized that it was just selfishness on my part. I was more concerned about how I looked than how the people around me looked. I didn't care about lifting others up. You know? It was an eye-opening realization. And I vowed that I was going to try to do my best to make sure that wherever I land, I'm not intimidating the people around me but am instead looking for opportunities to serve them."

"Well, I was a little intimidated when I opened the door and saw how...I don't know how to describe it. Sleek? Something like that. You just look like someone from the city, and I felt dumpy and frumpy when I opened the door and saw you."

"I'm sorry. I wanted to look nice. I... It wasn't necessarily about making a good impression as much as it was about making sure that you didn't think that I was a bum off the street that Vera picked up. Not that I thought that it would matter to you. It mattered to me."

They thought about that for a moment, then Vera said, "I think the way we dress often says a lot about ourselves. Maybe sometimes we put too much thought into it, rather than just making sure clothes fit, and maybe that they not look like they were taken out of the trash barrel. But we don't have to have the latest styles or be totally put together perfectly. Not that we want to worry about how our dress affects other people, but we don't want to spend so much time on looking good that we forget that we're here to serve people, not make sure our clothes are exactly what we want them to be."

"In other words, we should spend less time on how we look on the outside and spend more time making sure our hearts are shining from the inside."

"Yes, exactly. It's the Bible verse that we could talk about today, 'Whose adorning let it not be that outward adorning of plaiting the hair, and of wearing of gold, or of putting on of apparel; But let it be the hidden man of the heart, in that which is not corruptible, even the ornament of a meek and quiet spirit, which is in the sight of God of great price.'"

"So the Bible says that we're basically not supposed to care about how we look?"

"Or maybe God assumes that women have a natural tendency toward vanity. Because it almost reads like it assumes that we're going to make ourselves look as nice as we can. Regardless, I don't think that God thinks we should never brush our hair or take care of ourselves, but rather that it shouldn't be all-consuming."

"And maybe we shouldn't worry about the way other people look?" Norma Jean asked hesitantly. Taking it in, because her big concern wasn't how Laura had looked, and in reality, Laura had had years to work on being a good wife and being a good mother, so of course she was going to be doing better than Norma Jean, who just started.

"Yes. I agree. Or maybe, thinking that we need to do whatever Hollywood is doing. We have a tendency to look at the latest styles, and think we need to imitate them, and somehow think that's okay. But the latest styles are coming from Hollywood, who mostly are anti-Christian, anti-God, anti-modesty, pretty much anti-everything we stand for. Why would we allow them to dictate how we're going to do our makeup, how we're going to do our hair, how we're going to dress? It just... doesn't make sense that we would allow the world to dictate those things to us."

Norma Jean had never thought about why certain things looked good to her and certain things didn't. But it made sense. The fashion industry drove that.

"I think it behooves Hollywood to have us changing our looks all the time, because it needs to sell its products to make us look the way their ideal woman does."

"That's exactly right. We need to change our wardrobe every year because the clothes that we're wearing are sadly out of style and will look outdated if we don't keep up." Vera smiled sweetly. "Although, I want to look good just as much as the next woman does. But I think it probably makes more sense to get some timeless classics into your wardrobe, things that make you look slender and hide obvious flaws. Or things that are just comfortable and you can work in. Because that's really what we're supposed to be doing."

She opened her Bible and turned to a book toward the middle.

"That's pretty much what the Proverbs 31 woman is all about. I... was going to talk about her today. If you notice, the Proverbs 31 woman was very industrious. But the work she did wasn't something that she did outside of her home. It all had to do with taking care of her family. It talks about her buying a vineyard, but then she planted it. So taking care of a garden, even buying a plot of land in order to plant a garden, which is what the Proverbs 31 woman did. And people often point to this passage and say, well, it's a good idea for women to work outside the home because the Proverbs 31 woman did a lot of work. But everything that she did was for the ulterior motive of taking care of her family."

Norma Jean nodded. She wasn't terribly familiar with the Proverbs 31 woman, but that made sense to her. Motherhood was not something most women aspired to anymore, but it was God's plan for women.

"Sometimes I think it would be easier to work outside the home. I would love to drop my kid off with someone else at times. It's not that I don't love her. I love her so much it hurts sometimes, but sometimes I don't like her."

As though on cue, there was a crash in the room, and then Holly started screaming.

"I'm sorry. I thought this might happen. I'd really like to meet, but... it might be better to meet when my daughter is at school. We're less likely to get interrupted."

"You go ahead and take care of it," Vera said gently. "Children are why we're here. Half the reason. Maybe not quite half, because your relationship with your husband is the most important, but Jesus said 'Suffer little children, and forbid them not, to come unto me: for of such is the kingdom of heaven.' He valued children, and he wants us to too."

Norma Jean felt a little better about getting up from the table and going and dealing with Holly. She grabbed a box of Cheerios on her way out of the kitchen and figured that if she did this, it wouldn't be long before Holly wanted a drink. But maybe while she was getting the bread, she could get her a drink.

Holly wasn't terribly upset and had mostly stopped crying by the time Norma Jean got in the room. She hugged her tight and gave her a big pile of Cheerios, which seemed to satisfy her.

And then, because Vera had reminded her, she bent down and kissed her on her forehead and was gratified when Holly's hands came around her neck and squeezed tight.

"I love you, Mommy," she said softly.

"I love you too, sweetheart. So much."

She held her tight, until her arms loosened, and then she tapped her on the nose as she was pulling back.

Vera was right. This was why she was doing this.

Twenty-Two

Hobert had been going to Amara's house and helping to paint for a week and a half.

He had to mend some ropes and nets on Saturday, but he'd come on Sunday, and they worked all day.

"I wish the church was open. I... I always liked going when I was little, but I stopped since I've been in Chicago. I'd really love to get back in the habit. It...gives you a little shot in the arm."

"Yeah. When I was a kid, I would stare in the windows, looking in. Especially at Christmas, because we didn't have a tree. And they kind of fascinated me."

"Wow. Every story you tell from your childhood just makes me feel terrible," Amara said as she rolled paint at the bottom of the dining room wall.

They had painted the hall, moved all the furniture out of the living room, and did that room. The dining room was the last one. They had moved everything to the middle of the room and threw sheets over it.

She had enjoyed working with Hobert. He made things fun. It made time fly by quickly, and they never seemed to run out of things to talk about, although sometimes they did fall into silences that felt companionable and not awkward.

She never met anyone that she had so much fun with, especially while not doing fun things but just enjoying their company.

Her sisters were taking their good old time in coming, and Amara was thinking about heading upstairs and painting the upstairs if they didn't show up soon.

She was not going to go through everything by herself, since when her sisters got there, they would just have to go through it again.

"I don't mean for it to. I... I was agreeing with you. I wish there was a church. I would go. Beyond that, sometimes when the fish aren't biting, I'll pull up a YouTube video or something on my phone and listen to some Scripture and a sermon or someone teaching on the Bible. Which is just as good to me as a sermon."

"When Pastor Calvin ran the church, he mostly did preaching on Sunday mornings and teaching on Wednesday nights. Sunday night could be either-or, but I really appreciated that he did both. The exhortation with the preaching, and then the teaching, where you kind of learned what the Bible said and how you can apply it to your life. I suppose they both have the same effect, just different ways of getting through to people, and they both work for me."

"I heard a lot of good things about him, which is impressive, considering how little I'm in town."

He had been in town to help her with Fran's store. She had taken some mornings to work on arranging things, trying to leave the store so that it wasn't in a mess for the customers. She always left by noon, since Hobert would come help her sometime in the afternoon, and she didn't want to miss him. The mornings were for Fran, and then she had taken to sitting with Gertie for a little bit so Skyler could have a break.

Hobert had teased her that she had come to Raspberry Ridge and she was shaking things up, big-city girl that she was.

She laughed and said that she was just getting back in touch with her small-town roots.

He had given her a look that had warmed her to her toes and made her wish that there was more between them than banter and laughter and an occasional sunset.

"I don't think I'm gonna start anything new once we finish this room. It's going to be too late to watch the sunset today, but maybe you would want to sit out on the patio and just look at the stars or something with me?"

She held her breath. They hadn't done anything but work together for the last two weeks, and she didn't want to upset the apple cart, so to speak, but she longed for a little bit more.

She wanted to know that he did too.

"I'd love to. Maybe you'll come tomorrow afternoon and eat supper with us?"

"Sure." It was an easy yes.

"Probably around four? So it will mean that you won't get a whole lot of work done tomorrow."

"No, that would be great. And it's actually perfect. Since we're finishing up the painting, I can look at the upstairs and maybe run into town and grab some more paint. I'm not going through everything without my sisters being here."

"When are they coming?" he asked casually, although they had discussed it, and he knew that the last time they talked, she didn't know.

"I have no idea. They were supposed to be here two weeks ago. And they didn't show up."

"Well, if they do, bring them on down. Barry is making his shrimp and grits dressing, which is pretty much a meal in itself, and we'll probably have some fish to go along with it."

"Maybe I'll bring some vegetables. If I wrapped potatoes in foil, could we cook them in the fire?"

"Sure can," he said easily, and she took a minute to admire him, the broad shoulders, easy grin, the sparkling brown eyes that almost always had a hint of laughter or fun in them. The slight stubble on his jaw that said he'd been working and hadn't had time to shave.

She actually liked it when he went for a few days without shaving. She hadn't told him that, just admired it.

They finished up and rinsed out their brushes and rollers.

"You know, painting is hard work, but it's very satisfying. You can really see what you've done and accomplished."

"Feels good, doesn't it?" she said. "Although, that might have something to do with getting rid of those hideous colors that Mom picked out."

"I don't know. She's your mom."

"I definitely did not get my taste from her. It must have been from Dad."

"Must have been. Although he was a businessperson, wasn't he?"

"Yeah. They both were. So it's not too surprising with Mom, but who knows, maybe it skipped a generation somewhere."

They laughed, and she asked if he wanted anything to drink before they went outside.

"No thanks. I'm good. It's the company I'm interested in."

He said random things like that that made her toes curl and her neck warm. She didn't necessarily like for it to have that kind of effect on her, but it did.

"I guess we can turn the kitchen lights out," she said as they walked toward the door that led to the patio.

"You go first. I'll flip them off as I'm walking out."

She appreciated that he allowed her to walk out first, using the light to illuminate her way.

She walked over to the comfortable chairs and sat down in one.

She wished she would have thought to drag it a little closer to his, since there were probably four or six inches between it. But she didn't think about it until she had already sat down, and it would be too obvious if she tried to slide closer at that point.

The lights went out, and he walked over, stealthily, with catlike grace.

"I don't know where you learned to walk like that, but I enjoy watching you."

Maybe she shouldn't have started the conversation out like that. Not that she had any plans to say anything else. But that seemed like a very...personal comment. But no more personal than him saying he was here for the company.

Of course, a part of her said, why else would he be there? Painting every evening, after fishing all day.

But there was another part of her that said that he was just being neighborly and being a friend. Wasn't that what friends did? Made the burden easier for each other.

She really didn't know. Her friends in Chicago were the kind of friends that she called up if she wanted to go out to eat or out dancing or something. Not the kind of friends who came over and gave her a hand with anything.

They weren't the kind of friends who would volunteer to help her like she had volunteered him to help her with Fran.

And yet, Hobert had happily done whatever she asked him to.

He sat down beside her, and before he'd even settled, she felt his hand land on top of hers as it rested on her armrest.

Immediately she turned her hand over, palm up, so their hands met and their fingers entwined.

"Looks like a thunderstorm happening over the lake. Wonder if it'll make it to shore?"

She hadn't even noticed. She'd been so wrapped up in thinking of him, but as she looked across the horizon, she could see lightning occasionally lighting up the sky, showing the clouds, and reflecting off the lake water.

"That's funny. The stars are shining here."

"And it's not windy either. Doesn't feel like rain to me."

"Or me. But that sure is pretty."

She hadn't noticed until he said something, but now that she had, she enjoyed the lightning ripping through the sky, lighting up the clouds, putting on a show.

"I think I smell petrichor." He sniffed the air. "But still, I don't think it's gonna rain," he said, looking above them.

"I don't know. I really love thunder and lightning storms, but I'm not sure I want to be here by myself in one. It's one thing to have even one person beside you. But it's completely different when you're alone."

He seemed like he was thinking about that. And then he said, "I promise I won't leave if it starts to storm."

"I wouldn't have expected you to stay. Your relationship with Barry is better than a lot of people's relationship with their actual father. I love how you take care of him and cater to his needs."

"I've been neglecting him lately. I think he's been getting lonely. I'm glad you agreed to come tomorrow night."

"I'm looking forward to it," she said, and she meant that. "But I feel bad Barry can't always come with you."

"He's been sitting in his chair a lot and seems very tired. I don't think he's up to the walk." His voice sounded a little sad.

"I guess that's what happens when you get old."

"Being old is better than being young," he said, and she remembered the conversation they had the day they met.

"I'm pretty sure you feel like you won that argument, but I'm also fairly certain that I should have been the one to win that argument."

He laughed, like she thought he would. And then she said, "I'd like to go on the boat again with you. Not to invite myself or anything."

"I told you you're welcome to come out anytime. I'd love to have you."

"I can't do it tomorrow, because I have to finish up everything in Fran's, but...if my sisters don't come, maybe the next day?"

"That would be perfect. You're coming to eat tomorrow night, so you can just sleep on the boat. Unless that was too much for you? Do you need to sleep here?"

"No. That wasn't too much at all, and I'll definitely sleep on the boat. But maybe I'll bring a pillow. And a blanket and a mattress, and while I'm at it, why don't I just bring the whole bed."

"If it's nice enough, you can sleep on the deck."

"I don't think I want to do that by myself, and...I guess I assumed you were going to be on the boat too."

"Yeah. I'll be there." His voice was whisper soft. His thumb ran over the back of her hand, sending chills up her arm, and they landed somewhere in the vicinity of her heart, warming it the whole way through.

"Then yeah. Maybe I'll bring a blanket and a pillow, and we'll sleep on the deck. Actually, I'll bring two."

"I do own pillows and blankets."

"One blanket for the bottom, two pillows, and one blanket for the top. Or two blankets for the top. A comforter will be more comfortable on the bottom." She was rambling, because it was all she could do to not ask him to move closer. Her whole being was focused on their joined hands and how sweet that felt.

"However you set it up will work for me," he said easily. His thumb continued to stroke the back of her hand.

She closed her eyes, just focusing on the feeling of having that small, light touch. It was slow and languid, and she wasn't even sure he realized he was doing it.

"There is a part of me that wants to go back to Chicago with you."

"You couldn't do that! You belong here. You'd be...miserable in Chicago."

"You should see me when I'm not around you. I think I'm just as miserable without you as I would be if you weren't around. And I was thinking that I would be less miserable if I was in Chicago with you than if I were here by myself."

She was shocked. He had been considering moving to Chicago?

She couldn't believe it. But she didn't really live anywhere close to the lake, although she worked in downtown Chicago, and occasionally her commute gave her glimpses of it, but there weren't any affordable apartments that were anywhere close to where she lived. And she knew that Hobert would be miserable.

"You don't have to get worried. I told you, I promised Barry I wouldn't leave him. I guess maybe in the back of my head, I thought we could live on the boat or something, but he wants to just stay here. And I think that's what I need to do too. I...wasn't really invited to Chicago anyway, although I can move to the city if I want to, right?"

She smiled. "But you don't," she said easily, knowing it was true.

He squeezed her hand. "Maybe I was being presumptuous."

"You aren't. I've thought over and over about moving here. You know? I mean, in four weeks, I'm heading back, and I'm not going to have time to drive to Raspberry Ridge even on weekends. Most of the time, I work weekends. I've never heard good things about long-distance relationships anyway. I suppose you could call me when you're docking at Chicago to unload or whatever, but I don't get off work until five, and most of the time, I don't leave until six or seven."

"That's rough. Almost as rough as a fisherman's hours."

"Not nearly as rough as a fisherman's hours. I've experienced those and have a newfound respect for fishermen everywhere, but those are the hours I have to keep if I want to continue the path that I'm on, be promoted, get into the position of management, where I expect to be in the next ten years. After that, I have my eye on the top. The very top."

She didn't want to say that. She didn't really want that anymore. She might as well admit it.

"Lately, none of that excites me like it used to."

"Because of working for someone else?" he guessed, but she shook her head.

"No. Or maybe. I don't know. Just, it's so nice here. People welcomed me with open arms. I enjoy helping Fran, I love going with Vera to her Bible study, and I think we even might have someone coming to work at the church. I've heard rumors, and Vera said that she and Gertie's daughter-in-law, Homer's wife, were in touch with someone who was very interested in moving back to Raspberry Ridge."

"So he's from here? And he would be the pastor at the church?"

"That's what I understand. Now, I'm not on that committee, so I can't say for sure, but it looks very promising."

"It's exciting."

Another big bolt of lightning lit up the entire western sky, and they both stopped talking for a bit before she said in a soft voice, "Wow. That's pretty amazing."

Twenty-Three

Hobert watched the lightning flash across the sky. There was something elemental about it. Something that reached down into his soul. Or maybe it was the idea of watching it with Amara that changed everything. Their linked hands made him feel like they were connected, and he loved the fact that he could talk to her about anything. Even the idea of moving to Chicago, which of course he wasn't going to do. But she hadn't thought he was a crazy stalker or anything like that.

Thankfully.

A gust of wind blew, and he smiled. "Maybe we're going to get some rain after all. My fisherman's forecast isn't very good."

"Well, we're not on the lake. You can't be expected to be accurate, this far inland."

"Oh. So my fisherman's forecast is only accurate if I'm on the water?"

"Of course. You can't be expected to be proficient on land *and* sea," she said with a smile.

Her hand felt soft and right in his, but after the weeks of working with her, he wanted to be closer.

He could hardly ask her to stand up so he could put his arms around her.

That was probably not something that would go over very well. Or maybe it would. He wouldn't know unless he asked, but he didn't want to ruin whatever was growing between them by being too pushy or forward. Or asking her for more than she wanted to give. He knew for now that she was willing to hold his hand, and he supposed that if he were a reasonable man, he would be content with that. But somehow, he wasn't. He wanted more.

"Would you like to dance?" she said, her suggestion seeming to come out of nowhere, but it was exactly what he wanted.

"Watching storms makes you want to dance? Is that good music?" he asked as thunder rumbled in the distance.

"I don't know. Maybe I just want to be a little closer to you, because while I'm not exactly scared, there is a little bit of...anxiety?"

"I'm not going to argue with you. But I'm not gonna sing for you either. I don't think I probably know any songs that are appropriate for us to dance to anyway."

He wasn't quite sure exactly what kind of dancing she was talking about, and he had to admit he was a little nervous. He hadn't exactly danced a lot in his life.

And he didn't really listen to a whole lot of music, so he probably didn't know the songs that she knew.

She pulled out her phone and put on something slow and gentle.

She stood up, and he followed her.

"I've got to admit something."

"Okay," she said as she stepped closer. That was exactly where he wanted her. Well, he wouldn't mind having her even closer, but he almost jumped out of his skin when she put her hands on his waist.

"I've...never danced before."

"Oh," she said, like the thought had never occurred to her. Even though she knew his upbringing. Surely she would have guessed that this wasn't something that would be like second nature to him, the way it was to her.

"So... Do you still want to?" she asked softly.

"Yeah," he said. "If it gets me closer to you."

She laughed a little and then said, "Put your arms around me," and her arms went up to his shoulders, and she moved close enough that she could wrap her arms around his neck, touching the hair at the back that had grown long enough that she could thread her fingers through the back of it, twirling it around and giving him shivers he felt the whole way to his bones.

He didn't have a problem obeying her command, but he wasn't quite sure where he was supposed to put his arms around her, if he was supposed to wrap them around her neck, because he was gonna have a lot of arm left over if he did that. So he just wrapped them around her back and pulled her close, wanting to touch her everywhere at once but trying to content himself with playing with her hair, the way she had been doing with his. Hers flowed down her back longer than his, and he could reach it just fine.

"Wow. Yours is a lot softer than mine is."

She smiled. As though his words made her happy.

"Hasn't anyone complimented your hair before?" he asked.

"No one's ever seemed surprised it was soft. I...like what that says about you."

All it said was that he had grown up in a shack on the edge of town and had never really been a part of polite society. But for some reason, that made her happy.

"Why?" he finally asked, moving slowly as she did, just swaying back and forth, barely moving his feet. If this was dancing, he was all in. All. In.

"Because it means that you haven't stood around, dancing with a whole bunch of different girls. I...have always been very leery of guys who jump from girl to girl to girl, always breaking up and moving on. It...seems to show a lack of character. A lack of determination to stick. Or maybe a wanderlust I'm not interested in."

"That's what happened with Barry's wife."

"What?" she said, like he totally changed the subject.

"Barry's wife. Remember I told you that I asked him once what happened to her, and he wouldn't tell me? I asked him again not long ago, after you and I talked, and he told me. He had been out on the boat, working hard to support her, and she kept spending more and more money, and he kept working more and more, until one day he came home after being out for more than a week, and it was the middle of the day, and she was in bed with someone else."

"My goodness. That's terrible," she said, and her hands stopped moving in his hair.

He wished he could get her to start again. He'd liked it. He couldn't remember the last time he had a soft touch anywhere on him, but it felt particularly good on the back of his neck. Thumbing through his hair, like...he wasn't sure what. Just soothing. But at the same time, it didn't soothe all the parts of him.

Finally, he decided that he'd just say something. "Why did you quit moving your fingers through my hair?" He hoped he didn't sound too desperate.

"I'm sorry. Did you like that?" she asked, sounding hopeful and amused at the same time.

"Yeah. It...feels good."

He didn't want to say that he'd never felt anyone do that to him before. Then she would say, "I'm so sad; everything you say about your childhood sounds sad." And it wasn't his intention to make her sad.

"So did Barry leave?"

"Yes."

"Just turned around and left? Wasn't he angry?"

"I think he was angry, I think he was hurt more than anything, but he said he knew that there was no point in him doing the things that he wanted to, hurting the other man, even though he said the other man obviously wasn't as strong as he was and he could take him easily, but... she had made her decision. It was obvious. She didn't want Barry, she wanted that man. And she was pregnant."

"Barry left his child?" Amara said in a slightly louder voice, and her fingers stopped again.

"It wasn't his. She told him it was the other man's. At that point, he felt like he didn't have anything to lose, and so he walked out, got on the boat, found this place up here, and staked out the ground."

Her fingers had started moving again, and he closed his eyes, resting his cheek on the top of her head, breathing in her scent. It smelled wild like the lake and yet sweet, too.

He could breathe it all night. And he wanted to.

He wondered about the next night, when she said she would sleep on the boat with him. She said she would bring one blanket for the bottom.

He wasn't quite sure what she was planning on for that. Although, she had made sure to say two blankets for the top, but it sounded like they'd be sleeping side by side. All of a sudden, he couldn't wait until tomorrow night.

"I thought your dad had the shanty and the ground and Barry lived on the boat?" she said after a while as the song that had been playing flowed into another one.

She laid her head on his shoulder, and he could feel her breath against his neck. It messed with his thoughts, and it took a little bit to think about what she'd said and find the words to answer her.

"He did. I guess when my dad and my mom came, my dad and Barry built the shack together, and then for some reason, maybe because my dad had a wife and was going to have a kid, Barry moved to the boat.

"I guess my dad was too drunk to ever remember that it wasn't his to begin with, or Barry just didn't care. Regardless, Dad and I lived in the shack, and Barry lived on the boat, and I never had a clue that Barry owned everything until he told me about a week ago."

"Wow. Humble man."

"I guess a man who had everything ripped from him, and rather than trying to start again, he just...retreated."

"I don't know what I'd do if that happened to me."

"I can understand how he feels, I suppose. Not totally, of course, but it's...something I feel. Down to the deepest part of me, that whatever you do, there won't ever be anyone for me but you."

He could feel her breath stop. He hadn't meant to upset her, hadn't meant to say anything that was going to shift the delicate balance of whatever was between them, something between friendship and more. Something...tender and sweet, and he wanted to protect it with everything he had, but he also wanted more with everything he had as well.

"You don't mean that," she said softly, roughly, like he had taken her breath away.

"I do. Although, I didn't want to upset you. Sorry."

"No, you didn't upset me, I just... I guess I feel the same way, but I don't want to. Not really. Because...it's impossible. You're not going to Chicago. We already talked about that, and I'm not letting you. And even if I wanted to come back on weekends, what you just said about Barry's wife... Long-distance relationships just don't work."

"I don't think I would have to worry about you straying, and you know that I wouldn't. But it wouldn't be fair to you."

"What about you? You'd have a wife who was consumed with her work. You don't want that."

"I guess that's not really the way I see you."

"Then you don't know the real me," she said, and she sounded a little annoyed.

"I'm sorry. I should have kept my mouth shut." He turned his head, kissing her forehead. Although he hadn't meant to. It was just a natural thing that happened. Because no one had actually ever done it to him. Not that he remembered anyway. But it just seemed instinctive.

Her arms moved from around his neck, and her fingertips ran down his cheeks.

"Hobert," she whispered.

"Hmm?" he said, not wanting to talk. Just wanting to feel. She was touching him, and wherever she touched him left a trail of warmth that felt good clear from his head to his toes and every cell in between.

He didn't want her to stop.

"I... Kiss me?"

He just had. Right on the forehead. She wanted another kiss like that?

He gently touched his lips to a spot just beside where he kissed her before.

Then, as though that wasn't enough, he kissed her again, a little lower, and a little lower. She lifted her head up. Her eyes were closed.

He bent his head a little further and touched his lips to hers.

Something settled down into his soul, right and good, and he swallowed hard.

Her eyes opened just a little, and then she said, "More?"

He looked at her, her eyes under the stars, reflecting the light, and the sweet expression of her face, and it made him feel like maybe he wasn't worthy. Maybe he wanted more than what he deserved. Maybe she deserved someone who knew how to dance, how to kiss, how to treat a woman in the moonlight. As he obviously knew nothing.

"I want more too. But I'm not sure..." He let his words trail off.

"Not sure it's a good idea?" she asked softly.

"Not sure...how."

She narrowed her eyes a bit, and then to his surprise, she smiled. It was a smile that reminded him of Eve in the Garden of Eden.

She didn't say anything more, but moved closer to him, and put her mouth on his.

Her teeth nibbled on his bottom lip, and while it felt good, it also made him smile. She took advantage of that a little, and it didn't take him too long to catch on.

That was the kind of kissing that he wanted, although that kind of kissing made him want more than just kissing.

And he figured he was going to have to stop, and soon, or he wasn't going to want to.

The world seemed to shift around him, and he probably wouldn't have noticed if lightning struck right beside the house and a thunderclap exploded over top of his ear. But he finally lifted his head and laid his cheek on top of hers, breathing hard.

"You are amazing," he managed to say. Then he swallowed, taking a breath. "You should probably take it easy on me. I don't seem to have quite the experience you do."

It made him a little angry, a little jealous. But he couldn't help what she had done when he wasn't there.

And he was going to have to let her go and not think about what she was doing without him at that point either.

"I've only kissed a couple of guys, but I've seen movies, and I've read a few books."

"Books on kissing?" he asked, lifting his head and looking down at her, unable to believe people wrote such a thing.

"No. Romance books. Books where the main storyline is about two people falling in love."

"Wow. And kissing."

"Isn't that what people do when they're falling in love?"

"I don't know. Guess that's what I do when I'm holding you."

"I care for you. A lot," she said, sounding a little strained, like it was hard for her to say. "So much."

He swallowed. He wanted to tell her that he loved her. But it probably wasn't the right time.

He'd no sooner thought that than he said, "I love you. I always will."

Just then, a crack of lightning shot through the sky, feeling closer than all the others, although it still was out on the lake.

Thunder followed almost immediately.

"We should go inside. Actually, I probably should go home."

He didn't let her go but put his mouth to her ear, nibbling at the top of it after he spoke and feeling her shiver. It was good to know that he could make her have the same reaction that he did.

"I don't want you to walk home in that storm."

He smiled then, remembering what she had said about being alone during storms.

"How about we go in, and we'll sit on the couch. I'll wait until the storm's over before I go."

"Are you sure?" she asked, biting her lip as she looked up at him.

He nodded. Then he said, although he didn't want to, not even a little, "As long as you promise not to kiss me again. I don't think I can handle more than one of those a night. That was...amazing."

"You might have said that before."

"No. I called you amazing. The kiss... That was amazing too."

She smiled, then stepped back, her hand coming down and grabbing his, before she picked her phone off the table where she'd set it and led him into the house.

She didn't bother to turn on any lights but walked through the kitchen, careful to warn him if she thought he might bump into something, until they made it to the couch, which was still covered with a sheet, but it didn't matter, they just sat down on top of it.

Another streak of lightning lit up the entire sky, followed by another roar of thunder that seemed to rumble on and on.

"That was a big one," she said, and he could hear the fear in her voice.

She probably wasn't used to facing these alone. There were people everywhere in Chicago, not that people could save her, but humans seemed to find safety in numbers, the same way fish seemed to as well.

"It was a pretty one," he said, putting his arm around her and holding her close.

She shifted so that her head rested on his shoulder, and she must have kicked her shoes off, because she tucked her feet up on the couch, curling up beside him.

He could get used to this too. Kissing, curling up and snuggling, talking to her, laughing with her, working with her. Was there anything that they did that he didn't love and want to do more of with her?

He couldn't think of a single thing.

Maybe they would have disagreements. He couldn't imagine it. People disagree about things, but they could figure out how to work things out so that they didn't fight. Surely. He had lived with Barry for years, and they'd never said a cross word to each other.

Maybe that was Barry though. Maybe it wasn't because of him. But he'd try as hard as he could to figure out a way to get along with her, if... if she'd have him.

But she just said tonight that it was impossible. That kiss, this cuddling, the laughter and the banter, all of it was going to have to end.

By the time the storm was over, she was sleeping soundly against his chest.

He thought of Barry, hoped the old man had gone in the house and wasn't worried about him. He was going to have to stop in there before he went down to the ship, but he wasn't going to leave. He was going to stay here as long as he could, holding Amara, until the very last possible second. He might never get a chance again.

He fell asleep, but the internal clock in his head woke him up at exactly 1:50 according to his phone as he moved around, fumbling until he picked it up and looked at it.

It was time to leave.

He slipped out as best he could, setting her down gently as she murmured a protest, a soft one, sweet and low, before he slipped out the rest of the way.

He wished he had a blanket or something to cover her with, but he just bent down on one knee, pressed a kiss to her forehead, and then let himself out as quietly as he could.

Twenty-Four

Amara pretty much spent the next day dancing on air. She relived the kiss a million times, and while she knew that her imagination could not make it any better than the real thing, she had a hard time thinking about anything else.

She found herself stopping whatever she was doing, staring off into space, her fingers carefully touching her lips.

Wishing with all her heart that Hobert was still there.

What had the man turned her into? A silly schoolgirl, who couldn't think of anything but her latest crush. Except, Hobert did not feel like a crush. He felt like the real deal. Like everything she ever wanted in a man, honesty and integrity, tenderness and kindness, laughter and fun, and a special kind of something that was his and his alone.

An attraction that made her want to drop everything that she was doing and just be with him.

Of course, she felt like a fool in the hardware store, as she stood in the aisle, touching her lips with a dreamy smile on her face. Blueberry Beach was not a huge town, but it did have a hardware store, and she was able to order more paint.

If her sisters didn't show up, she was going to end up painting the outside of the house.

Except, she didn't think the kind of siding it had should be painted.

Well, they better show up soon, or they were going to find out.

She thanked the clerk as the teenage helper carried the eight gallons that she had bought out to her car. It wasn't enough to do every room in the upstairs, but it would get a good start.

She and Hobert would have lots to do together.

Of course, maybe she would ask him if they could spend a little time kissing too.

She smiled again at how sweet he had been the night before. Not just kissing her, and admitting that he didn't know how, but by staying, knowing that she was scared and didn't want to be alone, and leaving at some point, some point after she had fallen into a deep sleep and didn't even notice. She just woke up in the morning with the feeling of loss, but a smile on her face as well.

The man could make her smile, that was for sure.

And she couldn't wait until tonight. They would eat together and spend the night on the boat, looking at the stars. Of course, if it rained, they might have to adjust their plans, because she was not going to allow him to stay on the deck of the boat if it rained. But somehow, sleeping on the deck together didn't seem as...intimate as sleeping downstairs in the berth together.

She wasn't sure she wanted to examine why one was okay and one wasn't, but she didn't have any intentions of doing anything wrong. Except... Maybe quitting her job and moving to Raspberry Ridge. But that wasn't wrong. It actually felt more right than she could say.

Maybe she should talk to someone about it. Vera seemed like a good choice, or Fran.

But it turned out that all of her thoughts were in vain, because as she finished wrapping the last potato in aluminum foil and dropped it into her bag, she heard a car, which was unusual enough that it made her stop and listen. She heard gravel crunching, and then after a few seconds, the door slammed.

One of her sisters, no doubt.

She hurried to the door, going through the coatroom, in time to open the outside door for Mertie, who was digging in the flower bed for the key.

"Mertie!" she said, happy to see her oldest, serious sister and realizing how lonely it felt in the house when Hobert wasn't there.

Although she hadn't noticed it at all today.

She went down the steps, her arms out, as Mertie dropped her bag and strode forward with a smile.

They wrapped their arms around each other, Mertie composed as always but maybe just a little bit excited. It had been four months since they'd seen each other, since they finished cleaning out their parents' condo and sold it.

"I'm sorry I got delayed."

"It's no problem. But come on in and sit down. Are you hungry?" Amara said, praying that she would say yes. She didn't want to have to cancel on Hobert, but she supposed that she needed to at least welcome her sister into the house, although it was as much her sister's house as it was hers, so she supposed she didn't need to.

"I'm starved. Tell me you have supper ready. Even though it's only 3:30."

"I have supper ready. Except, we're going to the neighbors' to eat."

"We are?" Mertie said, looking every inch the Christian speaker, with her pressed slacks and her fitted sweater that buttoned the whole way to the top, and her serious eyeglasses and her hair that was perfectly coiffured, never a single strand out of place.

"Yes." Amara couldn't keep a smile from her face. "He's been helping me paint, and his adopted father is going to be cooking shrimp and grits dressing, whatever that is, and I just finished wrapping potatoes in foil, and it's going to be a great night. I know you're going to love it." And she was sure she would.

Mertie, serious and knowledgeable, and an admirer of all things upright and pure, would absolutely love Hobert. In fact, maybe she shouldn't introduce them. She wouldn't want Hobert to fall... No. That would never happen. Hobert was as straight as an arrow. He would never leave her. And her sister was also as straight as an arrow, and she would never do anything with Amara's boyfriend.

Whoa.

She brought herself up short, in the process of gathering up the potatoes. Was Hobert her boyfriend?

Well, what else did you call the man that you kissed in the moonlight, snuggled up with on the couch as a thunderstorm raged, and fell asleep on his lap while he held you, stroking your hair and making sure you were okay?

She couldn't think of another word for that. It definitely passed the line of a friend, blew by it.

Wow. She hadn't been expecting that and wasn't quite sure how to react.

"Amara? I thought you said we were leaving now?" Mertie said, standing by the door.

"I think you might want to wear different shoes. We're going to walk."

"We're going to walk?" Mertie asked, like she had said they were going to walk down Main Street with no clothes on or something.

"It's a beautiful night. Beautiful evening, warm, perfect lake breeze, and you will love it. Trust me."

"You need to quit saying that, because it makes me feel like I'm actually not going to like it," Mertie said as she gave Amara a look. "What should I wear? I only have these and six other pairs."

"A pair that you don't mind walking in," Amara said.

"Well, if I'm going to put sneakers on, I'll have to change my entire outfit."

"Mertie. This is not a big deal. These people are not pretentious, not in the slightest." She didn't want to give Mertie any preconceived notions, just allowing Hobert to do what he did best, which was be himself, honest and upright, a man of character, who obviously was someone that anyone could trust. But her sister was stressing when she didn't need to.

"Just put shoes on. Ones you don't mind walking in. Unless you want to walk in your bare feet and carry your shoes."

"My goodness. What has gotten into you? We don't walk in our bare feet anywhere. What are we, like six?" Mertie said, with a note of snobbery in her voice which made Amara want to laugh, but she knew she couldn't, or it would make Mertie mad.

She wanted to hurry Mertie out, but Mertie was the kind of person who the more you pushed them to go faster, the slower they went.

So, Amara passed the time by thinking of last night's kiss and whether or not she would be able to steal another one tonight.

Probably not with her sister there. Which...made her want to ask her sister if she'd rather just stay home.

But then Amara would feel bad and feel the need to hurry home to be with her sister.

Finally she was ready to go, and they stepped out the door together.

As they walked, Mertie talked about her trip and explained why she hadn't been able to come when she thought she was going to be able to, since a surprise meeting had come up, and she couldn't turn it down.

Amara understood. They all kind of had that work ethic. Well, she and Mertie did. Olive seemed to bounce around from place to place, but she was always so easygoing and always had a little bit of wanderlust.

She was a peacemaker and able to get along with anyone.

Still, she couldn't fault Mertie for trying to do her best at her job.

"We're walking away from town," Mertie said as they got to the end of the driveway and turned left instead of right.

"We are. And there is a beautiful healing garden that's been planted since the last time we were here. I'd love to show it to you, but I don't want to be late. So we're going to keep going."

"Down the bluffs?" Mertie asked as they made it to the end of the street.

"No. The opposite direction. Just trust me, you are going to have the best time tonight." Amara thought maybe she shouldn't work it up too much, because maybe Mertie really would be disappointed. It wasn't like they were going to do anything special, other than eat good food around the campfire, with great company, and she would see Barry from their childhood.

She was sure Mertie would remember.

She had a lot of other things she wanted to ask Mertie, specifically about her parents, but she listened to Mertie prattle on about her job and the things that she had coming up and try to explain why she wasn't going to be able to stay as long as she thought she was or why she might have to leave early.

"You don't want to stay?" Amara finally said.

"Oh no. It's not that I don't want to stay," Mertie said right away. Too quickly. And Amara narrowed her eyes.

But she knew her big sister. Mertie wasn't going to stay.

"Do you remember Barry?"

"The old fisherman who lived in the boat?"

"The very one."

"Sure. Is he still around?"

"He is, and we're going to see him tonight."

"Oh my goodness. That's the way down there. Does he still live on his boat? Are we...eating on a boat?" Mertie asked, sounding a little bit excited. It wasn't every day a person got to eat on a boat after all. Even her sister, who was old and mature, thought that was still special.

"No. We're going to his house. He shares it now with Hobert Gilcrest."

Mertie stopped.

"Did you say Hobert Gilcrest?" she asked, enunciating the name clearly.

"Yes. Come on. We're going to be late."

"But Mom told us that we were not allowed to associate with Hobert Gilcrest. Ever. For anything."

"Mertie. We were kids. We're not kids anymore, and Mom's gone."

"But..." Mertie started walking again. "I wonder why we weren't allowed?"

"I'm not sure. I suspect there's something deeper, but there's always the chance that it was just because his dad was an alcoholic, and they were poor."

"They were poor. I remember seeing him in bare feet, scrawny little kid, with his nose pressed against the church window." There was a pause as Mertie slowed down. "Come to think of it, I don't understand why no one ever let him in," Mertie said, sounding thoughtful.

"I didn't realize he was doing it, or I would have."

"It didn't occur to me that someone should have. At the time, I just knew who he was, because he rode the bus, and Mom told us not to associate with him, and I just thought he was up to no good. You know, sneaking around, waiting until he could, I don't know, steal an old lady's purse or something."

"And all because Mom said not to talk to him? Not because of anything that you'd ever seen him do?" Amara said, thinking about how biases started. If a person listened to someone talk badly about someone for long enough, they'd learn to hate them themself, even though there was no basis in fact to what the people were saying. Humans just started to believe the lies if they were told often and convincingly enough, and never thought about researching the information for themselves.

"Yeah. In fact, as I'm thinking about it, I can't remember anyone ever saying anything bad about him, other than he was poor and his dad was an alcoholic. I don't even remember anyone saying that they couldn't afford to pay their bills."

"Maybe that's because they didn't have any bills," Amara said, and it hit her for the first time that maybe her sister was going to be less than impressed.

She had been so overwhelmed with Hobert that she forgot that her reaction the first time she had seen the shack that he lived in was...not positive.

But it was too late, because they were going down the dirt road and headed toward the shack. Too late to turn back.

"Wow. That place is a dump," Mertie said, in a distracted tone of voice as though she was still thinking about what they had been talking about earlier about Hobert and how people had talked badly about him until both of them had disliked him, for absolutely no reason, other than people had said things and that they shouldn't like him.

"That's where we're eating."

"What are you trying to do, kill me?" Mertie said again, slowing and looking with irritation at her sister.

"At the very least, we can eat potatoes, but I promise you, you'll have a good time if you let yourself. Remember what we said? How we made assumptions that weren't true just based on what we saw and not what was actually there."

Twenty-Five

Mertie narrowed her eyes, but she picked up the pace again, until the campfire came into view, burning bright.

As though he had been watching for them, Hobert left the fire as soon as he saw them, murmuring a few words to Barry who still sat in the chair, before he hurried to close the distance between them, coming to Amara and wrapping his arms around her, and as she lifted her face, he kissed her right on the lips.

It was quick and not showy, but it still shocked her sister.

"Amara!" Mertie said, disapproval laced with shock and horror in her voice.

"Mertie, this is my boyfriend, Hobert." She prayed that he wasn't going to object to her use of that word. "And, Hobert, this is my sister, Mertie."

He held out his hand. "Pleased to meet you, Mertie. I think pretty highly of your sister."

He put his arm back around her and put his lips down to her ear.

"Boyfriend?" he said, and there was laughter and love in his voice, and she wanted to box up the sound and hold it close to her heart.

"Hobert. I remember you from our childhood. It's been a long time, and you've definitely changed."

"I remember you too. And you changed a bit as well. Gotten prettier, I suppose," he said easily. And Amara smiled.

She didn't think of Hobert as a charmer. But his words sounded charming and sweet, and it almost made her serious sister smile. Amara could see her lips quirking, but the smile just didn't quite win out over the disapproval that seemed to radiate off her.

If Hobert noticed, he didn't say anything.

"Hey, let's get these potatoes on the fire so they can get cooking. The shrimp and grits dressing is ready, and I figured I'd throw some fish on in a few minutes, after the potatoes get good and hot."

"I have no idea how to cook these over the fire, so I'm depending on you to let us know when they're done."

"I actually haven't done it too much, so we'll just use the best guess method."

"You can put a fork in them. That'll usually tell you," Barry said.

"Good idea." Hobert put an arm around Barry. "Mertie, this is Barry. Barry, Mertie. Amara remembered him from childhood, so maybe Mertie does too." He moved, putting the potatoes in the fire, then going back and standing with Barry.

Amara watched him. He moved with that catlike grace that she admired so much, but it was more than that which drew her eyes to him. It was his character that showed in everything that he did, the honesty in his eyes, the sincerity in his voice, the way he cared about people, and his loyalty. His desire to do things that helped her, and his willingness to sacrifice, his sleep, his comfort, whatever it was necessary to make her comfortable.

She'd never met anyone like him, and she realized that she would be a fool to let him go.

She had to figure something out. Maybe she could work from home. Work from the mansion. Maybe just travel down to Chicago once in a while.

That would mean that she was most likely giving up her path to the top, but she found that it wasn't really what she wanted anymore.

Barry and Mertie were catching up, and Amara noticed that another chair had appeared from somewhere.

She smiled. Someone had been thinking that perhaps her sister would show up after all. Just one more thing that made her smile about Hobert. He had heard her when she said that her sister might come, and he meant it when he offered for her to just go ahead and bring her along.

"She looks a lot more serious than you do," Hobert came over and murmured in her ear.

"She is. But I know she's going to love you. How could she not?"

"Easily. The same way she has never said a word to me in her entire life before, even though we lived in the same town."

He paused, then he lowered his voice even more and moved his lips to her ear. "Boyfriend? I've never been anyone's boyfriend before. Maybe you're going to have to explain to me exactly what this entails."

"No. I don't think I need to. All you need to know is that it entails a lot of kissing."

"I like it. I like it a lot. I'm all in for this boyfriend thing."

"Good. I'm sorry I kinda sprung it on you, but I realized earlier today that must be what you are. I mean, I don't slow dance with anyone else in the moonlight, or snuggle in anyone else's lap when a storm is brewing outside, or fall asleep with someone else's hands in my hair. And most of all, I don't kiss anyone else either. That must mean you're my boyfriend."

"You really thought about that."

"I thought about you all day. I couldn't stop. I felt like I was about fifteen, rather than almost thirty."

"Well, that makes two of us. The fishing was terrible today, which made my problem worse, because all I wanted to do was turn the boat around back to you. I...didn't, but I wanted to."

"I love you," she said softly, kissing his cheek.

"I love you too. Maybe we can get in some of that boyfriend kissing later."

"Yeah. You'll have to make sure of it," she said, her eyes crinkling. Then they dropped. "I guess you know I'm not going to be able to stay on the boat tonight and go with you tomorrow."

"I figured as much, and I'm disappointed, but I'm happy your sister finally showed up."

They stopped whispering to each other then, as everyone gathered around the fire.

Amara noticed that Barry didn't move a whole lot and seemed a little slower than he had even the last time she was here.

She wanted to suggest to Hobert that he ought to take him to the doctor, but she was willing to bet Barry wouldn't go.

Maybe they could talk about it later. But as they talked about the weather, and Mertie told them how they intended to sell the mansion, her eyes kept moving to him, and she worried a little. Not necessarily about Barry, who seemed relaxed and at ease, but at how Hobert was going to take it if he didn't pull through. Or if he continued to get worse. Hobert loved him like a father, and as hard as losing Amara's parents had been, she couldn't imagine losing someone as close to her as Barry was to Hobert.

She figured she'd pray about it and hope that the Lord would lend His strength and comfort to Hobert, if that's the way things went. Then she realized she was getting the cart ahead of the horse and tried to focus on the conversation around the fire.

"So this is where you live year-round?" Mertie asked, and Amara knew her well enough to know she was trying to keep the shock and horror out of her voice, but she wasn't very successful at it.

"Yep. Year-round."

"What about winter? Don't you get cold?" she asked, and Amara remembered her thinking the exact same thing and Hobert telling her that he just moved the bed closer to the stove.

Barry said something similar to Mertie, and Amara thought his voice sounded tired and weak.

As soon as Barry was done with his answer to Mertie, Amara said, "Hobert, I was absolutely fascinated with the fishing you did when I went with you. How do you determine where you're going to go each day?" she asked, knowing that he just went wherever he thought there might be good fishing and didn't really have any specific rhyme or reason, but at least it was getting the subject away from their house and Mertie's fascination with how they survived in such drab conditions.

It wasn't long after that that Barry announced that he thought the potatoes were probably almost done, and Hobert could get started cooking the fish.

"Are we setting the table anywhere? Do I need to help?" Mertie asked, standing up from her seat and taking a few steps, which made Amara smile. Mertie was the kind of person who just couldn't sit still, always had to be doing something, and if no one had organized it, she would.

"You can go ahead and sit back down, Mertie. We can just eat here in the chairs."

"So you've eaten here before?" Mertie said, her eyes narrowed, her gaze full of concern and suspicion and holding Amara's.

"I have. I had the best fish I've ever tasted here. You are going to be amazed. I keep hearing about this shrimp and grits dressing, so I have high expectations, just saying."

"I hope it's good. Wore me out to make it today," Barry said. "Used to be, when I was a young man, I could go all day long. And sometimes we did. Why there was this one time..."

And he went off on the story, much to Amara's relief. Mertie could hardly grill them on the level of their poverty if Barry was talking, and even though Amara had heard the story back when she was a child, and Barry had told it again not that long ago, it was a good one, and she thought it would probably keep her sister's attention. If not bring back the nostalgia for their childhood on the beach. Days of freedom, the wind and the surf, the pebble beach and lake views.

Days of freedom and happiness.

Maybe their family hadn't been the most loving family ever, but she had nothing but good memories of her childhood. At least here.

By the time Barry was done with his story, the fish were cooked, and the potatoes were ready as well.

"This is amazing," Amara said after she swallowed her first bite of the dressing. "It definitely lives up to its hype."

Barry smiled, but she noticed that he didn't eat much. Maybe cooking had worn him out, and she felt bad that they had asked him to.

Twenty-Six

They chatted around the campfire, Mertie finally getting off her kick of asking personal questions and enjoying the conversation which consisted of tales of the lake, fish they caught, and Mertie actually told a couple stories of their dad taking her and Olive fishing. Amara had been too young.

"I can't believe I missed that," Amara said.

"Yeah, by the time you were old enough, Dad and Mom were so wrapped up in their business that they didn't do it anymore, I guess. But Olive and I had a great time, and Olive caught that fish that was almost as big as she was. If Dad hadn't been holding onto her, she would have gotten pulled into the lake."

"Why is it that the smallest person on the boat always catches the biggest fish?" Hobert said, and they all laughed. It did seem to be true.

"Maybe that just shows you that fishing is a lot more about being in the right place at the right time, or maybe just being there, than it is about luck or skill or any of the things that people get so wrapped up about," Hobert said, and Amara met his eyes.

They were thinking about the sonar and all the things that modern fishermen used to figure out where the fish were and to try to catch them, and while it didn't exactly apply, she understood what he was saying. A person just had to put in the work if they wanted to succeed. Even if they didn't have all the big fancy tools and equipment, they couldn't be successful if they didn't work.

And it was work to get up at two o'clock in the morning every day to go out on the boat.

It was going on nine o'clock when Amara decided that even though she was having such a good time, Hobert needed to get up early. She felt bad that he was losing so much sleep because of her.

"I think it's time for us to go. I know these fellas have an early morning."

Mertie had already gotten up and rinsed out the dishes, although she'd been a little aghast when Hobert had said that he just used water from the hose and pointed to where he kept the dish detergent.

Thankfully, Mertie didn't throw up on the spot, and she actually did get up and wash dishes.

Amara thought maybe she should get up and offer to help, but she didn't. It only took a couple of minutes for Mertie to wash all four plates and spoons.

"You might as well take that dressing home with you if you liked it. I love it, but I'm not going to be here tomorrow, and Barry already put a little bit aside for him. Plus, we haven't had baked potatoes in a while, and I forgot how much he likes those."

"Just leave me a potato. That'll be plenty for me, one with that bit of fish," Barry said. "I don't have the appetite lately that I usually do."

"All right then. You get the potatoes and the fish, we get the dressing, although I feel like we got the better end of the deal," Amara said as Mertie stood up beside her, and Hobert put a wrap over the dressing.

"I'll carry it, and I'll walk you guys home," he said, and then he looked back at Barry. "I'll be back in an hour, tops."

Barry snorted. "Good night. I'll see you in the morning."

Hobert shook his head. "He's giving me a hard time because I stayed at your house the night of the storm."

"He stayed overnight at your house?" Mertie said as they walked away from the campfire, and to her credit, she said it in a low voice right beside Amara's ear.

Hobert walked on her other side, carrying the dressing in one hand, and he twined the fingers of his other hand through Amara's, tentatively at first as though he were asking if it was okay since her sister was with them.

She wasn't going to treat him one way when they were alone and treat him another way in front of her family or friends, but she was a little tempted to tone it down a bit, just to keep Mertie from asking them any more questions.

"It was storming. I was in the house by myself. He stayed because he knew I was afraid. But he gets up at two AM to go to work, so it wasn't like he stayed all night. Some people don't even go to bed until that hour."

She didn't know why she was trying to defend herself. She knew it was probably better to just not. Just let it go, let God take care of it. But it was her older sister, and she knew that Mertie worried about her. She wanted her to understand that there wasn't anything going on.

"We can talk later," Mertie said.

That did not make Amara feel any better at all, which might have been Mertie's point, she wasn't sure. Still, while the idea was still fresh in her head, she turned to Hobert.

"Barry doesn't look very good to me. Do you think he's okay? I mean, I would take him to a doctor's appointment if he makes one."

"I asked him a few days ago, because I noticed that he seemed like he was tired and all he's been doing is sitting in the chair sleeping. Which isn't exactly a massive change from what he did before, but it's still a change. He usually went down to the dock and went with me on the boat at least once or twice a week. He's been slacking off on going but..." He closed his mouth. "I guess I was rambling. I'm sorry. I asked him. I told him I'd make him a doctor's appointment, but...I think sometimes those of us who are living want to hold onto life so much that sometimes we try to drag the dying along with us, when...they're ready to go."

She didn't say anything. That was not exactly the kind of thoughts she normally thought.

"I guess what I'm saying is I want him to be able to do this on his own terms. And he told me that he didn't want to see a doctor. Not because he can't afford it, not because he's not in his right mind, but because...he wants to face death on his own terms, and those are his terms. No doctors."

It made sense. That was the type of man Barry was, but it was a little bit hard to swallow because she wanted him to try to take care of himself so he could stay with them longer.

"You could have a doctor come to see him. Some doctors are making house calls. It's starting to be a thing," Mertie said from beside Amara.

But that wasn't what Barry wanted either.

"I think I understand what he wants. He doesn't want to cling to life, letting go of his love of the lake and being shuffled from room to room and doctor to doctor and only half living." That wasn't exactly what she wanted to say. It didn't explain everything, but it explained enough she thought maybe Mertie would understand.

"Yeah. I suppose I can call a doctor and have one make a house call, if he was in pain, if he were desperate to try to cling to life, but he's content. He told me he lived his life, he used the time that God gave him, and while he has regrets, he doesn't want to lose his dignity trying to extend his life. That's what he said. Not me," Hobert added quickly, and Amara figured that he didn't want them to think that he was criticizing people who did everything they could to extend their time on earth.

"I think that takes courage. It's his decision. And I think that people need to respect that. That is a valuable and courageous thing, to decide that they want to face death the way nature intended perhaps."

"Without the pain. I think if he were in pain, it would be a lot harder to watch, and I would be begging him to at least take something for it."

"Yeah. I think...we're not used to seeing that anymore, because our mindset is death is bad, life is good, and there's only one side. But...I think there comes a time when dying is a mercy or a person is ready to go to heaven. And ready to leave the earth."

"I can't disagree."

They had made it up the trail and were at the bottom of their driveway.

"Someone left lights on," Hobert pointed out.

"That's Mertie. She takes care of everything, and I feel like a scatterbrain next to her." Sometimes her creative side overruled her organizational side, and things ended up seeming like they were in a huge mess.

But Mertie never had any creativity overruling anything. She was always very direct and exact.

"Well, of course I left the light on. Who wants to walk into their home in the dark? Especially since we're walking." It didn't sound like she was necessarily complaining, just being matter-of-fact Mertie.

They reached the door, and Mertie pulled the key out of her pocket.

"Would you like to come in?" Amara asked Hobert while Mertie was unlocking the door.

"I'd like to, but I better not. I do have to work in the morning."

"I'm sorry. Since you've met me, you've barely had any sleep."

"It's been worth it."

"I'm going in, but, Amara, I want to talk to you as soon as you are done there. It doesn't sound like it's going to be very long," Mertie said as she gave Amara a look and then walked in the house after bidding a short good night to Hobert.

She didn't give them a chance to reply before she closed the door.

"I think she's warming up to me," Hobert said with a bit of a laugh as he put his arms around Amara and drew her close.

She stepped into his arms willingly, wrapping hers around him, then running her fingers through the bottom of his hair which she knew he had loved the night before.

"She will. I knew that you would win her over, not because you're so charming, and not because everyone loves you necessarily, but because you just exude character and honesty and integrity, and even though Mertie can be a pill sometimes, she admires those attributes in people. And there's no way she couldn't see them in you."

"Wow. You have a lot of faith in me."

"That's right. I do. I also have a lot of faith that you're going to kiss me good night. I've been waiting all evening. That was probably the worst thing about Mertie coming. Because...I thought there would be a lot more kissing this evening than what there was."

He laughed. "Have I mentioned that I love you? Because I really, really love you."

"Same," she said, and she did.

She was disappointed, although breathless as well, when he lifted his head and put his forehead on hers.

"Every time, it gets better," he said, running his hands down her back and moving his head to kiss her temple, sounding breathless and amazed.

"How is that?"

"I guess we're practicing."

"And we're getting better?" she asked, smiling.

"That, or...I just fall deeper and deeper."

"Everyone says these feelings don't last. But they're so strong."

"I don't care what kind of feelings they are. I know what kind of person you are, and that's the important thing. Thank you for bringing your sister tonight, even though you knew it was going to be an uncomfortable evening, and thank you for trying to turn the conversation so that I wasn't defending myself the whole evening."

"You shouldn't need to. And she's going to see that."

"And thank you for your faith in me. I don't deserve it."

"You deserve that and more."

She wanted to stand there all night, just talking to him, holding him, having him hold her and run his fingers carefully down her neck and trace down her backbone, but she'd already kept him up longer than he should have been, and he really had lost a lot of sleep because of her.

"Are you coming tomorrow after work?" she asked.

"Do you think it's safe?" he returned with a little smile.

"I do. I know it's safe. I guarantee it."

"Then yes. And even if it wasn't, it is still yes."

He lowered his head and kissed her again, and she put her hand on his cheek, feeling the rough stubble beneath her fingers, using that to keep her grounded, when the world wanted to fly away.

When he finally lifted his head, she could hardly think.

"I love you," he said roughly.

"I love you too."

He backed up, and with a last glance at her and a lifted hand, he walked off the porch and into the night.

She stood there for a few moments, amused, her fingers going to her lips before she smiled with her eyes closed. A dreamy smile. The kind of smile a teenager might smile after her first date.

But...he was everything she ever wanted. Just that one, distance-related issue stood between them.

Unless a person counted their different economic statuses, but Amara did not.

So what if she lived in a mansion on a hill and he lived in a shack by the water. It didn't matter to her, and he didn't care either.

It shouldn't matter to either one of them.

And it wouldn't.

She smiled so big she could hardly stand it and walked into the house.

Twenty-Seven

Mertie peeked behind the curtains once more, relieved to see that the man who had been kissing her sister had finally left.

She took a breath and paced back and forth in the kitchen one more time. She had to marshal her arguments.

This was never going to work. And she had to convince Amara of that before Amara got terribly hurt.

Plus, Mertie could not stay here. She knew that and wasn't sure why exactly she had agreed to come in the first place. There were too many secrets here. Too many things that people knew about her that if they came out, she could lose the position that she worked for all her life. No one wanted a Christian speaker with skeletons in her closet. Especially the kind of skeletons that Mertie had.

"Wasn't it a great evening?" Amara said as she practically levitated into the kitchen.

Mertie looked at her sister, her eyes shining, her face beaming, her whole body seeming to say that life was good, and she couldn't be happier. And Mertie wanted that for her, she loved her sister, with all her heart. She wanted the very best for her.

But the very best for her was not a man who lived in a shack by the water, who took an eighty-year-old fishing boat out every day, and brought back enough food to keep from starving.

Although, the man did seem to have character and integrity and manners at least.

"It was. The food was really good," she said, and that was the honest truth.

"But you did have a good time?" Amara looked at her, her head tilted, her eyes searching Mertie's face as though she were trying to look into her soul for Mertie's secrets.

But Mertie knew how to hide her secrets. She knew how to keep the past buried so that she could protect her livelihood and continue to provide for herself, so that she never found herself in the predicament that she had almost found herself in back when she was a teenager.

If it hadn't been for Garnet.

She shook her head. No. She was not going to think about that now.

"I had a good time, but the kind of good time where you're having fun with people that you like, and you respect, but you don't want to spend too much time around."

"Why not?" Amara asked, sounding like she truly didn't understand.

"Amara. There had to have been a reason why Mother told us not to associate with them. Maybe there's some incest going on in their family, or maybe there was some abuse, whether it's physical or sexual, we don't want to have anything to do with that. You know that."

"You can't just throw out the whole family because one person was bad. And Hobert was just a kid. He didn't do anything wrong." Amara didn't sound angry, but it was obvious that she wasn't going to back down.

Olive was the peacekeeper in the family. Mertie had more confrontations with Amara than she ever had with her middle sister, because Amara was more headstrong. But it sounded like she'd mellowed.

"You've changed," she said, letting the argument go for now. She could come at it from a side attack and have better luck. Or maybe she should just find out why exactly their mother forbade them to have anything to do with the Gilcrest family, and then that should be enough to convince Amara that she was making a grave mistake.

"I think I have. I think it was something that was already happening before our parents died, but that kind of got me thinking, reflecting, wondering what exactly I wanted to have my life say. You know, we cleaned out the condo, and there wasn't much in the way of personal things. I think they had, what, one picture of our family?"

"They were busy. They were creating a business. I mean, we are going to see a significant amount of income from that business for years to come. You know you don't have to work."

Amara looked surprised. "When did that happen?"

"Oh, that's right. I got the mail, since I'm the executor, and I guess I just figured all three of us could talk about it when we met here."

"There is income?"

"Well, you got your share of the sale of the condo, right?"

"Yes."

"Their business is making money too. And they set it up so that if anything happened, then it would be managed through a trust, and if the business stops making money, the trust is commanded to sell it so you shouldn't have to lift a finger, and you're going to get a nice, tidy six-figure income every year."

"I see."

"Amara, Hobert isn't the kind of man who is going to want to move to Chicago and climb the corporate ladder with you. Even if he doesn't have to fish every day. He...loves living in his shack next to the lake," Mertie said, and she tried not to make shack sound like a dirty word, but she didn't think she was quite successful when she saw her sister flinch.

"But he's a good man. It doesn't matter how much money he has. It doesn't matter where he lives. He's honest and has integrity and has a good work ethic, what more could I want?"

"Heat in the winter perhaps?" Mertie said, trying not to sound sarcastic.

"He has a woodstove. It's cozy in there."

"It wouldn't be cozy for your teenage kids, who have to go there after school and have all their classmates making fun of them because they don't live like everyone else."

"Maybe I'd homeschool. Maybe I don't want to live like everyone else. Maybe the way everyone else lives is wrong. Doesn't the Bible say that the wrong way is wide and there are a lot of people on it?"

Mertie pressed her lips closed. Amara was hitting a little too close to the truth. Probably it was wise to homeschool her kids. With the way public schools were going.

She sighed, pulling her thoughts from that direction before she got really upset.

"Listen, you don't have to admit I'm right. I'm not asking for that. I just... I love him. And I've been seriously considering quitting my job in Chicago and moving here. I'll buy your share of the mansion, and Olive's share, if I can afford it, and we'll live here, and if I can't afford it, we'll live down there. Maybe we'll build something, maybe we won't, and I don't care. Where we live doesn't matter. It's how we live and that we're together."

Mertie crossed her arms over her chest and walked to the window looking out. Maybe Amara was the one who should be the Christian speaker, and she should be the marketing exec, because Amara was saying the things that she should have been saying. Because she was exactly right. It didn't matter where they lived. It mattered what was in their hearts. And that should be the truth whether she was picking a husband, or friends, or living a life for herself.

"I'm sorry. You're right. I really want to find out what's going on, why Mother told us not to talk to him, just to make sure that there's nothing wrong." She said that determinedly, because there had to be something, it had to be more than just because they were poor and not considered important in society. Her parents were perhaps a little snotty, but they wouldn't have been that bad.

"But you're right. I know that. And I guess I needed that reminder. I was very judgmental today. Very. And I shouldn't have been. I'm sorry." She looked at her sister. "I'll apologize to Hobert the next time I see him. He seems like a really good man. I just... I want the best for you. The best of everything."

"Then you want me to put my treasure in heaven. And it doesn't matter whether I have a big house here on earth or not. Heaven is where it's at."

"You're right. And I knew that. I'm sorry." She dropped her hands and took one step, but she didn't have to take any more because Amara hurried to her and threw her arms around her.

"I love you," Amara said. "I'm sorry I upset you tonight. But I want more than anything to have a relationship with you and Olive. To me, as I've been thinking about things, that's the most important thing in my life. You and Olive and Hobert too if he'll have me."

"What do you mean if he'll have you? He is so stinking blessed that you even gave him the time of day."

"No. You have it backward. I'm the one who's blessed. You would not believe how amazing he is."

There was a part of Mertie that was a little bit jealous. She had given up her right to have an amazing, wonderful man like that. She couldn't undo the sins of her past, and she didn't want to saddle someone with a wife with history like hers. Plus, there was always the chance that the skeleton in her closet would fall out at some point. She couldn't do that to a man. Not a good, godly man who was trying to have a ministry like she was.

And she wanted to marry a man in the ministry. Actually, if she were going to get married, she would marry a man in the ministry. But that ship had sailed for her.

"I'm so happy for you. But would you do me a favor?" she asked as she pulled back away from Amara and held her at arm's length. "Please, wait to make any permanent future plans until I figure out what was going on with Mom."

"How can you figure that out? It was years ago. I wondered that myself whenever I first realized who Hobert was, but they're not here to ask anymore."

"Mom had a journal. I looked for it in the condo, but I didn't see it. I assume it's here. I...have been dragging my feet a little bit, because it feels like being sneaky behind our parent's back to look for her journal intending to read it, but at the same time, it might have the answers to our questions."

"I didn't realize she had a journal."

"I was the night owl. I was often awake at night walking around, and I would see her writing in it sometimes. But she never left it lying around. Which made me feel like it probably had secrets in it that she didn't want people to know. And I never saw her writing in it when Dad was around either. Which also made me very suspicious."

"Well. I just bebopped around my own little world, and I had no clue that Mom had this whole life going on that could have been sideways from what her family was."

"It could have been. And it could have been just nothing too. Maybe her hopes and dreams of being a businesswoman, or mother, or whatever. I don't know. But I'm tired, and I'm not going to look it up tonight, but maybe tomorrow. Okay?"

"All right. Since I've already started on painting, I'm going to do that, and Hobert's going to be here afterward. Anywhere from two o'clock to six, and he'll help me until nine or ten. You're welcome to paint too if you want to."

"All right. Yeah. I think I would like to get to know Hobert a little better. It sounds like he's going to be around for a while."

Amara smiled huge, and Mertie silently said a prayer of thanks that God had shown her her arrogance before it was too late. At least, too late for her sister. Hopefully Hobert didn't hate her for the way she acted tonight. She hadn't been terrible, but she had given him a little bit of a hard time, and she shouldn't have.

In the meantime, she'd figure out where her mother's journal was and see what she could find there.

She just hoped that her mother didn't have the kind of skeletons in her closet that Mertie had in hers.

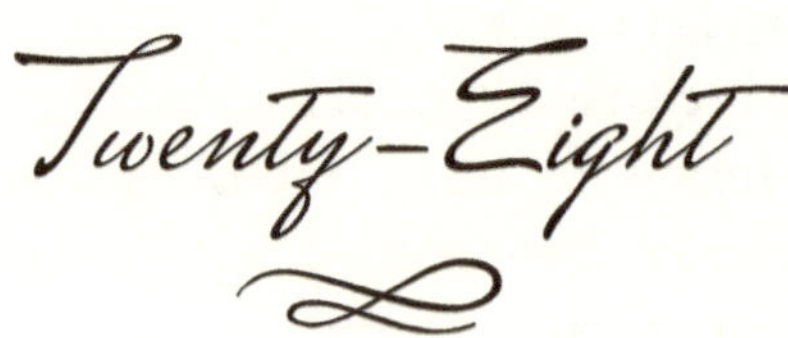

Twenty-Eight

Hobert eased the boat to the dock and tied it up, whistling and hurrying with his work.

He had a decent day of fishing, but the fish quit biting around noon, and he'd come in.

He couldn't wait to get back to Amara. Maybe this was what being in love was like, unable to stand the amount of time a person had to stay away and counting the minutes until he could get back to the one he loved.

Whether that was it, or whether it was just an infatuation that would eventually simmer down, the embers would burn under the actual actions of love that he intended to do for Amara, every single day that she would allow him, until she left him, he didn't know, and he didn't care. He just knew he wanted to see her again.

But as he walked off the dock, he thought that maybe he ought to spend half an hour or so with Barry. He hadn't seen him much at all lately, and he suspected that Barry's time on earth was not going to be long. But as he walked back, he noticed that there were tire prints in the road.

It had been so long since anyone who drove a car had been back, the prints were obvious.

It looked like there were two. So either two cars came back, or one car came back and then left.

He picked up his pace, although he hadn't been slouching to begin with, unable to figure out what in the world might have been going on. Who would have come back? Did Barry decide to call an ambulance?

He had an old flip phone that worked most of the time and that he could use in an emergency, but he couldn't believe that Barry wouldn't have called him to let him know what was going on. Unless he just didn't have time.

Walking so fast he was practically running, he stopped when the shed came into view, and Barry was sitting on the chair like he normally was. Slouched and had a blanket over him. Which was new.

It was like he was sitting in the sun, trying to get warm, and just never could. He even started a fire the other day when it had been cloudy and a little drizzly out.

Hobert hadn't said anything, but he just helped Barry get closer to the fire, close enough to get warm, without burning anything.

He wished he could do more for him, but Barry didn't seem uncomfortable.

"Hey there," he said, coming in beside Barry and scrunching down on the stump that sat by his chair, his hands on the arm of Barry's chair, looking up into the older man's eyes.

They opened slowly.

"Hobert. You're back."

"Yes. I quit a little early today, because the fish quit biting. I had a pretty good day though."

"Good. I...had a visitor. I need to talk to you." His voice was soft and tired, a little slow.

Hobert felt a twinge of fear claw in his stomach. "All right."

Barry opened one eye, gave him a look, then he closed it. "It was your mother."

What?

Hobert stood up, looking around, wanting to see her. What did she look like? He never even saw a picture of her. He didn't have a single idea of what she looked like, what kind of person she was, who she was.

"She's gone," Barry said. And then he sighed. "And she won't be coming back."

"She left?" Hobert asked, disbelief heavy in his words. "She left without...even seeing me? Did you tell her I was coming back?"

"She knew. I told her. She left twenty minutes ago, I told her you'd be back soon. But...I don't think she wanted to see you. Sorry."

"No. It's okay. It's not your fault. Of course she didn't want to see me. She knows where I live. She could have been here anytime, and she chose not to be."

"Yeah. I wouldn't be telling you, but I don't want the secrets to die with me." Barry sounded tired and weak.

Hobert wanted to say, *you're not dying*, but it would have been a lie. And he didn't want to lie to Barry.

"I don't want to face that," he said instead, which was the absolute truth.

"Lots of things in life we don't want to face, boy, but lots of things we have to anyway," Barry said, his voice raspy, and he was a little out of breath, like just talking made him breathless.

"What is it you want to tell me?" Hobert asked, hoping he could just get the bad stuff out of the way so they could deal with anything else they needed to, like getting him warm, making sure he was comfortable, and finding out if there was anything else he wanted to do before the end of his life.

"When she left, she threw her rings at your father. The wedding ring wasn't much, just a gold band, worth probably a hundred bucks if that. But the diamond ring. Your dad paid good money for it, took him ten years to pay it off."

"Ten years? Like ten years while I was born?"

Barry nodded. "He bought it maybe two years before you were born. It took him more time to pay that thing off than they spent together."

"And he had it all the time? He could have sold it for money?"

"Sometimes I wondered if he didn't sell it to buy booze, but he didn't."

"So you still had it?"

"I did. I guess she's hard up for money and came back for it."

She came back for her engagement ring, because she needed money, but she didn't even stay an extra twenty minutes to see her son.

Hobert stood, biting his lips together and turning away. His heart hurt.

But it shouldn't. He'd known his whole life his mother didn't give a flip about him. If he needed proof, here it was, but he supposed there was just something in every little boy that wanted his mom to love him.

Regardless, he had to let it go. She didn't love him, and there wasn't anything he was going to be able to do to make her. That wasn't his fault. He just couldn't...be bitter and angry about that.

"She took the ring, but that reminded me about the question you'd asked me not that long ago, and I wanted to answer before I go."

"My question about why Amara's family wouldn't allow the girls to speak with me?"

"Yeah. Your mom, Nancy, is a selfish person."

Hobert wanted to shout a big amen to that, but he supposed there were times where he was selfish as well.

"Okay."

Barry opened one eye, a little bit of amusement on his face. "You can agree with me."

"I suppose I do, but I didn't see any point in it. She is what she is, and I can't really fix that. I just...have to work on not being bitter and angry against her. And I suppose I have to work on forgiving her, even though she's never going to ask for it. That's the hardest thing, she doesn't even admit that she did something wrong."

"Yeah. Today, she didn't care. All she cared about was the ring. Not about you, not about me, not about your dad. He was gone, she didn't give a flip."

"She didn't realize he died?"

"I don't think so. All she's been doing is living her life. But she's not with the same guy she left him for. But that's not my story. Years ago, Amara's mom had her best friend and her husband visiting her here in Raspberry Ridge."

Barry took a breath. It wasn't going to be a long story, because sentences tired him out, but Hobert appreciated him taking the time to tell him.

"Apparently, the husband of Amara's mom's best friend, I don't remember what her name was, saw your mom. And he fell for her. Hard. I don't know. Your dad thought she was skinny-dipping, and he saw her then. Maybe a David and Bathsheba type thing. Regardless, they had a pretty torrid love affair."

Good to know his mom was a woman of character, Hobert thought to himself, with not a little bit of sarcasm.

"And Dad found them?"

"Yeah. But he loved your mom so much, he would have taken her back. In fact, he did. But your mom broke up Amara's mom's best friend's marriage. Of course, the wife was heartbroken, and Amara's mom was extremely angry and blamed everyone down here. She didn't care, she just thought we were all trash. And this proved it." Barry's lips thinned. "Anyway, your mom got pregnant from it."

"I have a sibling?" Hobert said, hope in his voice. Maybe it didn't matter about his mom, if he had a sibling. He had family.

"That was you."

"No." His eyes opened wide again. His dad was not his dad. "Is that man still alive?"

"I don't know. I asked your mom, and she said she left him about two years after they left here. She snorted derisively like she thought it was good riddance or something, but the thing that matters is, your mom stayed here until she had you, then, not even a week after you were born, she was running after him."

"I wasn't even a week old?"

"That's right. She left your dad here with a newborn baby and went to find her lover. Apparently she did, and apparently they stayed together for a couple of years, but neither of them could stay true. Your dad was such a softy for her that he raised you."

"What else was he going to do?"

"He could have given you to the police. Said she abandoned you or something, I don't know. He didn't seem to resent it though, even though you weren't his."

"He was too drunk to know."

"I don't think that was because of you, necessarily, although maybe looking at you might have been a little bit painful. We never really saw the man. It wasn't like he hung around here. She just ran off with him. I think they were here for four weeks or something. They took a month to stay at the beach with their good friends. Broke up the lady's marriage, and Amara's mom never forgave us."

After that long speech, he sat, panting.

Hobert wasn't exactly panting, but he felt like someone had poked his heart with linchpins. He just hurt all over.

"So Dad became an alcoholic because he lost Mom, and somehow I managed to survive, despite that and everything else."

"There were a couple of times I rushed you to the ER in the middle of the night, where you got sick and spiked a fever and your dad was passed out."

"You were always more like a dad to me than he was."

"I'm sorry I can't give you the name of your real dad."

"Biological dad. Biological mom, but they weren't parents."

"No. I'm sorry."

"No point apologizing. It's not your fault, but I guess I've heard enough. She came today and didn't want to talk to me, so that pretty much says that she's not interested in a relationship."

"I'd tell you to reach out to her, if I thought it would make any difference, but I doubt it. I gave her the ring, and she won't be back." Barry took another breath. "One more thing. Under my pillow, I have all the information you need after I die. Okay?"

"You didn't have to tell me that."

"Son, we never know when we're going. You need to live each day like it's your last. I wouldn't want to be your mom, or your dad, or anyone in that situation, on Judgment Day. They're going to have a lot of explaining to do. In the meantime, I have some good words for you."

"I sure hope so. But I suppose I could do more."

"You've been taking care of me like I've been your own."

"That's how you took care of me. I'm just repaying."

"A lot of people don't repay their parents. A lot of people just walk away, wash their hands of it, because it's too hard. They don't want to be bothered. I don't think the Lord's going to look on that very well."

"I think you might be right," Hobert said, although he said it more to get his mind off the fact that Barry had told him to look under his pillow when he passed.

"Now don't you have a little girl you need to go see?"

"I don't want to leave you."

"Maybe I don't want you around here bugging me all afternoon. I got a nap to take, and I can't hardly do it with you hovered over me, like I'm an old lady."

"I'll be back early tonight, okay?"

"Don't come back early for me."

"You want me to make a fire in the stove before I go?" he asked, even though the temperature was in the high seventies.

"No. I'm fine." He coughed, a deep, hacking cough, and then the old, gnarled hand, dark from years of working in the sun, lifted from his lap and came down on Hobert's hand. He squeezed.

Hobert swallowed, his eyes pricking.

"I love you, son."

"I love you too," he choked out. He wanted to beg him not to go, tell him not to give up. Ask him to at least go to the doctor and extend his life a little, because Hobert wasn't ready to let go, but it didn't really matter whether he was ready or not. Life moved on. People were born, they died, and the people who were left needed to accept that and keep living their life the best they could, until it was their turn to go. Maybe giving a little hint for the people who came behind on how to die with grace and dignity, with honor for their creator, and with courage, facing the unknown.

"Are you sure you don't want me to stay here? Hold your hand?" His voice cracked.

"No. Jesus goes with me. Sometimes, it's best to just be Jesus and me," Barry said, looking at Hobert from underneath his lowered eyelids.

"All right. I'll leave you in Jesus's hands. That's a better place to be than mine anyway."

"You take care of that little girl. Name one of your kids after me."

"All right. We'll do that," Hobert said, figuring that if Amara didn't want to, they'd have to cross that bridge when they came to it, but he hardly thought that Amara would turn down Barry's last request.

"I love you," Hobert said again. He'd said that more in the last two weeks than he'd said it in his entire life.

"You too." Barry closed his eyes, and his chest rose and fell slowly.

Hobert waited until he was sure the old man was asleep before he stood up, pulling his hand out from underneath Barry's and putting Barry's hand back on his chest, over top of the blanket.

He swallowed again, thinking about the years that Barry had spent with him, teaching him to fish, teaching him character, teaching him manners and the skills that he needed in order to live. Never pretentious, never angry, never impatient. Just...always there.

He wasn't sure how many more days they would have together. Weeks, months, some people lived for years, after they thought they were on their way to the next world.

Maybe that would be Barry.

Hobert hoped so. But in the meantime, he stood, looked around the camp, couldn't believe that his mother was there and hadn't waited to say something to him, and then walked down the dirt road, toward Amara's house. He wanted to see her and tell her everything.

Twenty-Nine

"That's almost unbelievable," Amara said, sitting on the couch holding Hobert's hand after he had just told them everything that Barry had told him that morning.

Her heart ached for him. He had told them without too much emotion, but she knew how much that had to hurt. The fact that his mother had been there, in Raspberry Ridge, his house no less, and had not cared to see him. All she wanted was money.

"You know. That probably won't be the last time she's around. If she needed money now and came back for it, she'll be back, hoping she can get more." Mertie spoke the obvious truth, which Amara hadn't even thought of yet, but as soon as she said it, she knew Mertie was right.

"You're probably right. Maybe I will end up seeing her again. I'll... have to work on forgiveness," he said, looking down at their joined hands, almost as though he could draw strength from that.

"Well, forgiveness is not easy, but it's as much about you as it is about the person who wronged you," Mertie said, sounding like the Christian speaker and author that she was.

Hobert nodded but didn't speak.

"I looked early this morning, and I found my mother's journal. I was waiting until you came before I discussed this with Amara, but it basically said the same thing. I mean, she went through a lot of her anger and her absolute hatred for someone who would break up a marriage, but I felt like she was unreasonably angry at your...not father, but your mother's husband at the time, because it was her who made the choice. And just for the record, in her diary it does say that she was skinny-dipping."

"Good reason not to go skinny-dipping, not like I've ever been tempted," Amara said.

"You just have to do it with the right person," Hobert said, and Amara almost laughed as Mertie flinched.

"Please. Spare us," she said, putting a hand up and turning her face away.

"All right. I just wanted to tell you guys what I knew, but apparently Mertie already knew everything anyway."

"You added some details that weren't in Mom's diary, and she had some things that you didn't say, but it all adds up to the same truth. It was a mess, but it certainly wasn't your fault and certainly no reason for Mom to forbid us to talk to you, other than she was angry for her friend."

"That's too bad," Amara said. "But I don't think it changes anything now, do you?" she asked, looking at Hobert, her hand still clenching his, hoping that this didn't change anything for them.

"No. Not for me."

"All right. I'm going to go back up and continue to go through Mom's things. I will help you guys paint when you get started, if you have enough brushes or rollers or whatever."

Mertie stood up and walked out of the living room, leaving Hobert and Amara sitting there.

Amara sat with him in silence for a bit, figuring this was a lot to process and knowing that it would be hard for her heart, if it had been her. As it was, she felt pain, even though it wasn't even her mom.

"I wish I could do something. You don't deserve to have a mom like that. You deserve to have a mom who cherishes you and loves you," she said, knowing that she hadn't really had that.

"If I got what I deserved, I'd be in hell. I guess... Anything we get that's better than that, we should be grateful for, but we have a tendency to look at our lives and see what we don't have rather than what we do."

"That's very wise," she said, nodding.

He grinned.

"I know that it's been a hard day for you, but what you said about Barry makes me want to go see him and...just say goodbye, I guess."

"We could do that now," he said, lifting his brows. "I don't want to keep you from your work if that's what you want to do, but I'm willing to walk down if you really want to say goodbye. Maybe we have months, I don't know." He lifted his shoulders.

"Yeah. It's better to do it now than to wait and have it be too late."

Although she didn't feel bad with the way she left last night. She had thanked Barry and given him a hug before she left. He had looked a little embarrassed about the hug, but he also looked pleased. And if that was her last memory, she wouldn't be upset. But the fact that he was hinting that he wasn't going to be for this world long made her want to go and talk to him one last time.

She and Hobert held hands as they walked out of the house and down the driveway. They didn't say much, and she figured that Hobert was still deep in contemplation over the way things had gone.

It had taken her a while after her parents' death to reconcile what would never be between them.

But she had never been rejected so solidly. And her heart just bled for Hobert.

As they went down the dirt road and came to the trail and the shack came into view, she could see Barry sitting in the chair just the way Hobert had described him. His hands on his stomach, his body slightly slouched, the blanket tucked in around him.

There was something off.

"I think he's gone," Hobert said softly.

Amara wanted to cry, more for Hobert, and the things that he had been through that day, than for herself. First his mother soundly rejected him, and now he lost the man who was more like a father to him than anyone else in the world.

"It feels like I have no family," he said softly.

"You have me. And we can talk about it later, but I sent my

resignation to my job in Chicago. I'm done the last day of my vacation. I might have to go down to Chicago and clean out my office, but...even if I don't, there's nothing there I want. I am hoping to sublease my apartment, and I'm planning on staying in Raspberry Ridge."

She didn't tell him that she might not be staying in the mansion if she couldn't afford it, and she also didn't tell him that her sister had said that she should have a six-figure income for the foreseeable future. Maybe she'd be able to pay off the mansion. She didn't know what electricity would be or property taxes or anything like that. The future was fuzzy and uncertain, but she knew what she wanted, and that was Hobert.

A smart girl didn't pass up a man like him, not for a job, not for a house, not for anything.

He smiled as he looked down at her. "Are you serious?"

She nodded, looking up at him, a little bit of a smile on her face, and she knew hope was shining from her eyes.

"I don't want you to give that up for me."

"I didn't. I mean, yes, I wouldn't have thought about it if it hadn't been for you, although I wasn't happy in my job, wasn't happy doing anything in Chicago. And I love it here. So, I'm not giving things up for you, I'm gaining a better life because of you."

He swallowed, closing his eyes and then smiling. "I'd better check."

"I'm here," she said, squeezing the hand she held.

He nodded and then strode forward, but it didn't take long to tell that there was no heartbeat, and the old, frail chest was no longer rising and falling.

"If I get a choice of the way I want to go, this is exactly it. Yesterday, he made his shrimp and grits dressing, slowly, with help, but still, and then today, he slipped into the arms of Jesus. I can't think of a better way to go."

"Me, either. No pain, no tears, just a happy reunion."

"After living a full life." He took a shaky breath. "But it still hurts."

"I know."

He turned, gathering her in his arms, and she wrapped herself around him, holding him close, as he squeezed her tight, burying his face in her neck and breathing out.

"I didn't know it was going to be this hard," he said.

"I think it surprises us. Every time."

She thought maybe mentally, they couldn't stand the idea of the pain that losing someone so precious to a person felt, and so subconsciously, they pushed it aside.

At least she'd been shocked when her parents had passed. Of course, it had been unexpected too. Although Barry's decline had been rapid in the last two weeks.

Regardless, Amara marveled at the timing of the Lord. Hobert could have been alone at this point. After finding out about his mother and losing Barry. But the way God orchestrated it, her vacation, meeting Hobert, and even the whirlwind romance that they'd had. It had all worked together, for this moment, for her to be standing here, offering her support, knowing her sisters were coming, and they, imperfect as they all were, would be a family together.

She couldn't ask for anything better.

Thirty

T he funeral had been short and small. They'd opened up the Raspberry Ridge church, and Pastor Calvin, who had baptized him years ago, had come to do the service.

There had just been people from Raspberry Ridge there. Maybe twenty-five in all. The whole town had hoped that the new pastor, Garnet Irving, would be there to help officiate the ceremony, but he had been delayed.

For some reason, Mertie had seemed especially upset every time someone mentioned the new pastor.

Anxious, like she wanted to leave.

Amara had told Hobert that Mertie was just high strung and always in control, but Hobert thought there might be something else going on.

But what did he know? He really hadn't been around a whole lot of women in his life, and maybe Amara was right. Regardless, he and Amara now walked down to the shack. He'd asked her to marry him, and she happily said yes, and they'd agreed that they didn't want to wait. So, they'd be planning a wedding soon, but after the funeral, he remembered that Barry had told him to look under his pillow after he passed.

With the funeral, helping the sisters to finish painting the mansion, trying to keep himself busy, and going out every day to fish, he hadn't really thought about it.

So, Amara was going with him on a bright Sunday afternoon, after they'd looked at the grave that Barry had been placed in yesterday after the service.

"What do you think is under there?" she asked.

"I don't know. Maybe an envelope with hundred-dollar bills in it. I always gave him what was left after I paid for my fuel and insurance and bought the groceries. Sometimes it was a good bit. Sometimes it wasn't much. But I figured he deserved it. I don't know if he ever spent it or not. Sometimes I wondered if he had someone somewhere else that he sent money to. He was that kind of guy, you know?"

"Always taking care of people?"

"Exactly," Hobert said as he opened the door to the shack, and Amara stepped in first.

It was dim inside, but light enough that they didn't need a light, and he looked around, at the neatly made beds and the rustic and rough but clean room.

He spent his entire life here. And it looked like home to him.

But to other people, he understood that it looked like poverty. Abject and miserable.

But he'd been happy. For the most part. Sometimes his dad's drunken sprees had made things uncomfortable. But when his dad was sleeping it off or not quite to the point where he was making everyone miserable, life hadn't been bad.

He'd really enjoyed it after his dad passed away and it had been him and Barry. He hadn't felt like he needed anything else.

Until Amara came along, and he realized he was missing a whole piece of himself that he hadn't even noticed.

"You want me to get it?" she asked from beside him.

He put his arm around her and pulled her close to him. "I guess I just... I don't know. Sometimes when you don't know something, it's better than knowing it. Like, if I hadn't noticed the tire tracks, I wouldn't have known that my mom came, was here, and didn't want to see me. That's one of those things I'd be better off not knowing. Now, God gave that to me so I could work on getting over it. Forgiving and loving anyway."

"This seems to be a theme in your life."

"I should be better at it than anybody else?" he said with a little grin.

He didn't know why God kept giving him that lesson, but his prayer had been that he would learn it so he didn't have to go through it again. Someone had said that God kept giving lessons until the person who was learning the lesson finally went through the trial the way they were supposed to. And then they passed.

He wasn't sure whether that was true or not, but he was trying. He was trying.

"All right. Let's see what it is. None of this melancholy, let's be sad stuff. Barry didn't want us to be sad. He was ready to go, and he didn't want to try to stay. So, we're not going to be morose, but we'll focus on just trying to be happy."

"It's a choice, but sometimes it's a hard one."

"Amen to that," he said as he went over to Barry's neatly made bed and lifted the pillow. He wasn't sure what he thought he was going to find, but the two letters were not it.

"Looks like a bank statement and an investment portfolio or something," he said, wrinkling his brows and looking down at the paper in his hand.

"All right. No big packet of hundred-dollar bills."

"Yeah. I guess... Barry must have gone to the bank. Or... I don't know. That's kind of a mystery."

Amara didn't say anything as he opened the bank statement.

He blinked and looked at it again. "All right. I wasn't expecting that."

"What's that?" Amara said, not sounding the slightest bit impatient. But calm and like she could wait all day for him to talk.

"There is one million in it. I... Well."

He closed his eyes and shook his head, looked at it again, and then he handed it to Amara. "Am I looking at that right?"

It didn't take her nearly as long as it took him.

Her brows went way up, her eyes opened wide, but she nodded her head. "You sure are."

"Well," he said, and then while she was still holding the bank statement, he opened the other letter.

It was a letter naming a lawyer for Hobert to get in touch with in order to have his name put on the bank account and the investment account listed below. For the amount of two point three million dollars.

"Okay, if that made your heart beat funny, this is really going to make it go weird."

"Okay?" Amara said, looking at his face. "Must be good news, you don't look upset," she said slowly, like she was trying to figure it out while she was talking it through.

"Two point three million in the investment account. Barry has given me power of attorney for that and the account that you're holding."

"Holy smokes. You're...rich."

He laughed. "I'm no different now than I was five minutes ago. I just...have a little bit more that God entrusted me with. Maybe I passed those tests okay."

"I'd say. He's definitely given you a good bit to be a steward over. And that's a good way to look at it."

"All right." He looked around the room again. Happy that Barry hadn't spent the money. He might have been a different person if he had. If Barry had used the money to make his life easier, better, then he wouldn't have had to work so hard, wouldn't have had to suffer through the time of his broken leg, realizing that he needed a nest egg of his own. Barry had been wise.

"I don't know that I would recommend that anyone grow up like this, but can I say that I'm really glad that Barry put the money in an account and saved it and didn't spend it on me?"

"Well, you wouldn't have nearly what you have now, because investments grow over time, and if you had spent it, you wouldn't have had it. But... I kinda think that maybe it's because he knew that when he was gone, you weren't going to have any family. And not that money takes the place of family, but he wanted to leave you with something."

"Wow." He swallowed, and then he said, "I guess you can have a little bigger wedding than what we were thinking about if you want to," he said, lifting up his eyes, wondering what she would say about that.

But she smiled and shook her head. "No. Weddings are frivolous things to waste money on. And the important thing is that the people that you love are there. Although, maybe we'll spend a little bit extra and put a special bouquet at the altar, in memory of Barry."

"Yeah. Because he's someone we loved."

She nodded, and he came back, the paper still in hand as he wrapped his arms around her and hugged her. Loving that the money hadn't changed her. That she didn't want to go blow a big wad of it on something crazy but just wanted to be unpretentious, and that was probably the reason that she wanted to move to Raspberry Ridge. Because she didn't like that big-city lifestyle either.

"Have I told you today that I love you?" he asked softly, his lips by her ear as he trailed them across her temple and down her cheek.

"I'm not sure. You better say it again, just in case," she said, closing her eyes as he trailed his lips along the edge of her jaw.

"Amara. You're the best thing that's ever happened to me."

"I love you, Hobert. And I might want to disagree with that, but I can definitely say that it's true for me. You've helped me make choices that were the best choices, and I am excited to spend my life with you."

<u>Join Jessie's list and be the first to know about new releases and sales on her books!</u>

Read Around the Next Bend, the next book in the Raspberry Ridge series where Mertie Jerdine reunites with her childhood best friend, only her deepest secret threatens to make her leave Raspberry Ridge, and her blossoming romance, for good. Keep reading for a sneak peek now.

Sneak Peek of Around the Next Bend

This might have been the biggest mistake of his life.

"We're looking forward to hearing you speak tomorrow, Garnet," Mrs. Brandstetter said as she shook his hand. Her husband, Mr. Brandstetter, stood silently behind her, looking stern and serious. As he should.

Picking any pastor was not something that should be done on a whim. But a small-town church, especially one in a town as tiny as Raspberry Ridge, presented its own set of problems. The least of which was whether or not the church was going to be able to pay the pastor's salary.

Garnet still wasn't sure that was actually going to happen. The pastoral committee had warned him that he was going to need to retain his full-time job even after they voted him in.

Garnet didn't tell them that he had already given his two-week notice and his last day was yesterday. He'd spent years going to Bible school around a full-time job, studying, learning and finally receiving a degree from a respected school in pastoral studies. He'd been ordained in his denomination and had served as an unpaid assistant pastor in his church in Indiana, before leaving it all behind. It wasn't a spur of the moment decision. He truly believed the Lord wanted him here, and not just for the church.

His eyes drifted to his daughter, Dabney, fourteen years old and not very happy to be pulled out of the homeschool they had been a part of on the other side of the Michigan line, in Indiana, and to be moved two hundred miles away to the small town of Raspberry Ridge. The fact that it was directly beside Lake Michigan, and she'd basically be almost living in a beach house, had made the move only marginally better. Dabney, while mature for her age, was still a typical fourteen-year-old, and her life revolved around her friends.

The fact that he had homeschooled her from the very beginning, and that the "school" she was leaving there was the homeschool co-op where she had grown up with other homeschooled children, didn't matter to a teen. Moving was moving.

She sat outside the window, on one of the church benches overlooking the wide expanse of Lake Michigan, with a book in her hand, her head bent, her legs tucked up around her.

She must have inherited her father's personality, since her mother was a real go-getter. Nothing stood in Mertie's way when Mertie wanted to get something, not even the inconvenience of a child.

Garnet smiled at the next person who waited to shake his hand. He wanted to make a good impression on the pastoral committee, even though they'd already voted to allow him to come candidate. He would preach two Sundays in a row, and then the church would vote on whether or not they wanted to retain him.

He didn't want to think about Mertie, but how could he not? She had been his best friend as they'd grown up in Raspberry Ridge. And when she'd come to him asking for his help, he hadn't been able to turn her down.

But he also hadn't been able to do what she wanted him to do.

Because of that, he hadn't been able to see her since. And he wasn't sure seeing her now was such a good idea. He hadn't expected her to be back in town to close up and sell the mansion her parents had left to her and her sisters when they had been tragically killed in a car accident earlier in the year.

"Welcome to Raspberry Ridge." Homer Aiken stood in front of him, his hand out. Homer had impressed him as an intelligent man with a discernment for truth and a desire to do right. He had been slow to speak and always quick to listen.

"Thank you. It's good to be back in my hometown."

He and Homer hadn't grown up together, although they knew each other. Homer was a good bit younger than Garnet.

"I've been leading a Bible study on my front porch at seven o'clock every morning. Even on Sundays, since there is no church. I...haven't talked it over with the people who've been attending, but I think we'd be honored to have you attend, and if you'd like to lead it, it would be even better."

Garnet appreciated this gesture of hospitality. In his experience, small towns were notoriously difficult to assimilate in. A person always felt like an outsider. Even after they'd been there for forty years. The small town he lived in in northern Indiana had been exactly like that. People had accepted him, they'd been kind to him, but they'd always considered him an outsider.

Of course, Raspberry Ridge was his hometown, although he'd been away for years.

"I'd love to," he said immediately. If they were going to ask him, he was going to do it. He had quit his day job in order to move back to Raspberry Ridge. He hadn't really enjoyed the sales position that he had at the company he worked for since he moved to Indiana and wasn't going to miss the little cubicle and monotonous workday, followed by as much time as he could get with his daughter.

It had been hard to squeeze in the time he needed to homeschool her since he'd been promoted from his administrative position four years ago. Back then, he had worked from home, and his hours were flexible.

"We've been reading through the Bible, and we're in the book of Deuteronomy, chapter 10, but you can teach from wherever you want. My wife and I started the Bible study when she said she wanted to know what the Bible said but had never read it through. So, we typically read a few chapters and talk about them. Sometimes we get through one, sometimes more than that. I usually have Matthew Henry's commentary and maybe a few other resources I pull up on my phone."

"Thanks for the heads-up. I'm happy to do it, and I'll just continue doing what you do. I'll get a few things together so I can say a few words about that chapter and possibly up to four others." It felt good to be given a job. To have something concrete in front of him to do.

He did have the blog that he had been working on building for the last ten years. Blogs had not quite gone the way of rotary phones, but they weren't as profitable as they had been in their heyday.

He'd also been working on starting a TikTok channel, but in his experience, people on TikTok weren't exactly interested in God's word. Maybe he just hadn't found his people yet, or maybe it was a mission field and he should keep working on it. God hadn't shown him for sure, yet.

He shook the hand of the next person in line, nodded as they welcomed him, speaking some words about how they were looking forward to hearing him speak on Sunday. He responded and tried to project confidence.

Lord, I'm trusting this is the right thing to do. I was sure this was all Your plan, but now that I'm here, I feel lost and a little nervous. Please don't let Dabney suffer because I made a mistake.

That summed up his years of being a dad. Everything that he did, he did with Dabney in mind.

Of course, he always had to follow the Lord's leading, but it was always with an eye toward his daughter.

Lord, You know I had no idea that Mertie was in town.

He broke off with that thought. It had been in his mind that he needed to avoid her at all costs. As much as he didn't want to. Over the years, it had gotten easier, and sometimes he even almost forgot about her. Although with Dabney in his home, it was almost impossible, since she was a carbon copy of her mother. In her features, anyway. Personality wise, she couldn't have been more different.

Garnet had always appreciated the fact that God had given him a laid-back, easygoing daughter who had never been demanding, even as a baby. Her toddler years had been a dream. He watched as other parents had struggled with their children, temper tantrums and attitude were common, and at times, Garnet was tempted to believe it was his parenting skills that had kept Dabney from going down the same road, but he knew better.

He had no idea how to be a parent and had flown by the seat of his pants, reading as many books as he could on the subject and occasionally going back to talk to his parents.

Being that the only child his parents had raised was him, they weren't a lot of help, although, according to them, he had been as easy as Dabney.

Until this point, though, he had tried to avoid being in Raspberry Ridge as much as he possibly could without being obvious about it. He hadn't wanted to run into Mertie. Although from what he'd seen, she hadn't gone back much, if at all.

So what were the odds that he felt the Lord had led him to come back for good, and she was here?

"Looking forward to seeing what you do with the church. I'm just as excited as the rest of the town to have it open again. It's perfect timing for us," Hobert Gilcrest spoke as he shook Garnet's hand.

Hobert had told Garnet that he and his fiancée were interested in getting married. They intended to build a small house down by the dock where Hobert kept his boat and start a family.

Coincidentally, or maybe not so much so, Hobert's fiancée was Mertie's sister. Amara recognized him, knew him, but did not realize that Dabney was her sister's child.

Thankfully, Dabney was always happy to sit somewhere with her nose in a book, and while people had met her, she hadn't hung around. As far as Garnet knew, Amara had not looked Dabney full in the face. If she had, there was no way she wouldn't see the family resemblance.

Nervousness tightened his muscles, and he had to deliberately relax his face into a smile.

"I love it when God's timing works that way," he said, meaning it. Obviously Hobert and Amara were starting a family here in Raspberry Ridge, and having a church, not just where they could hear the preaching of the word several times a week, but also where they could go to enjoy fellowship with their church family, would be helpful in keeping them on the straight and narrow, raising their family for God's glory.

"I appreciate the fact that you know the importance of the church and intend to include that in your daily life. It's encouraging to me," Garnet said, knowing that he sounded serious and possibly even boring. People had accused him of that. He wasn't quite sure how he had been able to become a good salesperson. After all, most of the top salespeople were jovial people pleasers with the ability to talk to anyone and with a joke always on the ready.

Garnet was pretty much the opposite of all that. But maybe it was his reliability. The way people seemed to be able to look at him and feel like he was honest and trustworthy. He just had a way about him, people said, that made them think that whatever he was saying was the absolute truth.

As well they should, since he made it a point to always speak the truth.

"Welcome to Raspberry Ridge. I'm confident that our little congregation is going to love you, and you're going to be a part of it for a long time. Of course, you have some big shoes to fill."

Dominic Miller stood in front of him shaking his hand. Dominic was the head deacon and the leader of the small pastoral committee. He was the one that Garnet needed to impress, not that Garnet was keeping track or making an effort to be anything other than himself. He was just going to be who he was and allow the Lord to work things out. At least, that was his plan. Sometimes things didn't go according to plan, but God had the ability to straighten anything out.

"Pastor Calvin was a good man. You know he was my preacher throughout my growing-up years. He definitely shaped my personality and my thinking. I am forever indebted to him for preaching solely from the Bible and not trying to slant his sermons to preach what he wanted to say or support his political opinions."

Very few people did that anymore. They took out the things they didn't like or ignored them. And then put in things that suited their social narrative. That was part of the reason Garnet had decided to become a minister. People didn't know what the Bible said anymore.

And yet, how could they be Christians if they didn't know what a Christian was? What a Christian was supposed to do?

The questions had bothered him, until he finally realized that God was prompting him, Garnet Irving, to become a preacher of the word.

How beautiful upon the mountains are the feet of him that bringeth good tidings, that publisheth peace; that bringeth good tidings of good, that publisheth salvation; that saith unto Zion, Thy God reigneth!

He remembered quite clearly the day he'd read that verse and realized that God wasn't just prompting him to study more, He was prompting him to study so that he could teach others.

Sometimes the idea that God was using him, a studious kid from a small town—so small it didn't even have a stoplight—in Michigan, to spread the gospel to his people, still brought Garnet up short.

But there was also the verse that said that a pastor should be the husband of one wife.

That verse could be interpreted to mean that a pastor should only have one wife - that he shouldn't be divorced and remarried or polygamous. Or it could indicate that a pastor should be married. He chose to believe it meant that he needed a wife. After all, God created him to need a help meet. Others might disagree, and he would not say they were wrong, but he was not going to take a pastorate without a wife.

Lord, You said if I go, You would provide what I need. I can't be a pastor if I don't have a wife. It's right there in Your word.

He and God had been having this conversation for a while. Garnet had been listening as well as he could, knowing that God sometimes didn't move until the last minute. But Garnet had determined in his heart that he would not accept the pastorate on a permanent basis if he did not have a wife.

You're cutting things a little close, Lord.

He figured that's the way Daniel must have felt, when he got thrown in the lion's den. Perhaps it was the way Shadrach, Meshach, and Abednego felt when they had been put in the fiery furnace. He thought about other men through history who must have wondered at God's timing and whether God was really going to come through. But a person's faith couldn't be tested if God did everything on the human timeframe, because if it had been up to Garnet, he would have had a wife fifteen years ago.

Sign up for Jessie's newsletter! Get a free book, access to exclusive bonus content, get fun and funny updates on her life on the farm and more!

View this code through your smart phone camera to be taken to a page where you can download a FREE ebook when you sign up to get updates from Jessie Gussman! Find out why people say, "Jessie's is the only newsletter I open and read" and "You make my day brighter. Love, love, love reading your newsletters. I don't know where you find time to write books. You are so busy living life. A true blessing." and "I know from now on that I can't be drinking my morning coffee while reading your newsletter – I laughed so hard I sprayed it out all over the table!"

Claim your free book from Jessie!

Escape to more faith-filled romance series by Jessie Gussman!

The Complete Sweet Water, North Dakota Reading Order:

Series One: Sweet Water Ranch Western Cowboy Romance (11 book series)

Series Two: Coming Home to North Dakota (12 book series)

Series Three: Flyboys of Sweet Briar Ranch in North Dakota (13 book series)

Series Four: Sweet View Ranch Western Cowboy Romance (10 book series)

Spinoffs and More! Additional Series You'll Love:

Jessie's First Series: Sweet Haven Farm (4 book series)

Small-Town Romance: The Baxter Boys (5 book series)

Bad-Boy Sweet Romance: Richmond Rebels Sweet Romance (3 book series)

Sweet Water Spinoff: Cowboy Crossing (9 book series)

Small Town Romantic Comedy: Good Grief, Idaho (5 book series)

True Stories from Jessie's Farm: Stories from Jessie Gussman's Newsletter (3 book series)

Reader-Favorite! Sweet Beach Romance: Blueberry Beach (8 book series)

Blueberry Beach Spinoff: Strawberry Sands (10 book series)

From Strawberry Sands to: Raspberry Ridge (12 book series)

Swoonfully Jolly Holiday Stories:

Holiday Romance: Cowboy Mountain Christmas (6 book series)

Cowboy Mountain Christmas Spinoff: A Heartland Cowboy Christmas (9 book series)

New and Much Loved: Mistletoe Meadows (4 books and counting!)

Laughing Through the Snow: Christmas Tree, PA Sweet Romcoms (6 short reads)